SERAPHIM ACADEMY 2: SINFUL THINGS

ELIZABETH BRIGGS

Cover Designed by Jessica Allain

ISBN (paperback) 9798625738156

ISBN (ebook) 9781948456210

www.elizabethbriggs.net

Chapter One

OLIVIA

Some days I forget I'm half demon and I live on light like any other angel. Other days I wake with a raging hunger for sex and remember there's no escaping my succubus side.

Today is one of those days.

I held off for as long as I could, and then debated going back to bars to pick up strangers, but in the end, I contacted Bastien for help—again. I've been using him to feed over the last few months, and he's never questioned or commented on my sudden requests. I'm sure he's only here out of some sense of obligation to my brother, but I'll take whatever I can get.

I suck all the lust and desire out of him as I stare at my soft yellow bedroom walls. Allowing myself to get into the feeding isn't an option, so I turn off all my emotions, even the raging anger I feel toward him. It's still a good meal because Bastien is incredibly powerful and damn good in bed, but there's a reason I called him and not Marcus. With Bastien, sex is a quick and easy business transaction between two people, and nothing more. That wouldn't be the case with Marcus—and sex with emotions is an *entirely* different experience.

For a second the emotions manage to creep back in anyway, and my heart pangs as I think about how it could've been if the Princes had been honest with me instead of trying to bully me off campus. Damn it, now I'm mad again.

Bastien must sense the change in me, because he stops pounding into me from behind and flips me over. He takes my chin and turns it to the side, then presses his face against my neck almost tenderly. He breathes me in deeply like he can't resist, but then his cock plunges into me hard, and the moment is over. We're back to business, and it's a relief to lose myself in the feel of him thrusting in and out of me.

He never lets me go unsatisfied, even though it's not part of our deal, and he reaches between us and finds my clit with his very talented fingers. I can't help but groan as he strokes me in the right way to drive me wild. By now, he knows exactly what it takes to get me off, and he doesn't hesitate or delay. I don't want to feel, but for a few seconds all I do is feel, feel, feel, and my legs tighten around his hips to draw him further inside me. The climax ripples through me, and he joins me moments later, hitting me with a rush of power. His face is right beside mine, and I start to turn my head to kiss his perfect lips, before I remember who we are and what we're doing and why I very much do *not* want to kiss Bastien.

When I've soaked up all the energy I can from him, I push him off me and straighten my clothes, avoiding his eyes. Bastien stands and pulls up his slacks, which we only yanked down to his knees in our haste. He buttons them as he walks toward the bedroom door, and I watch his tight ass as he moves away. At least the view is nice.

"I appreciate your assistance," I say in a stiff voice. Nice views don't cancel out what he did to me.

"Are you sufficiently sated?" he asks, his voice equally stiff.

"Yes, thank you."

He nods and then walks down the hall with his nose in the air. *You think you're doing me this huge favor, you ass.* But I don't say it out loud, because technically he is doing me a favor. Of course, he also gets to sleep with a hot succubus as part of the deal, so I think he's doing pretty well for himself.

I open the front door for him, and the beautiful sunset streams through with the still-crisp air. It's the beginning of March, which means school starts in a few weeks. I've been living in my father's house in Angel Peak for the last few months over the break, and although it's been nice to finally have a home, I'm eager to head back to Seraphim Academy.

Bastien pauses in the doorway, while the sun makes his black hair shine like raven feathers. "We'll be in school the next time you need to feed. I'm sure Marcus will be willing to provide that meal."

I cross my arms. "Not going to happen."

Marcus would want to grovel and apologize and tell me how much he cares about me, and I am so not in the mood for that right now. I'm far too pissed to give him an inch, and I doubt he'll be okay with me using his body and sending him on his way, like I'm doing with Bastien now.

Bastien scowls. "We both know feeding on one person alone isn't going to cut it."

"Have a good night," I say in my coldest voice, and begin closing the door on him. He's right, of course, even though I hate to admit it. I'll have to find another solution soon, or risk draining Bastien dry.

He clamps his mouth shut and walks outside. *Finally.* I watch him head down the porch steps, where he spreads his dark silvery wings and launches into the air in the direction of campus. When he's gone, I breathe deeply, trying to calm myself down. My anger is hard to swallow when the Princes are around. Even though Callan was the true instigator of the events last year, Bastien and Marcus were just as complicit. I won't let them off easily, if at all.

Over the break, I've been plotting my revenge. I have several tricks up my sleeve for the coming school year to get payback for what the Princes did to me. All three of them need to be knocked down a peg, not just for my own pleasure, but because they have to realize they don't rule the school anymore. And forgiveness? That's not in the cards. Not unless they convince me they're really sorry. The only one who might succeed is Marcus. Bastien is good for a quick meal, at least. But Callan? He's a lost cause. I picture him on his knees, begging for my forgiveness. Not a chance.

They deserve what I have planned for them.

Other than plotting my revenge, I've spent my winter break trying to figure out how to rescue Jonah. He's been missing over a year now, and my heart aches every time I think of him, but I refuse to believe he's dead. By infiltrating Seraphim Academy's secret society, the Order of the Golden Throne, I learned that Jonah went into Faerie to find the Staff of Eternity, the magical object used by Michael and Lucifer to end the great war, close off Heaven and Hell, and bring all angels and demons to Earth permanently. The Order wants to use the Staff to send all the demons back to Hell and reopen Heaven so they can try to rebuild it. I have no idea why my brother volunteered to get the Staff, but something bad must have happened once he got to Faerie, or he would have returned by now. My guess is the fae found him and have him locked up somewhere—and I won't rest until I bring him back to Earth.

Seraphim Academy has a spectacular library, and over my break I spent much of my time there searching for information on how to get to Faerie or on the Staff of Eternity. Sometimes I ran into Kassiel there, but I tried to avoid him as much as possible. After the kiss we shared at the end of last semester, the sexual tension between us has only grown stronger. The attraction popped and sizzled between us whenever we were in each other's presence, but we've both agreed we can't give in to our lust again, not until I graduate anyway. Teacher-student relationships are forbidden at Seraphim Academy, and I don't want to do anything to put his job in danger. Especially since he's my only true ally at the moment, and I'm going to need his help if I'm going to find Jonah and stop the Order.

I have a huge journal full of notes, but no clear plan yet. I'm hoping that once I take Fae Studies this year I'll be able to fill in all the gaps in my knowledge. It might take me some time, but I won't give up until I find my brother and bring him home. *I'm coming for you, Jonah. Stay alive for me. Please.*

I take a quick shower to wash Bastien off me, and put all the Princes and Kassiel out of my mind. The less I think about them, the better.

Chapter Two

OLIVIA

*I*n the morning, I head into the kitchen to fix myself something for breakfast, but groan when I open the fridge. Almost empty. I'll have to head to the store for one last supply run before it's time to return to campus. At least I still have plenty of money left from the allowance Aerie Industries provides students for attending Seraphim Academy. I barely spent any of it last year, so most of it is hidden in my bedroom here under a loose floor board. I keep my new golden robes from the Order in there too.

I grab a slightly stale croissant off the counter and munch on it as I walk into my bedroom, then look around with satisfaction. My room was pretty sparse when I moved in, and I've managed to decorate it on a tight budget with some cute pillows, flowing curtains, and a few little trinkets here and there. The room feels like mine now. For the first time, I belong somewhere. I just wish Jonah could be here too.

I dig my boots out of my closet, where they've been buried under a few days of laundry. With a sigh, I pick up the clothes and drop them in the hamper. No reason to be a total slob just because I'm here on my own without anyone popping in to judge me.

Gabriel comes to visit me every few weeks, but things are always a little awkward between us. We spent Christmas together, but it was a sad affair, between the lack of Jonah and the fact that Gabriel and I have barely had anything to do with each other for the last twenty-two years. He did get me a new winter coat though, which was nice, and I could tell he was trying, at least. He stayed for a week then, and it was almost a relief see him go at the end of it. I appreciate that he's claimed me and is making an effort to be a true parent for once, but we'll need some time to figure out how to be a family.

Especially since Gabriel still doesn't believe me about Jonah being in Faerie. I explained everything about the Order —which he knew about, of course, and said he's been monitoring for years—but he claimed he already spoke with the High King of Faerie, who assured him Jonah wasn't there. Which means the king doesn't know, or he's lying.

Honestly? I think it's easier for Gabriel to believe Jonah has run away, rather than to face the truth that he might be imprisoned...or worse.

I grab the coat he got me, which is bright, lipstick red with white fake fur trim around the neck. It's big and loud and practically screams, *I'm done hiding, deal with it.* I love it, especially because it shows Father does know me, at least a little bit.

Not having to hide who I am has been a welcome change, along with all the snow over the winter. I was in no way prepared for living in the mountains of northern California, but loved it all the same. Every time I wanted to go out, I layered on pretty much all of my wardrobe, but the coat helps with that.

There's no snow now though, and the sun is shining high, filling me with light as I fly into the main part of Angel Peak, the small town near Seraphim Academy that only angels can visit. It's been pretty empty all winter, since angels hate the cold and tend to migrate into warmer climates like birds. But with Seraphim Academy starting in only a few days, people are returning to town, and the quaint little shops are busy again.

I land on the sidewalk and retract my black wings into my back. The entire street seems to pause all at once in order to stop and stare at me, and I can't tell if the looks are angry or fearful. Now that everyone knows I'm both half-demon and the daughter of an Archangel, people treat me differently. No one is outright rude, because no one dares to insult Gabriel's daughter, but some move out of the way quickly to avoid me, and others cast me hateful glares, like I'm tainting their town by being in it. I can't decide which is worse.

I quickly hurry into the local coffee shop, and it's probably my imagination, but I think I hear a collective sigh of relief from the street as the door shuts behind me. It's a relief to be away from their judgmental looks too, except when I move to the counter to order, I see someone who makes me nervous all over again. Araceli.

Things didn't end great between us last semester, and I'm still riddled with guilt over that because I know it was all my fault. Araceli was my roommate and my best friend—sometimes my only real friend—during my first year at Seraphim Academy, but when she found out I lied to her the entire time about who and what I am, she was pretty upset. I tried to mend the relationship as best I could, but she said she needed space, and I respected that.

I debate rushing out of the place, but then she spots me, and it's too late. I have to face her now. She's wearing her lime green combat boots, and has that purple streak in her dark brown hair, and I have to admit, it's really good to see her. I just don't know if she feels the same about seeing me.

I approach her at the counter and we stare at each other awkwardly, before I finally ask, "How was your break?"

Araceli surprises me by throwing her arms around me. I instantly have tears in my eyes as I hug her back. "Oh, Liv," she says. "I missed you."

"I missed you too." My voice only cracks a tiny bit. "Are we...good?"

She pulls back and smiles at me. "We're good. Like I said, you're still my best friend. I just needed some space." She pokes her finger at my chest. "And you better not lie to me ever again."

I let out a long breath as the tension leaves my body. "I won't. I promise."

"Good. I'll get a table so we can catch up."

She grabs her coffee and heads off to a round table in the corner, while I step up to the counter. The barista doesn't meet my eyes, even though I've been coming here once a week for months now. She knows my order by heart though, and hands it to me immediately, then takes my payment quickly before darting off to be anywhere else. I give her a big smile and drop a few coins in the tip jar anyway.

With my giant cup of liquid heaven—yes, the coffee here really is that good—I sit down across from Araceli. "How have you been?" I ask, with more confidence this time.

"Good. I spent the break with my mom, and that was nice, but I came back a little early to get settled in before school starts. I'm staying with my aunt now. She has a five-year-old, and he's cute, but a total monster, so I came here for an escape." She takes a sip of her coffee. "What about you? How was your break?"

I shrug as I warm my hands on the coffee mug. "It was okay. I spent a lot of time researching and learning about the fae. I don't feel like I'm any closer to finding my brother, but I should ace Fae Studies this year at least."

She laughs. "You better, with me as your roommate. I took that last year to see if I could learn anything new about my heritage."

"And did you?"

"A little, yeah. My dad told me some things of course, but he left out a lot. It was good to have an outside perspective on it all too."

Araceli rarely mentions her half-fae dad, and I guess I was too self-absorbed before to notice that. Worst. Friend. Ever. But I'm totally going to do better this year—it's one of my goals, along with getting revenge on the Princes and finding my brother. "You don't talk about him much."

She stares into her coffee mug. "My parents separated a few years ago and things got weird after that. At first he came to visit me every weekend, but then it became more like every month, and now it's like once a year."

"Does he live in Faerie?" I ask. "Have you ever been there?" The Order wanted to use Araceli to get into Faerie to find Jonah. I won't use her like that, but she did offer to help me however she could.

"No. Dad was a messenger between the fae and the angels,

and both sides grudgingly accepted him because he was useful. Then he met mom, they fell in love, and then I was born. The fae excommunicated him after that. I guess having a child with another angel was the final straw for them. He can't go back to Faerie without being killed, and I'm not welcome there either."

"I'm sorry. I had no idea."

She shifts uncomfortably and shrugs. "I don't like to talk about it. I'm only a quarter fae anyway, so I just focus on my angel side and don't worry about the rest."

I take a bite of my burrito and nod, even though I think she might be making a mistake. Try as she might to deny her fae heritage, Araceli will always have some of their blood. There's no escaping it. I know that more than anyone.

"Anyway, Dad lives in Florida now, and we don't talk much. When I do see him, it's pretty awkward."

I snort. "I know all about awkward encounters with dads. Christmas with my father was definitely uncomfortable at times."

"I bet. But hey, at least he's trying."

I nod and take a sip of my coffee. "He is, and I appreciate that. Maybe once Jonah is back it won't be so awkward anymore."

She gives me a pitying look. Like everyone else, she probably believes Jonah is dead. "I'll do whatever I can to help you find him."

"Thanks. I appreciate that."

She sips her drink again before raising her eyebrows at me. "How's the, ah, *eating* situation going?"

I lower my voice, even though there's no one sitting near us. "I've been using Bastien for a quick meal. It's working for now, but I'll need to figure something else out soon."

"What about Marcus?"

"I'm not sure I want to open up that can of worms again." I sigh and sip my coffee. "Marcus would grovel, and try to win me back, and tell me how much he cares, and I'm not interested in any of that. Bastien is an emotionless bastard, and that's exactly what I need right now."

"And Callan?"

My eyes narrow. "Callan deserves what's coming for him."

"What do you mean?"

"I've been thinking about ways to bring them down a notch or two, and I have a plan."

Araceli grins and leans forward. "I'm in. Whatever it is, I'm in."

Chapter Three

KASSIEL

I land in front of Gabriel's house in Angel Peak, silently retract my black and silver wings, and adjust my tie. I'm wearing a heavy coat, even though the cold doesn't bother me at all, but I have to keep up the appearance that I'm an angel. Only two people at Seraphim Academy know what I truly am—Uriel and Olivia. Perhaps that's why the Archangel sent me to collect Olivia, and when he asks me to do something, I have little choice but to obey. As a Fallen, I don't need to bow to his authority, but as a professor at Seraphim Academy, I have to respect the headmaster. I'm only allowed to teach at the school because of his good will, and I appreciate that he keeps my secret for me. If the angels found out a demon was teaching their students, they'd have me fired...or worse.

And if anyone finds out about me and Olivia? It would be just as bad.

Not that anything is happening with Olivia at the moment. We slept together before I became her professor, and there's nothing we can do about that. The kissing at the end of last semester is another story, but nothing like that will happen again, not as long as she's a student. We've both agreed to keep things strictly professional between us while we work together to take down the Order of the Golden Throne.

That's the true reason I'm at Seraphim Academy, and I spent the break trying to research them, along with the Staff of Eternity. Of course, that only brought me closer to Olivia, since she was also researching the same things. That's how we ended up at the library together several times this winter. And every time I saw her, it grew harder to deny my feelings for her.

I'm determined not to let my desire for Olivia alter the way I treat her, though. She's my student, and I want her to get the most out of what I can teach her while she's at Seraphim Academy. Even though I have an ulterior motive for being a professor, I take my teaching very seriously, and in Angelic History classes I try to present the past as neutrally as possible. Angels and demons have fought for centuries, but now that the war is over, I hope the new generations can grow up in peace, without the old stereotypes and hatreds. I took this job as a special assignment from Lucifer himself, but I've come to enjoy it, and I care about my students. Especially one in particular.

But I won't take advantage of her, or show favoritism, or anything else that men in authority positions have a tendency to do. Especially human men.

My hand freezes before I strike the door. Coming to Olivia's house feels like a major violation, and an even bigger temptation. I remind myself I'd do this errand of Uriel's for any student, no matter who they were. I raise my fist and knock on her door.

Olivia answers wearing a tight tank top that is trying desperately to hold her large breasts flat and failing, with some matching yoga pants. Her hair is tied back and there's a sheen of sweat on her face that makes me think she was exercising. I can't help but remember when I had that body pressed up against the wall as I pounded into her, and she had that same sheen of sweat as she clenched around my cock.

"Kassiel?" she asks, leaning against the doorway. "What are you doing here?"

I force my gaze upward, away from the allure of her upper thighs. It takes me a moment to remember why I'm here. "Uriel sent me to fetch you. He wants to speak with you immediately."

Concern floods her features. "Why?"

"I don't know, but he said it was urgent."

"Come in, please."

My eyes can't help but travel the length of her body again. "I'd rather not."

She rolls her eyes. "I won't jump your bones, I promise. I just need a few minutes to change into something else."

"Probably a good idea." I step inside the house. Archangel Gabriel's house. If he knew there was a Fallen standing in his living room, he'd probably teleport here in an instant to eject me from his land. And if he knew I'd slept with his daughter once, he'd probably have my head.

Olivia slips away, and I stand in the living room awkwardly while I wait. The big windows offer a gorgeous view, but I'm more interested in the bookshelves, which are full of human novels. Old classics, written before I was born, and new bestsellers too. The spines on most of them look worn, as if they've been read many times.

"My dad loves to read human books," Olivia says. "Everything from the tawdriest romance novel to the driest of the classics."

I turn as if barely interested and see she's put on a pair of jeans that hug her curves and a black sweater that dips down in a V and accentuates her breasts. I'm not sure she could wear anything unflattering. All succubi are incredibly sexy, and Olivia is the most alluring one I've ever met.

She opens a closet and pulls out a bright red coat with a white fur collar. "Let's go."

I can't help but chuckle. "You can't be that cold, not with demon blood in you."

"I'm not overly sensitive to the cold, like an angel, or the heat, like a demon. I'm more like a human in that way. But I grew up in LA, so I'm still kind of a wimp about the cold." She heads outside and locks the door behind us. "Ready?"

"Are you nervous?"

"A little." She looks up at me with those mysterious eyes. "I'd be more nervous without you at my side."

My chest tightens, and I have to look away before I grab her, kiss her, and tell her everything will be okay, I'll make sure of it. I can't do that, but as much as I can be there for her, I will. She's still my student, I remind myself. The most attractive student I've ever seen in my life, but still. Just a student, for two more years anyway.

I have a feeling they'll be the longest two years of my life.

Chapter Four

OLIVIA

lying next to Kassiel is a wonderful kind of torture. He's the only other person I've met with black wings, which are rare but not unheard-of among angels, and common among the Fallen. Most of the angels in last year's Flight class had white, gray, or brown wings, and Araceli has the most beautiful wings of all—white with purple, the same color as the streak in her hair. Along with her pointed ears, they're the only thing marking her as part fae.

As we fly, it's hard not to steal glances of Kassiel in his sexy black suit, with those silver and black wings spreading from his back, especially when I can still feel his lust for me. His reaction to seeing me in my yoga clothes washed over me before either of us had time to utter a word. His desire for me has given me nice snacks in between meals from Bastien. In all the time we spent together over the break, I never felt him crave any other woman in the library, even though there were several very attractive angels shooting him obvious come-hither looks. He never even noticed.

But he's not mine. He can't be mine, not until I graduate from Seraphim Academy in two years. Not unless we want to put his job and everything we're trying to do in jeopardy.

I'm just not sure how we'll be able to resist each other that long.

Now I'm flying toward campus with him right beside me, with his lust hovering between us. I'm starting to think facing Uriel might be easier than being around Kassiel without acting on our feelings for each other. Because it's not just lust we share, but something more. Something I definitely can't think about right now.

The forest below us gives way, and the gleaming white buildings of the campus greet us, along with the sparkling lake. Spring is in the air and the grounds are a verdant green, with flowers beginning to bloom along the walkways. I draw in a deep breath. I came to Seraphim Academy under false pretenses in order to find my brother, but to my surprise I came to love it here over the last year. When the Princes tried to get me expelled, I pleaded my case so I could stay, and it wasn't only because of my hunt for Jonah. I wanted to stay here for me, too.

As we approach the headmaster's house, my stomach twists. Why does Uriel want to see me two days before class starts? Is it to tell me he's changed his mind, and I'm not welcome at the school anymore? What else could it be?

We land in front of Uriel's Victorian house, which looks too quaint to be a part of the campus. I've been in his office a few times before, and it was never a pleasant experience. I hesitate and turn to Kassiel. "Are you coming too?"

"I am," he says, as he leads the way inside.

That's a relief. Going at it all alone has been my MO my

entire life, and it's nice to have someone in my corner for once. Someone other than Jonah, anyway. My brother's the only one who ever had my back—and now it's my turn to return the favor by rescuing him.

Kassiel opens the office door and stands to the side so I can enter. As soon as I get a view of the room, my blood runs cold. Uriel isn't alone. Sitting across from his desk in one of the wingback leather chairs is a man so coldly handsome it takes my breath away. With long black hair casually draped around his broad shoulders, piercing blue eyes, and sharp cheekbones, he looks like the kind of man who'd haul you over his shoulder and take you back to his evil lair.

"Please come in," Uriel says, and indicates the chair beside the other man. "This is Baal, the headmaster of Hellspawn Academy."

My eyes widen. Baal is the Archdemon of the vampires. Whatever this is, it can't be good.

"I'm pleased to meet you, Olivia." The vampire stands and holds out his hand. Like Kassiel, he has an English accent, except his sounds more formal. Older. Ancient.

I reach out and shake his hand. I expect it to be cold and clammy, like a dead person's, but then remind myself that just about everything in movies and TV shows about vampires is wrong. They're not dead, they can go out in sunlight, and garlic does nothing to them except give them bad breath. It's only his eyes that are cold as death, even as he gives me a charming smile.

"Please, have a seat. I don't bite." He winks at me with those ice-blue eyes.

Oh, yes you do. I'm reasonably sure he won't do that in

front of Uriel though, so I sit at the edge of the leather chair. Kassiel moves to stand directly behind me.

Baal lifts his gaze over my head and narrows his eyes. "Kassiel."

"Baal." Kassiel's voice is flat, and I glance back to see him crossing his arms and staring the Archdemon down. I wonder how they know each other, and if it's safe for Kassiel to be here with me. I appreciate his support, but I don't want him to get in trouble on my behalf.

Baal's gaze returns to my face. "Olivia, I'm here to secure your enrollment at Hellspawn Academy."

I nearly fall out of my seat. "My enrollment?"

"As the first angel-demon hybrid, it's only right you spend half your time at Hellspawn Academy." He smiles at me, but it's the smile of a lord looking down at one of his minions and expecting them to drop into a bow.

"I appreciate the offer..." I swallow. How can I word this delicately? "But I'd prefer to stay here."

"I'm not sure you have a choice." Baal is still the epitome of polite, but he's got a strong undercurrent of darkness too, and it's clear he expects to get his way.

I don't look behind me to see how Kassiel reacts, but he shifts and his hand brushes against my back. I'm pretty sure he's gripped the top of the chair.

Uriel clasps his hands in front of him on his big mahogany desk. "If Olivia wishes to stay here, then she shall. We can assure her safety here."

Thank you, Uriel.

Baal leans forward. "She will be perfectly safe at Hellspawn Academy too. I can promise you that. It's important she learn about her demon side, as much as her angel side. Not only so that she can know our history from our point of view, but so that she can learn to control her powers and not be a threat to others."

"I've been trained," I interject. "My mother spent a considerable amount of time with me when I came of age so I could learn to use my succubus powers safely."

Baal arches an eyebrow. "And your mother is...?"

I shrug casually, and hope my necklace protects me from lying to Archdemons too. "A succubus named Laylah. I don't know much about her."

"Hmm." Baal's face turns thoughtful. "Nevertheless, there are many things we can teach you that the angels can't."

I'm intrigued, I will admit. I do want to learn more about my demon side. But I need to stay here to find Jonah and take down the Order. I can't do that from Hellspawn Academy. "Sorry, but my place is here."

"Would it be an acceptable compromise if a demon taught her about your kind here on campus?" Uriel asks. "I already have one of the Fallen in place who can do that."

Kassiel adds, "It would be my honor to teach her about our ways."

Baal doesn't look happy about this, but he doesn't object either. He shifts in his seat and crosses his long, muscular legs. He really is hot, but his age radiates off of him like a heatwave. He's thousands of years old, as old as my parents. Not for me, thanks.

"Fine," he drawls. "Kassiel can teach her about our history and our laws, but I want a succubus to test her to make sure she is properly trained in that area, as well." I start to protest, and Baal shoots me a hard look that instantly renders me silent. "Even though you say you've been trained, let us be the judge of that. We cannot have an untrained succubus draining humans dry all over California. You'll meet with a succubus of my choosing, or you'll attend Hellspawn Academy. Your choice."

I want to argue that it hasn't been a problem for that last four years, but I guess I understand his need to be cautious. I'm not super excited about more classes with Kassiel either. It's going to be a lesson in restraint for both of us, at least.

"All right," I reluctantly agree. "Anything else?"

"That will be all." Baal stands to his tall height and flashes me a dangerous smile. "It has been an absolute delight, Ms. Monroe. Archangel Uriel." He purses his lips. "Kassiel."

"An honor to see you again, Archdemon Baal," Uriel says.

The vampire gives Uriel a nod, and then walks out of the room. I relax in the leather seat as soon as he's gone, and my eyes wander around Uriel's office. I spot the shadowy black feather floating in a glass case, and wonder again whose wings are missing it. I also eye his private bookshelf and the forbidden book I stole from it last year. I feel a little guilty about that, but I had to do it to get into the Order. At least it got returned at some point.

Uriel steeples his fingers and meets my eyes. "Olivia, as I'm sure you've surmised, Kassiel is a Fallen and not an angel. He's working here as part of an initiative to improve angel-demon relations, but we're not ready to reveal what he is yet to the school. I trust you to keep this secret as part of the condition for remaining at Seraphim Academy."

I nod and pretend this is news to me. "I understand. I won't tell anyone."

"Good. I'll add weekly training sessions with Kassiel to your schedule. I'm not sure when the succubus will arrive, but you'll have to find time for her lessons as well. Do you have any other questions or concerns for me?"

"No," I say. "But I appreciate your support. Thank you for letting me stay here."

"Of course," Uriel says. "You belong here as much as anyone does. I'll see you at orientation tomorrow."

That sounds like a dismissal, so I nod and leave the room, with Kassiel right behind me. Once we're outside, I give him a smile. "Thanks for staying with me."

"You're welcome." Kassiel frowns and stares down the road away from the house, before looking back at me with a warning in his eyes. "This deal with Baal is the best we could have hoped for, although the succubus will obviously be spying on the school for the Archdemons."

"Uriel must realize that," I say. "Otherwise he wouldn't have agreed."

"I'm sure he does, and he probably has a spy of his own at Hellspawn. Just be careful, Olivia."

"I'm always careful. It's how I've stayed alive this long on my own."

"I know, but things are different now. Everyone knows who—and what—you are, and both angels and demons will want to use you." His mouth twists. "Or they'll want you dead."

Chapter Five

OLIVIA

$\mathscr{I}$t's the first day of school...and time to face the Princes.

Araceli and I moved back into our dorm room yesterday, and then went to Uriel's orientation, where he went over the rules and introduced us to the new teachers. I was relieved to see I'd never slept with any of them this time.

As I head outside into the sunshine and breathe in the crisp air, I glance at the bell tower. It's a habit to look for the Princes' shining metallic wings, even though I dread the idea of seeing them. Luckily, the bell tower appears empty.

Unfortunately, my first class of the day is Combat Training, which means I'll have to face Callan. The one saving grace is that Araceli shares the class with me, so I don't have to walk into the danger zone alone.

I keep my head high and my shoulders square as I walk into the gym with my friend at my side. I spot Tanwen first, who is playing with her straw-colored ponytail, and she gives me a little nod. It's unexpected, and I'm not sure what to do in return. Then my eyes land on Callan.

Somehow over the last few months I forgot just how incredibly handsome he is, and I nearly stumble as it hits me all over again. Short golden hair. Bright blue eyes. Muscles for miles. He's delicious. And I should know—I've kissed him twice now.

My eyes narrow as I remember how he played the video of our second kiss to the entire school to show I was a succubus. The bastard betrayed my trust and revealed my deepest secret in an attempt to get me expelled. He said it was for my own good, that he was doing it because my brother told him to keep me away from the school, but I don't buy it. He did it because he wanted me, and he couldn't handle wanting a demon. Even one who's half angel.

His eyes are hard as he stares back at me, and he crosses his arms. It feels like a challenge, but he should know by now that I'm not going to back down. I move to stand along the wall, still meeting his eyes, and only look away when Professor Hilda's voice announces the start of class.

"Welcome back, Second Years," Hilda says with a grim smile. She's one of the Valkyries and looks like she could tear a man in half with her bare hands. I pity anyone who would try to mess with her. "This semester, we're learning weapons."

She indicates the far wall, where a myriad of different types of weapons are displayed on several tables. "Callan is going to help me demonstrate the proper use of each of these weapons over the next few classes, and then you're going to try each of them out. Over time, you'll find an affinity for one of them. By the end of the year, I expect you to be able to pick up any weapon and use it without injuring yourself in the process, and to be well-trained in the weapon of your choice."

Callan walks over to one of the tables and picks up the first weapon, a huge two-handed sword. My mouth waters a little as he lifts the heavy blade with ease. Hating him would be a lot easier if he wasn't such a perfect specimen of masculinity.

"Sit," Hilda says. "Get comfortable."

The wrestling mats are on the ground, and Araceli and I settle down behind the Valkyries. Tanwen shoots me a look as I pass by her, and I wonder what her deal is this year. Is she preparing her next verbal attack, now that she knows I'm part demon? I realize she wasn't behind the notes and vandalism last year, like I initially suspected, but it's not like she's ever been nice to me either—and that was back when she thought I was half-human. How much worse will it be this year?

Hilda talks about the proper use of the sword, including stance, grip, and footwork. I try to pay attention to everything she says, but it's hard to keep my eyes off of Callan. Every time that asshole swings his sword, he makes sure to do it while looking directly at me. As if he's imagining thrusting the blade into me with every strike.

Or maybe he's thinking about thrusting something else into me.

I shift a little on the mat at that thought, trying to ignore the growing heat between my thighs. It's hard though, when Callan keeps swinging that sword like some kind of sexy barbarian warrior. I'm a modern woman who doesn't need a man to save her, but sometimes it's pretty hot knowing a guy *could* save you if you were in danger. Even if I hate him.

He glares at me like he knows what I'm thinking about,

and I give him a seductive wink in return because I know it will annoy him. He practically seethes, and I only smile wider. I can't wait 'til he sees what I have planned for him.

By the time class is over, I could use a cold shower. The good news is, I'm pretty sure which weapon I'm going to focus on this year—the dagger. It's a weapon of stealth and skill, perfectly suited for me, whereas Callan is more attuned to weapons that require brute strength. Maybe Hilda will be the one training me, instead of him.

As the class heads out of the gym in a big group, someone moves past me and bumps my shoulder hard.

"Sorry," I mutter, the apology coming automatically.

"Why don't you watch where you're going?" The guy that plowed into me jerks away and stares at me as if I've just vomited on him. "Don't touch me again, demon filth."

I blink at the guy as he rushes away, and it takes me a second to remember his name. Jeremy. He was in my Flight class last year, and I never really paid him any attention. He didn't seem interested in being my friend, but he wasn't particularly rude or anything. He never gave me a reason to think badly of him, until now.

"Whoa," Araceli says. "What was that about? He's never acted like that before."

"He obviously has a strong opinion about demons, and I'm sure he's not the only one." I push the door open to go out toward the lake and pretend the encounter didn't hurt my feelings. I'm still the same person I was last year, but not everyone is going to see that. They were already standoffish before when they thought I was half human, and I imagine it will only get worse now.

"Don't sweat it," Araceli says. "Not everyone will be a dick, I promise."

Probably not. But if I expected my second year at Seraphim Academy to be any easier than my first, I'm already being proved wrong.

Chapter Six

OLIVIA

I'm relieved to see Raziel is teaching Fae Studies this year, and even happier when he gives me a kind smile as I step into his classroom. He looks exactly the same as he did last year, with his friendly face, salt and pepper hair, and quirky bowties. Today's is white with black Scottie dogs on it.

I got an A last year in Demon Studies, naturally, and I'm hoping to do just as well in this class. Thanks to my research over the summer, I know more than the average angel or demon about the fae. I'm hoping this class either reinforces that knowledge or teaches me something I don't know already. I trust that Raziel will keep things fairly unbiased, like he did in Demon Studies, even though the things I most want to know probably won't be covered in the class. Like what the fae do with their prisoners, and how to rescue one.

I take a seat at the front of the classroom and get out my notebook, then groan out loud when Bastien walks in. I should have known I'd share this class with at least one of the Princes.

He doesn't even give me a glance. We might as well be strangers, except he sits at the desk beside me even though most of the classroom is still empty. I arch an eyebrow at him, but he ignores me as he pulls out a black Moleskin journal and a pen. As he slowly flips to a blank page, I glimpse very precise handwriting in black ink, with no doodles or anything else. It's all so very Bastien.

"Welcome to Fae Studies," Raziel says in his cheerful voice once class starts. "I'm so happy to see some familiar faces here. This year we're going to learn all about the reclusive fae, along with the world they live in, Faerie. Though most of you probably won't have any encounters with the fae other than at the school's sports games, it's still important to learn about them, because you never know when things might change."

I lean forward, pen poised, greedy for whatever knowledge Raziel can impart upon me—and not just because I hope it will help me find Jonah. Surprisingly, I'm actually really curious about the fae. The Olivia of a year ago would have laughed at the person I've become. I never cared all that much about school before coming to Seraphim Academy.

"Just like there are different types of angels and demons, there are different types of fae," Raziel continues. "They're divided into four Courts, based on the seasons. Each Court has its own king or queen, but they're all ruled by the High King of Faerie, who united the courts after the Faerie Wars. We'll talk more about those wars in upcoming weeks, but first let's go over some basics. What do you know about the fae already?"

Jeremy raises his hand. Ugh, he's in this class too? "They have pointed ears."

Raziel nods. "Yes, they do, and a few of them even have

wings, although that's pretty rare and mostly found in the royal families. What else?"

"They're weak against iron," another student calls out.

"They can't lie," someone else adds.

"All very true," Raziel says. "Although they're very good at misdirection and twisting their words, so that even though they're speaking the truth, they're not actually being honest. You must be very careful to never make any bargains with them, especially since they're famous for being tricksters. They're also known for being cruel and inhuman, mainly because they see themselves as better than all other races, which makes them somewhat callous."

I could say the same thing about some of the angels I've met so far, like the ones in the Order. I wouldn't be surprised if there are demons like that too. Then again, even among humans there are people with superiority complexes and hatred of people who are different. Discrimination and prejudice seem to be universal traits, unfortunately.

Raziel continues giving a basic introduction and overview of the fae, until our time is up and the students begin to file out. I'm starting to think Bastien and I might ignore each other forever, but as we exit the room he gives me a little nod. "See you in class tomorrow."

Before I can reply, he turns on his heel and stalks away. I check out his ass again, because hey, why not. A succubus can look, can't she?

My next class is Ishim Training, taught by Nariel. I met him briefly last year, and he tested my Ishim abilities about a week ago. I debated playing inexperienced again, but decided I didn't want to get stuck in the First Year class with the newbies. Thanks to my father's training, I suspect I could have been placed with the Third Years in skill level, but I'm happy to be in this class with the other Second Years.

When I enter the room, I'm surprised to see Grace there, since she's a year ahead of me. Her normally pale skin has a nice tan, and her strawberry blond hair seems especially bright, like all the Florida sunshine over the holidays made her even more beautiful.

She gives me a kind smile and a light hug. "How have you been?"

"Good. How was your trip to Disney World?"

"So much fun," she says. "My little brother loved it, and it was a nice distraction from everything that happened last year."

Grace was my brother's girlfriend, and she seemed to really care about him and worry about his disappearance. However, she's also a member of the Order of the Golden Throne, so I can't entirely trust her, even though I wish I could. She knew he went to Faerie, and knew I was his half-sister, and didn't tell me anything until I found out on my own. I can't forget that, even though she might have had her reasons.

"What are you doing in this class?" I ask.

"Nariel let me test out of the Third Year class, and now I'm working as his teacher's assistant in the hopes of becoming a professor someday. With the way the school is growing every year, they're going to need a lot more teachers soon."

"That's great. It'll be nice to have a friendly face in the class." The only other student I've heard of testing out of classes is Callan with Combat Training. I bet it helps that Nariel is Grace's uncle. I don't see any resemblance between the two of them though. Nariel almost looks like an albino, with very light hair and very pale skin. He must have lathered on the sunblock while in Florida, because he didn't get even a hint of a tan while they were there.

Ishim class goes by quickly, and after a small lunch in my dorm, I head to my fourth class of the day—Angelic History. Kassiel gives me the subtlest of nods when I walk in, and I raise my eyebrows at him. Last year he only taught the 101 class, but now he must be teaching this one instead. Did he switch to 102 because I'm in it? It feels arrogant to think so, but it feels right too. I'm pretty sure he did it to be close to me, even though it would be a lot easier for us if he wasn't my teacher anymore—no more sexual tension distracting me in class, for one thing. But at the same time, I'm relieved to see him standing at the chalkboard. He's a good teacher, and I like being around him, even if it's torture of the best kind—his classes are always a mixture of barely contained desire and interesting stories.

I sit in the front row and cross my legs, and his green eyes drop down to them. He swallows hard and looks away for a moment, but then he looks back, like he can't help himself.

Oh yeah, he likes the torture just as much as I do.

Light Control is my last class of the day, and it's out by the lake, probably so we can soak up the sunlight. They chose this mountain in northern California for Seraphim Academy because it's one of the sunniest places in America, and today doesn't disappoint. My angel side wants to stretch her wings and soar over the lake, but I settle for taking off my sweater and letting the light sink into my skin.

The teacher, Eileen, is a red-haired angel with freckles on her nose, and her eyes widen with a hint of fear when she sees me. Great, even a professor is scared of me now.

"Angels and demons both use life force to fuel their

powers, and they need to recharge that in different ways," she explains. "Angels use light, and demons have different ways of doing this depending on their type. The Fallen use darkness, vampires use blood—"

"And succubi use sex," a Valkyrie I don't know says with a smirk.

Eileen's face turns bright red and she glances at me quickly before looking away. "Um, well, yes. As I was saying, in this class you'll learn how to best recharge yourselves, and how to use your light magic in ways you might not have thought of before."

Like my other classes, this one is mostly an overview of what to expect during the year, and I find my attention wandering. My gaze drifts over the lake, watching the breeze make tiny ripples in the water, and then I spot Marcus standing on the other side. Looking directly at me.

I'm going to have to face him soon—and I'm so not ready.

Chapter Seven
MARCUS

I'm going to be late to my Human Studies class, but I can't keep myself from stopping to watch Liv in her Light Control class. It's outside next to the lake, and her dark brown hair shines under the bright sun as she listens to the professor. She's so beautiful it makes my chest hurt, and I long to go to her and beg her to take me back.

I managed to stay away from her over the winter, even though it was hard. Especially when I found out she continued sleeping with Bastien, even though she's still pissed at him. I understand why she did it, but they both know she needs to feed on more than one person, and dammit, it should be me helping her, not anyone else.

I'm filled with guilt at the thought. Now that I know she's Jonah's sister, I can't look at her the same way without feeling like I've betrayed my best friend somehow. Jonah would kill me if he knew what happened last year, although maybe he'd cut me some slack if he knew I slept with her to keep her safe and healthy. Does that make it okay to sleep with your best friend's sister? Could he ever forgive me?

Of course, that's not the only thing I'm going to have to answer for, if we ever find Jonah. In a moment of weakness, when it was clear Jonah wasn't coming back, I slept with his girlfriend, Grace. It was a monumental mistake and we both regretted it immediately and swore we'd never bring it up again. I've avoided Grace ever since then, but I'll have to own up to that with Jonah, and tell him how sorry I am.

I head to my Human Studies class, but I find it hard to concentrate on anything the professor says. Callan is in it too, but I shoot him a cold look and sit on the other side of the room. I haven't spoken to him or Bastien after they betrayed Liv, and although I miss them, I'm still pissed at them too.

Afterwards, I head back to my dorm to get ready for soccer practice. It's going to be intense, because the fae always kick Seraphim's ass at the sport, but I consider skipping it anyway because I just don't care. Ever since school ended last year, I've been feeling...lost.

I step into the elevator to my dorm, the one I still share with Jonah even though he's been gone more than a year. I hate going back there. It's too empty, and every time I glance at his door, I'm reminded that he's gone and probably never coming back.

Olivia steps into the elevator just before the door closes, and she stiffens when she sees me. For a few seconds we're alone, and I have to say something. I have to try.

"Liv," I say. "I missed you."

She doesn't answer, but just stares at the elevator door. It's going to open any moment now and she's going to leave. Before

I know what I'm doing, I hit the STOP button and the elevator jerks to a halt.

"I'm sorry," I continue. "I never meant to hurt you, and everything I did last year was to protect you."

Her unusual green eyes cut to me sharply. "Trashing my room was protecting me?"

I cringe, but at least she's talking to me now. "Yes, in our own way, or at least we thought so at the time. It was stupid though, and I should have stopped Callan and Bastien. We should have been honest with you from the beginning."

"Yes, you should have."

"But you weren't honest with us either. You could have told us Jonah was your brother."

She props her hands on her hips. "I had no reason to trust you. And then I *did* trust you, and Callan betrayed me anyway."

"Callan is a dick, and I haven't spoken to him in months. I'm pissed at him too, but I had nothing to do with him betraying you. You have to know I'd never do anything to hurt you." I draw in a deep breath. "I am sorry for what I did though. I'll say it a hundred times, if necessary, until you believe me. A thousand times. A million."

She glances away, her shoulders dropping. Maybe I'm finally getting through to her. But then she pushes the STOP button again, and the elevator hits the second floor.

"I believe you're sorry," she says, as she walks out. "But I just don't care."

The door shuts with a thud after that, and the hollowness inside me feels like a black hole I can't escape from. I've never felt this way about a woman before. In fact, before Olivia I slept with a new angel every month, and they all knew it was just a bit of fun and nothing serious. Then Liv came into my life, and nothing was ever the same again.

All I can do is keep trying to win her back. I screwed up last year, but I'll make it up to her, somehow. And I think I have an idea how.

*M*y first week of classes is pretty uneventful, other than the constant looks from other students. Most of them avoid me, which is fine by me. At least Araceli still treats me the same. It's good to be living with her again, even if she insists on waking up at the crack of dawn, something I doubt I'll ever get used to.

On Friday, it's time for my first demon lesson with Kassiel, and it's held in his office in the professor's building, with their housing on the floors above. I wonder what his apartment is like. Is it all organized and refined, like he is in class? Or is it super messy, a way of letting himself go in his own private space? I long to find out.

When I step into his office, he's taking off his suit jacket and loosening his tie. I stop in the doorway to admire him as he relaxes a little. When he rolls up his sleeves, I have a hard time not unbuttoning his shirt one pearly white button at a time. I have a feeling these lessons are going to be even more torture than his classes.

Kassiel is off-limits, I remind myself.

"Hello, Olivia. How was your first week of school?" His voice is so formal. I might as well be any other student, not one who's tasted him before.

"Fine," I say, trying to keep my tone even too. I sit in the chair in front of his desk.

He sits across from me. "After what happened the other week, I thought I'd begin our lessons with a little about the Archdemons, starting with Baal."

"Probably a good idea. I know a little about them from Demon Studies already, but I'd like to hear your side of things." Mother also told me about them, but she didn't spend much time talking about demonic history. She focused on how to be a succubus. How I would survive without getting caught and without killing anyone.

"As you probably know, Baal is the leader of the vampires and the headmaster of Hellspawn Academy. What you probably don't know is how well-respected he is among the demons."

"I guess that makes sense, if they trust him to teach their children. Just like Uriel is well-respected among angels."

"Exactly. Plus vampires are a charming bunch at their worst, and Baal is the most powerful vampire there is. He has the power to dominate entire groups of people and bend them to his will, and he's ruthless and determined. I can't be sure he doesn't want to supplant Lucifer as leader of the demons, but if so, he's got another think coming."

"It's 'another thing coming,'" I mutter absently as I remember the darkness in Baal's eyes.

Kassiel opens his mouth to continue talking, but then closes it and stares at me. "No, it's 'another *think*.'"

I roll my eyes. "There's a whole song about it. It's 'thing.'"

"I've been alive for more than a century, and you want to question me?" he asks, with a hint of teasing in his voice.

I tease him back, unable to stop myself. "This has nothing to do with age. I've lived among humans all my life. I know what I'm talking about."

"Let's find out." He opens his laptop, presumably to search online for the answer. It doesn't take him long to find it. "Ha! I was right."

He turns the screen toward me, and I read about the phrase, which has suddenly become the most important thing in the world.

The phrase was originally 'think,' but... "No." I shake my head. "I'm right. Modern slang has changed the phrase to 'thing.' So there." I close his laptop with a click and cross my arms.

"Maybe we're both right, but I was right first because originally it *was* 'think.'" He sits back in his desk chair and grins like he just ate a big canary.

I lean forward and grin even wider. "And I'm right *now*, because we live in this century and not the previous one."

As we stare at each other, something shifts between us, and our fun argument seems more like verbal foreplay. His eyes drop down to my cleavage, which is on display as I lean forward on his desk. I sit up quickly, my cheeks flushed with heat.

He tugs on the collar of his shirt and looks away pointedly. "This is dangerous."

"It doesn't have to be." I fold my hands in my lap like a proper student who is not thinking about banging her professor right here on his desk, nope, definitely not. "We got sidetracked by the argument. Tell me more about the Archdemons. What about the Fallen one?"

Kassiel clears his throat as he gets back into professor-mode. "The Fallen are technically led by Lucifer, but since he's the leader of all demons, Samael acts as his second in command and handles most Fallen issues."

"What's Lucifer like?" I ask. "You must have met him before, since you're here on a mission for him."

"He's...intense. It's hard to say no to him." He stares off into space, and then shakes himself and comes back to reality. "In Demon Studies, did they mention that Las Vegas is a hotbed of demon activity?"

"Yes, and they said that Lucifer controls most of the casinos there."

"He does. In Vegas, demons can feed without drawing too much attention to themselves. What they didn't tell you is that Lucifer set everything up to take over the casinos almost imme-diately after the Earth Accords were signed. He'd been plan-ning it for a while."

"That's definitely not in the textbooks."

"I'm not surprised. Few know that Lucifer and Michael privately debated for a long time on how to best end the wars. The Earth Accords were in development for many years before they actually happened."

"Really?" I raise my eyebrows at him. "Do you think Lucifer killed Michael?"

Kassiel's eyes narrow. "No. I know he didn't. And why would he? Lucifer and Michael were friends, or as close to friends as they could be, considering the circumstances. What reason would he have for killing Michael now that the war is over, anyway?"

"I don't know." Unlike the angels at the school, I don't have an opinion on the matter. It does seem odd to me that Lucifer would kill Michael now that angels and demons are at peace, but maybe I don't have all the facts either.

Kassiel's face darkens. "The angels want to believe he did it, but they're rarely rational when it comes to demons. It's easy for them to blame Lucifer for everything bad that happens. They've been doing it for centuries, after all. Why stop now?"

He has a point. How many sayings are there about Lucifer? *The devil made me do it.* A convenient excuse, for sure.

Kassiel seems pretty worked up about this topic though, so it might be time to change the subject. "What about Fenrir?" I ask. "The shifter Archdemon?"

"He's angry, as most shifters tend to be, but he's good at controlling it. He's also one of the few Archdemons who doesn't live in Vegas. He prefers to be in the background, usually in the wild, staying out of sight and controlling his kind from the shadows. Lilith is like that, too. A true nomad."

I sit up a little at the mention of the Lilim's Archdemon. "What can you tell me about Lilith?"

Kassiel pauses, like he's considering what exactly to tell me. "She's very old and very powerful. Also, she's smart. Probably one of the most intelligent creatures I've ever met."

"Oh, really?" I've never heard anyone talk about her except with a negative connotation. Her reputation is almost as bad as Lucifer's, but maybe that's more angel propaganda.

"She's very mysterious as well, and is always on the move. I'm told she's impossible to track down, unless she wants to be found. Even though she's technically the Archdemon of the Lilim, she lets Asmodeus handle most matters for her."

"Asmodeus?"

"Her son."

My mouth falls open, although I quickly close it. "She has a son?"

"Yes. I believe she's had a few children over the years. I'm not sure how many are still living though."

"That's unusual, isn't it?" I ask. "For one of our kind to have so many children?"

"It is, although she does get around a lot, if you get my meaning."

I do. I very much do. "Why does she move around so much?"

He shrugs. "Most Lilim are nomadic. They can't take a human lover for more than one night, and they would need multiple demon lovers to survive, so most don't bother with that. Traveling allows them to feed without repercussions." He pauses and his brow furrows. "Speaking of that, are you...? No, never mind, inappropriate question."

I'm very tempted to ask if he wants to give me a snack. The truth is, I'm hungry, and I'm going to need to feed soon, and not on Bastien again—but I can't tell Kassiel that. So all I say is, "I'm surviving."

He nods slowly. "Good." A moment of awkwardness hangs between us before he says, "I think our time is up."

I practically jump to my feet, because now that I've started thinking about feeding on Kassiel, it's hard to stop. "Thanks for this lesson. I wasn't sure if I'd learn anything from these meetings, but I did."

"I'm glad," Kassiel says, as he walks me to the door. My arm brushes against his, and a bolt of lust shoots through me.

I'm not sure if it's from me or him. "We'll meet next week at the same time."

As soon as I escape the room, I breathe a sigh of relief—and regret.

I'm starting to think going to Hellspawn Academy would have been easier than this.

*I*t's becoming increasingly obvious that people are terrified of me. Grace usually has a table full of people sitting with her at dinner, but the minute I sit down, the place becomes a ghost town. Students who would've come to eat with Grace veer off in a different direction. But Grace doesn't seem to mind, and I'm used to people treating me like dirt. At least they aren't actively trying to kill me. Yet.

When I get back to my dorm, there's an invitation to the next meeting of the Order of the Golden Throne sitting on my bed. My first one as a true member.

I still can't believe they kept me in, but I suspect they have ulterior motives. Their main purpose is to rid the world of demons, after all. How can they do that and allow a half-demon in their midst?

Kassiel's words come back to me. *"Be careful. Everyone knows who—and what—you are, and both angels and demons will want to use you...or they'll want you dead."*

Good thing I'm always careful.

The next night, I pull my new golden robes out of my hiding spot behind my desk, along with my mask. Last year I was only an initiate of the Order of the Golden Throne and wore a white robe for these meetings. As I pull the shimmering material over my head, I'm reminded of how far I've come since then. I passed all their tests and proved myself to them, even with my demon blood. I don't agree with the Order's beliefs or their methods, but I infiltrated their ranks in order to find my brother, and now I hope to learn more about their plans and to uncover the identities of their members. I know Kassiel is a member—he was sent by Lucifer himself to infiltrate the Order and see if they're a threat. We've already agreed to work together to stop their grand plan—to retrieve the Staff of Eternity to send demons back to hell.

I need to find out who their leader is, most importantly. He or she is the one who ordered Araceli's boyfriend, Darel, killed. They made it look like a demon murdered him in an attempt to get her to join the Order, but I convinced her to stay far away from them. They want to use her fae blood to get into Faerie, although neither of us is sure how exactly—something else I hope to learn from the Order.

The meeting tonight is earlier than the ones last year, and it's in their secret lair under the lake. I make myself invisible using my Ishim powers, and fly to the large boulder in the forest. As I fly lower, I spot another golden-robed member appear out of the night, as if made of shadow. That must be Kassiel. As a Fallen, he can control darkness, although I've never seen him use his powers before. It eases my nerves to know he's going to be with me at the meeting tonight, that I have an ally among the other masked members.

Of course, I know some of the other people in the Order

already. Grace. Cyrus. The Princes. But I'm not sure I can call any of them allies.

Kassiel opens the boulder, and I follow him down into the dark, damp stone tunnels leading under the lake. At the end of the tunnel, far below the surface, is a large cavern with over a dozen people sitting in a circle, all wearing gold robes and matching masks. Kassiel and I take a seat on the last empty stone bench.

The leader of the Order wears a gold crown and stands before us, in front of an ancient gold throne carved with depictions of angels and demons in battle. I've never seen our leader sit on the throne before, but maybe that will happen tonight. Otherwise, who is meant to sit there?

The leader speaks, but the masks are magically enchanted to distort voices, so I can't tell if it's a man or a woman. "Welcome, members of the Order of the Golden Throne. I'm pleased to see you all back with us for another year. We have much work to do."

He or she strides forward, and a shoe peeks out from under the robes. Black loafers, too big to be female, although some of the Valkyries have pretty big feet. It's impossible to tell from the voluminous robes, but I get the sense it's a man.

"As this is the first meeting of the year, let me remind everyone of our three basic tenets. One, angels are superior beings, meant to guide Earth and humanity to a brighter future. Two, demons are evil and must be eradicated from Earth to protect humanity. And three, loyalty to the Order is paramount, along with discretion. Anyone who speaks of the Order outside of these chambers will face dire consequences."

He continues on about the Order's long history, and I

glance around at the other members, wondering which is Grace. I look for feminine builds, but the robes are very good at concealing body types, which I'm sure isn't an accident. Everyone else is a mystery. There are three large figures sitting together, who could be the Princes, but it's hard to tell for certain. Cyrus must be here somewhere, probably at Grace's side. I wonder if Jeremy, who hates demons so much, is here too. If so, he'd probably lose his shit if he discovered I was a member. It's probably a good thing my identity remains hidden from most members of the Order at this meeting. Only when people graduate do they learn who else is in the Order.

"Has anyone made any progress in our goal to retrieve the Staff of Eternity from Faerie?" the leader asks, drawing my attention once again. I hold my breath, but no one answers. Good.

Finally one person speaks up, their voice unreadable due to the mask. "Perhaps we should try to get that fae-blooded girl to join us again."

Another person adds, "Or we could kidnap her and force her to help us. She must know how to get into Faerie."

"She doesn't," I speak up, even though it draws attention to me. I don't care though—I can't let them hurt Araceli. "She was raised among angels and knows nothing about her fae side."

"I agree," says one of the people in the cluster that could be the Princes. "She is worthless. We must find another way."

"We could use the fae at one of the upcoming soccer games," a person across the room says. "Perhaps we can kidnap one of them and force them to open a portal."

I have to bite my lip to stop from speaking out against this idea. This is exactly why I'm here—to learn their plans. Even if I disagree with them.

"A valid idea," the leader says. "One that we must ponder. However, getting to Faerie is only the first step. We must find the Staff once we are there, and Faerie is large and dangerous. It won't be easy."

"And we need to find Jonah too," another of the Princes says. My bet is Marcus.

The leader inclines his head slightly. Not really an answer, I notice. "Continue your research," he says instead. "You will also be sent an individual task throughout the year, which you must complete. Do not fail us, or your punishment will be swift and severe."

His chilling words wash over me. What kind of things do they want us to do? Last year they had us manipulate humans and torture demons as tests, so I'm not looking forward to whatever these new tasks are.

"We will meet again soon," the leader continues. "For now, we must welcome the new initiates in the woods. They should be there by now, and we will form a circle around them. Do not speak. I will address them and assign them their first test."

He turns and walks up the pathway to the exit, and the circle follows in single-file silence. Once outside in the cool night air, we move through the forest to surround the initiates in their white robes. I have no idea who they are, but they peer around the clearing and wring their hands. I remember exactly what it felt like to be in their shoes.

Our leader gives the same speech he gave last year, and ends with giving the initiates the task to steal an important object from one of the professors. We're all dismissed, and we disperse silently into the shadows, slipping away like eels into the dark night.

I attempt to follow one of the other members for a short time, hoping to uncover who they are, like I did with Cyrus last year, but they turn invisible and I lose them. And when I get back to my room and remove my mask, only then do I realize that I didn't really learn anything new at the meeting. Dammit.

Chapter Ten
OLIVIA

On Sunday, the school's yoga classes on the lawn start up again, and it feels good to settle into the familiar poses. The combination of yoga and sunlight help keep my hunger to a low simmer, which is easy to ignore as long as I don't let my gaze settle on Kassiel...or one of the Princes.

Tanwen's in my yoga class too, and I cringe a little as I remember our big fight last year. I keep expecting some of her bitchy commentary now that she knows I'm a demon and has even more material to work with. Surely she must hate me—she's a Valkyrie, after all. They're raised from childhood to fight in the Angelic Army against demons, and she probably considers me an abomination, like many others do. My very existence is forbidden, after all.

I wait for the insults or taunts the entire class, but all she does is give me a little nod at the end, when we all grab our things and walk away.

Odd.

I spend the rest of the afternoon doing my homework and

reading, which is light since classes just started. Araceli and I order in pizza from Angel Peak and watch old episodes of Friends. Every time I spot the purple streak in her hair—which I know now is not dyed, but part of her fae heritage—I'm reminded of what the Order said and how they want to use her. I'm doubly glad I'm her roommate again so I can protect her from them. I'm not letting anyone hurt my best friend.

After we say goodnight, I glance out the window toward the bell tower. Are the Princes up there tonight? Do they still gather there to lord over the rest of the school like kings? A pit hardens in my stomach at the memory of being up there with them. When they found out I was a succubus. When they threw me a birthday party. When they betrayed me.

It's time to begin my revenge.

I throw on a hoodie and slip outside, using my Ishim powers to go invisible. The necklace my mother gave me protects me from any Ofanim who might see through my angelic powers, but it hardly matters because there isn't another soul out tonight. Not at this late hour. Angels are definitely not night owls...and I definitely am.

I stroll toward the parking lot with a bag over my shoulder containing the means of my revenge. This is only stage one, my opening shot, and after tonight, they'll know its war between us.

My poor, battered Honda sits on one end of the parking lot. Last year, Callan broke my windshield and left me a note telling me I didn't belong at Seraphim Academy. It wasn't cheap getting it fixed, and now it's time to get even.

Callan's convertible Audi stands out from the rest of the cars, with its ostentatious red color and shiny silver rims. I slowly run my hands along the side of it, knowing no one will see me, not even the video cameras that are trained on this lot. Is Bastien watching them now, wondering if I'll sneak out again for a quick meal? Probably. But he won't see anything tonight.

I remove the canister from my bag and put on a mask over my mouth and nose. Still invisible, I begin my work, and can't help but grin as it comes out even better than I expected.

It takes me hours, but it's worth it. So very worth it.

I can't wait to see Callan's face in the morning.

———

"*Y*ou're up early," Araceli says, when she exits her room in the morning to grab a cup of coffee.

I'm already dressed and getting my bag ready. "I want to get to the cafeteria early. Care to join me?"

"Sure," she says. "Any particular reason why?"

"It might be entertaining," I say with a sly smile.

Araceli raises her eyebrows. "You started, didn't you?"

"Maaaaybe."

She lets out a whoop and runs back into her room to throw on some clothes. Five minutes later, we're heading out of our dorm, and I'm pleased to see there's already a crowd gathering in the parking lot. We join it, along with other students who can't help but be drawn to the spectacle. No one is outright laughing, but I see a lot of grins and hear hushed whispers and giggles, like we're all sharing an amusing secret. And in the center of the crowd is the thing we're all staring at—Callan's convertible Audi, no longer bright red, but now a glittery hot pink that sparkles under the morning light. Across the top of the windshield, pink and white letters spell out PRETTY PRINCESS. It looks like a real-life Barbie car.

"I can't believe you actually did it," Araceli says. "Respect, girl."

A hush comes over the crowd, and even though I don't turn my head, I know the Princes have arrived. Two of them, anyway.

Callan stomps through the parking lot, practically shoving people out of the way. The crowd parts like water, and when he gets that first view of his car, his whole body tightens with fury. His rage is beautiful in its intensity, and the students in the crowd no longer think it's funny. They step back and duck their heads, as if they're afraid to be caught looking at my prank.

"Who did this?" Callan roars, glancing around, sending people scurrying like pigeons.

Bastien leans over and says something quietly in Callan's ear, and then the two of them turn toward me as one. Pure hatred fills Callan's eyes as he glares at me, and an aura of angry white light surrounds him. Bastien rests a hand on his shoulder, and I wonder what would happen if he wasn't there to hold the beast back. Would Callan shoot me with his burning light? Would he run over and throttle me right here, in front of all these other students?

I stare Callan down, meeting his challenge head on, and give him a sinful smile. His face is absolutely priceless as his fury only grows, but I'm not afraid of him. He's already done his worst to me, and now it's my turn.

I turn on my heels, toss my hair, and walk away. If he wants to retaliate, he'll have to come after me.

Bring it, baby.

———

*C*allan skips Combat Training that morning. Maybe he's too angry to face me. Maybe he's trying to figure out how to get the pink sparkly paint off his car. Whatever the reason, Hilda isn't pleased by his absence, but shows us how to wield an axe with practiced ease anyway.

"I used this move to cleave through an incubus once," she says with a wicked grin, while she slices the heavy axe through the air. Then she glances at me and her smile drops, like she's worried she's insulted me somehow.

When class ends, I tell Araceli I'll see her later and start to head to Fae Studies. Tanwen passes by me, slinging her bag over her shoulder, and says, "That was dirty. He loves that car more than anything."

I shrug. "He deserved it."

"Probably," she says. "But you better watch your back."

My eyes narrow. Last year she had a thing for Callan, even though he only had eyes for me, and she's probably still pissed about it. "Is that a threat?"

"No, just a warning."

I put my hands on my hips. "If you have something you want to say to me, just spit it out already."

Tanwen tugs on her long straw-colored braid and laughs. "I think I'd rather keep you in suspense for now. Besides, someone else is here to talk to you. Good luck with that."

She walks away, and I turn around to see what she's talking about.

Callan stands behind me, his hands still clenched. Everyone else has vanished. We're alone outside the gym, in the same spot where we kissed.

This is where he betrayed me.

"What the fuck was that?" he growls.

"Payback," I reply. "You messed with my car, and I've messed with yours. Now we're even."

"You think this is a game?" His angry eyes search mine, but he doesn't make a move toward me.

"Isn't it?" I poke a finger at his chest, hitting hard muscle. "A game you started, but one I intend to finish."

"Everything I did was to protect you." He grabs my hand, and I tense, waiting to see what he'll do next. He holds it a second longer than I expect as he stares into my eyes, and then he drops it in disgust. "Just stay away from me, demon."

"Half-demon," I remind him sweetly. "Don't worry, I intend to keep my distance from you. But this game? It's only just begun." I lean close, so close my lips almost brush his. "Make no mistake, this is war."

Chapter Eleven

I sink into the desk beside Olivia and give her a long look. I hoped to get through my final year as a student at Seraphim Academy without any problems, but clearly that isn't going to happen, not with our little half-succubus around. That prank this morning was clever, I'll admit, and a fitting punishment for what Callan did to her, but it was also unwise. Callan is a formidable opponent, and he does not forgive easily. If I hadn't been there, I'm not sure what he would have done.

Olivia ignores me as she pulls out her notebook and pens, while Raziel talks to another student just outside the classroom door. We have a few minutes before our Fae Studies class will begin.

"What do you think you're doing?" I ask Olivia in a low voice.

"I have no idea what you mean," she says with a smile. The picture of innocence.

"Even your necklace can't hide that lie." She goes back to

ignoring me, and I pinch my brow before starting again. "Tell me this is a one-time thing. A single prank to get back at Callan, and now it's over."

"I can't do that."

My eyes narrow. "What are you planning next?"

She tilts her head with a taunting smile. "I'm sure you'd love to know."

There has never been a more infuriating woman than Olivia Monroe. Raziel walks in and starts going through some papers on his desk. I pin Olivia with a stern look. "Be careful. Callan is not someone you want to cross. Neither am I."

She drops her smile. "I'm getting really tired of everyone telling me to be careful all the time."

I lean forward and hiss, "Then maybe you should stop being so reckless."

She leans forward too, her face very close to mine. "Or maybe you should treat me like a grown woman who can take care of herself for once."

"I'm only trying to protect you, but you do make it difficult."

She places a hand over her heart. "Aw, Bastien, for a second it almost sounded like you cared."

I scowl at her. "I care about keeping my promise to Jonah. Nothing more."

She bats her long lashes at me, but then Raziel moves to the front of class and clears his throat. He glances at us like he's worried he's interrupting, and I sit back in my chair and gesture for him to begin his lecture.

"Today we're going to start discussing the different Faerie courts, beginning with Summer and Spring," Raziel says. "Together, they're known as the Seelie courts, and in history they've often been depicted as the 'good' fae, although this isn't really correct. They can be just as kind or cruel as any of the Unseelie fae. The Summer court is known for being both brave and volatile, while Spring court members can be both kind and capricious."

He continues on, but I already know everything he's discussing, so I take few notes. Instead, I wonder what else Olivia has planned. Is she going to exact revenge for every-thing we did to her last year, tit for tat? If so, she'll probably go after our rooms next. Or the bell tower.

As class comes to a close, Raziel says, "Before I forget, I want to pair everyone up for your class project. If you've been in one of my other classes before, this should be familiar to you. You and your partner will write a paper on a topic related to the fae, and this year I've decided to let you choose it."

He begins assigning partners, and when he calls Olivia, he pairs her up with me, exactly as I instructed him. I got the idea from Marcus, who did the same thing last year in Demon Stud-ies. Raziel is a good professor, but he's a weak-willed fool, and like most people, he has no desire to go up against the Princes. Olivia's the only person who has ever tried.

She lets out an audible groan when she hears she's assigned to me, and it sounds just like the one she makes when I'm fucking her. I'm instantly hard, and she glances my way. Can she feel it, my desire for her? I shove it to the back of my mind, along with my other emotions. I feel nothing for her. Nothing at all.

When class ends, she turns toward me in the hallway. "What a coincidence that we're paired together."

"Indeed. What shall we pick for our topic?"

"Magical objects." She touches the gold and aquamarine

necklace hanging above her breasts. "I'd like to know more about how they're made."

"Good choice. Let's meet on Mondays in the same time and place as we did last year."

She makes a disgusted face. "Right, when you performed tests on me like a lab rat."

"That was Uriel's decision, and if you'd been honest about your Choir, we wouldn't have had to do that."

"If I'd been honest, they would have kicked me out of school." She shakes her head. "Let's just try to get this paper over with quickly so I can go back to avoiding you as much as possible."

"As you wish." I take her chin as I stare into her green eyes. "But don't forget who provides you with your meals. Unless you want to go back to feeding on strangers?"

She opens her mouth, but can't seem to form a reply, and I gaze down at her perfect red lips. My cock hardens as I imagine what I'd like to do with that mouth. She senses my desire and her breathing hitches, while her eyes glaze over a bit.

"You seem rather hungry," I ask, stroking her soft skin. "Should I come by tonight?"

"Yes, fine," she says with a sigh, before jerking away. "But only for a quickie."

"I'll be there at nine." A satisfied smile crosses my lips as she walks away. She needs me, even if she won't admit it...and I'm more than happy to give her what she wants.

Chapter Twelve

OLIVIA

My classes keep me busy, and two weeks pass by in what seems like only minutes. I avoid the Princes, and they stay out of my way too. My hunger grows, since I took as little from Bastien as possible during our last encounter. I ignore it as best I can, and spend extra time soaking up sunlight to give me strength. That won't last forever though, and I know it. But I can't keep feeding on Bastien either. Sooner or later he's going to start to grow weak, and it'll be my fault.

I receive a message from Uriel that my succubus testing will begin on Wednesday after my normal classes, and that I'll meet with her in one of the rooms in his house. I'm excited to meet another succubus other than my mother, although I'm not sure what kind of tests she'll have for me. I hope I pass.

At the appointed time, Bastien opens the door to Uriel's house and instructs me to follow him. He leads me past the office and deep into the house, where I've never been before. We step into some kind of old-fashioned parlor, where Uriel sits in a chair with curled wood arms, sipping tea across from a woman in a red dress. She's the most beautiful woman I've ever seen other than my mother, with dark brown skin, luscious curls, perfectly pouty lips, and amazing curves. All angels and demons are attractive, but the Lilim have something else, something irresistible that makes it hard to take your eyes off them, and this succubus is no exception.

"Ah, there's Olivia now," Uriel says, as I step inside the room. Will Uriel be attending these sessions too? That could get very awkward. Especially if we start talking about my sex life. Or how I'm sleeping with his son for sustenance. I glance at Bastien in a panic, but he discreetly exits the room and closes the door as Uriel begins speaking again. "This is Delilah. She'll be handling your succubus testing, per Baal's request."

"It's a pleasure to meet you," Delilah says, and even her voice is alluring.

Uriel stands. "I'll leave you two to get started. Feel free to enjoy some tea and cakes."

He exits the room, and I hesitate a second before sitting in the chair he vacated. On the table beside me there are tiny little yellow teacups and a steaming tea pot, along with some cute mini cakes with pastel frosting. I pour myself some tea, even though the whole moment feels like something from a dream.

"How strange to be having tea in an Archangel's house," Delilah says, before bringing her cup to her lips for a delicate sip. "I look forward to teaching you here, in Uriel's quaint little parlor. It's so very chaste, and what we'll discuss is definitely not."

"Teach me?" I ask, confused. "I'm not sure how much Baal told you, but I already know how to control my succubus hunger and how to feed without hurting anyone. I don't think there's much more you could teach me."

Delilah's laugh floats through the air like butterflies with gossamer wings. "My dear, you don't know a quarter of what I have to teach you. Besides, that's not why I'm really here, now is it? We both know I've been sent to evaluate you for Baal. Now, what Baal doesn't know is that I'm also here to watch over you, at the behest of your mother."

My eyes widen. "You know who my mother is?"

"I do. I'm one of your cousins. But don't worry, I won't tell anyone who your mother is." She gives me a wink that could bring humans to their knees.

I sit back with a sigh of relief. It's forbidden for angels and demons to have relationships, and Mother's life could be in danger if anyone found out she gave birth to me. Then the other part of her statement registers, and my eyes widen. "We're cousins?"

"Yes, we share closer blood than most."

I want to ask more, but I get the sense she is being purpose-fully vague, and likely won't tell me anything else. Instead, I ask, "Are you going to test me?"

She picks up one of the little cakes and takes a bite. "No, I already know enough just by looking at you. For one thing, I can tell you're not feeding enough."

"It's not exactly easy on a campus full of angels," I mutter.

She waves a dismissive hand. "There are plenty of places nearby you could go to find prey."

"I tried that last year and it was...challenging. I also got attacked by demons, which didn't make it any easier." I don't mention that I would prefer not to feed on strangers anymore, for fear it will make me seem weak or something.

"You don't need to worry about that anymore. There were rumors of a rogue succubus in the area and a bounty was placed on your head, but that's all over now that you're not in hiding anymore. No demon will attack you, not without facing the wrath of the Archdemons."

That's good to know.

She cocks her head. "If you're not feeing from humans, who are you feeding from?"

"Right now, one of the angels on campus."

"That's it?" She blinks at me. "No wonder you're half-starved. You can't survive on one angel alone—your mother must have taught you that. Not only because it won't sustain you over a long period, but because eventually you will kill this person, just as you would a human."

I stare down into my tea. As much as I dislike Bastien, I don't want to hurt him. "Can we never have a long-term super-natural lover then?"

"No, you can, however you would need many of them. Ideally six to eight, unless they're very powerful, then you might get away with fewer. That way, when you feed regu-larly from all of them, you take less of their life force and don't put them in any danger." Her lips curl. "Of course, the tricky part is finding multiple supernaturals who agree to share you."

"Have you done it?"

"I have in the past, but it never lasts. In the Lilim world we call it a harem, and many young idealistic succubi and incubi try to create one, but find it challenging to maintain. Lovers get jealous and fickle over time. Personalities clash. People leave." Her eyes go distant, and I sense that she's remembering some-thing in her own past. After a moment, she shakes her head.

"It's a lot easier to keep traveling and feeding on human strangers, as you'll soon learn."

I take a sip of my tea and think over her words. She's saying nothing I haven't heard before from Mother, but I foolishly hoped another succubus would have better answers for me. But as Mother said, love isn't for our kind.

"I'll figure something out." I'll have to either start trolling nearby bars again for truckers to bang, or I'll have to take Marcus into my bed again. And probably a few other angels too. But who? Kassiel is off-limits. Callan hates me, and the feeling is mutual. I can't think of anyone else on campus I'd sleep with, unfortunately.

Delilah scrutinizes me. "Have you figured out how to feed off of lust not directed at you?"

"I have." I remember the snacks I used to get from Araceli and Darel, before he was killed anyway. That's not an option now.

"Good. That should help sustain you. One thing you could try is going to a strip club to feed on the lust in the air, but that can only do so much. You could also incite lust in people around you. You do know how to do that, don't you?"

"Yes, but I don't do it often, especially here on campus."

"That's understandable, but I have an idea for how you can do it without getting caught. I assume you sleep in dorms, as they do at Hellspawn Academy?" she asks, and I nod. "When all the little angels are asleep in their beds, send out a wave of lust through the building. You'll give every student in your dorm a sexy dream that will sustain you for a short time."

I sit up straighter. "That's a good idea. Nobody discusses their sex dreams, right?"

She smiles, pleased at my enthusiasm. "Indeed. You'll have

to start small though. A few rooms at a time at first. But that should tide you over until you find more lovers, at least."

"Nothing replaces sex though, does it?" I ask.

"No, but we do what we must to survive." She finishes the last of her tea and sets it down, then rises with the elegance of a queen. "I'll return in a few months to check on your progress. I hope to see signs that you're feeding better by then."

I jump to my feet with a lot less grace. "I'll try."

Delilah reaches out and strokes my cheek tenderly with her red nails for a fleeting moment. I catch a quick glimpse of a gold ring set with rubies, and for some reason it reminds me of the necklace I wear, but then I'm ensnared by her mysterious green eyes, which look just like mine. She's only the fourth member of my family I've ever met, and I almost beg her to stay longer. I have so many questions, but more than that, I just want to spend time with her. But the moment ends as quickly as it began, and she draws herself up and walks out of the room, moving with such confidence you'd think this is her house and not Uriel's.

I stare at the empty doorway with a hollowness in my chest, but then collect myself and set out for the dorms. I have something new to try tonight.

Chapter Thirteen

OLIVIA

When I get back to my dorm, there's a piece of blue paper taped to the door, announcing something new called Family Day in June. I rip it off and scan it quickly. It says all parents will be invited to explore the campus and attend classes with us that day, plus there will be a big feast out on the lawn. I doubt Father will bother showing up, so I leave the paper on the kitchen counter in case Araceli wants it. Her mom will definitely come, but I'm not sure about her dad.

I head into my bedroom, drop my bag on my bed, peel off my cardigan, and then freeze. There's a gold envelope on my desk, like the ones the Order sends...but it's too soon for another meeting, isn't it? Although last year I was only an initiate, maybe now that I'm a full member, I'll be expected to attend more meetings. But when I rip it open, I see it's not an invitation, but something that sends a chill down my spine.

Find a way to bring your roommate's father to campus

before the end of the year. Failure to complete your task will result in the punishment of a loved one.

I ball up the paper in my fist, and then notice my hands are shaking. I should have known the Order would want to manipulate me to achieve their goals. I just didn't expect them to do something like this, or with such an open threat. Then again, they got away with murder last year—what *won't* they do?

I sit on the edge of my bed as I consider my options. I think Araceli wants to reconnect with her dad, and after doing the same with my father, I believe it will be good for her. Convincing her to invite him to Family Day or one of the upcoming soccer games won't be too hard, and I'll be doing it for her benefit, not for the Order. Plus, he must know something about getting to Faerie...which is probably why the Order wants him, of course.

If they want him, it can't be for anything good. What will they do to him if he comes to campus? Kidnap him and force him to open a portal to Faerie? I can't let anything happen to one of Araceli's parents. Then again, it will be easier to stop the Order if we can set up a trap for them, and her father's arrival would be perfect for that. And maybe if he comes to school, he can help us find Jonah too.

My head spins, trying to decide what to do. Manipulate my best friend, and risk her father's life with the best of intentions? Or ignore the Order's task, and put someone I care about—possibly Araceli herself—in danger?

I hear the front door open and Araceli's combat boots stomping through the living room and the kitchen. She pauses, and I imagine she's looking at the Family Day flyer. Probably debating whether or not to invite her father. All I have to do is go out there and convince her it's a good idea. Easy.

No. I've resolved to be a better friend this year, and that means no more lying or deception. The old Liv didn't trust anyone and relied on no one but herself, but I'm trying to change. It's hard for me to accept that I don't have all the answers, and even harder for me to put my trust in someone else, especially after the Princes betrayed me, but Araceli has never done anything to make me question her loyalty.

I touch my mother's necklace. Its purpose is to help me lie and conceal, and I'm very good at both of those things. As an Ishim and a succubus, my nature is to work from the shadows. But maybe truth is the answer sometimes.

I head out into our shared living room, where Araceli is plopping down on the couch and grabbing the TV remote. I pick up the Family Day flyer off the kitchen counter and bring it over to her, questioning my decision with each step.

"Hey, Liv," she says, glancing up at me. She sees the look on my face and sits up a little. "Everything okay?"

"Did you see this flyer?" I hold up the Family Day notice.

"Yep. My mom is going to go nuts when she finds out. I'll never get her to leave." She rolls her eyes. "Are you worried about your dad coming?"

"No, that's not it." I sit beside her on the couch. "You know I joined the Order of the Golden Throne so I could find my brother, and now I'm trying to stop them from the inside."

"Yeah..." Her nose wrinkles in confusion. "After what they did to Darel, I told you I'd help."

"They want all their members to perform tasks this year. I just got mine." I hand her the letter from the Order, which she carefully unfolds.

Her eyes widen as she reads it. "Holy shit."

I let out a long breath. "I told you I was going to be honest and open with you about everything from now on, and I'm trying to do that. I want to know what you think we should do."

She reads the paper again and then looks up at me. "I'm really glad you showed me this, and I know it probably wasn't an easy decision." She chews on her lip a little, and then tugs on her purple strand of hair. "Okay, I'll ask him to come to Family Day."

"Are you sure? It could be dangerous for him."

"I know, but there's no guarantee he'll come anyway, and if he does, then we'll know to watch out for an attack." She hands me the gold letter. "Besides, we have to try. If we don't, they could hurt someone else."

I throw my arms around her. "Thank you, Araceli. I'm so sorry you're mixed up in all this. If I could protect you from it, I would."

She pulls back from my hug and pokes me in the arm. "I'm not the one who needs protecting, girl. You're getting involved with some dangerous people, people who know what you really are now, I might add. Good thing you've got me to watch your back."

I can't help but smile, especially since her words remind me of something Jonah once said. Here I am, trying to protect her from the people who want to use her fae blood, and she's trying to do the same for me. "Yes, good thing."

She rips up the Order's note with her nails, and for a second I think I catch a glimpse of that infamous fae cruelty in her eyes. "Whatever the Order has planned, we'll stop them."

Chapter Fourteen

OLIVIA

The next month passes in a blur of spring, sunshine, classes, and homework. My classes are harder this year than last, and combined with my extra meetings with Bastien and Kassiel, I barely have time to breathe.

Callan finishes his demonstration of all the different weapons in Combat Training, and now we're starting to try them out ourselves. As expected, I find daggers the easiest to work with, and plan to pick them when the time comes. We still seethe at each other during every class, but otherwise pretend the other doesn't exist, which suits me just fine.

The most curious thing is I don't feel any lust from Tanwen toward him anymore. I wonder what changed? Maybe she found someone else over the break? Or has she finally realized he is the actual worst?

In Fae Studies, we move from learning about the Seelie courts to the Unseelie courts, and on Mondays, Bastien and I do research on famous magical objects throughout history and mythology, like Excalibur. He's not as fun a partner as Marcus was, but he gets the job done at least. Meanwhile, I keep hoping to find clues about how to find Jonah, but always end up disappointed.

In Angelic History, Kassiel has started talking about migrations of angels and demons to Earth in the past, like during the Renaissance. Did you know Leonardo Da Vinci was an angel? No, me neither. Then, during our private sessions, Kassiel gives me the demons' perspective on the same lessons—like how they believe Mona Lisa was Leonardo's secret succubus lover. Kassiel knows all the good gossip, for sure.

In Ishim class, we study how to conceal other people and large objects, which is something I hadn't learned yet, and it takes a lot of energy. As does everything in Light Control, where we started out by creating little hovering lights to guide us in the dark, and are now making big flashes that can temporarily blind our enemies. It's exhausting, and all it does is make me hungrier.

Delilah's trick helps. Every night I set an alarm for 2 AM, and then I practice what we talked about during our meeting. I started with a few rooms on my floor, sending a wave of lust to my sleeping peers, while avoiding Araceli, of course. That topped me off nicely, but it didn't last long. The next few nights, I spread my powers to other floors, being careful to skip around a lot so no one suspects me. I have no idea what the dreams are about, but I can feel their intensity as I feed on the desire they create. I hope the dreamers enjoy it as much as I do. It's not as satisfying as sex, but it does the job. For now.

I'm so busy with schoolwork and trying to stay sated that it's easy to forget about my plan to get revenge on the Princes. Then, on a Friday night, there's a knock on my door while I'm reading my Angelic History textbook. Araceli is out having dinner with her aunt, and I'm careful when I open the door—but it's just Marcus on the other side.

"Hey," he says, leaning on the doorway and looking good enough to eat. "How are you?"

I cross my arms. "What are you doing here, Marcus?"

"I just came to see if you wanted to grab a bite to eat with me. We could even go to Angel Peak. Or maybe order in..."

I raise my eyebrows. "Like on a date?"

"Sure, if you want to call it that."

I'm actually tempted by his offer—we don't have any classes together this year, and I sort of miss him a tiny bit—but I shake my head. "That's not a good idea."

"Are you sure?" He reaches out and brushes a piece of hair back from my face. "You look like you need to eat. I can help you."

His voice dips low, and I know he doesn't mean food. His desire rolls over me like a wave, and it's delicious and irresistible, because it's different from the normal lust I get from people. There's real emotion behind it, which isn't something I feel often. Maybe it's because of that emotion that I grab his shirt and pull him into the room, then shut the door behind him.

We're on each other instantly, lips locked, hands roaming, bodies pressed together. Damn, I really missed kissing Marcus. The boy knows what he's doing with his mouth, that's for sure. And his fingers. And everything else. After surviving on nothing but dreams and light for weeks, I can't get enough of this real desire directed at me. I know I should stop this immediately, and that sex with Marcus can only lead to drama, but I can't do it. I'm so hungry I'm physically unable to tear myself away from the man in my arms, even as he leads me to my bedroom.

Once we're inside, Marcus doesn't hesitate. He pushes me down on the bed and yanks my skirt up, then rips my panties off like they're made of tissue paper. His eyes are determined and a little wild, before he drops to his knees and buries his head between my thighs. His mouth and tongue conduct a little symphony on my clit, and I grab onto his thick, luscious brown hair and moan. It's so good, but I need more. To really feed I need his pleasure too, and I need it now.

"Fuck me," I command him. "Hard and fast. Hurry."

"Someone's feeling a little desperate, isn't she?" he asks, as he slides a finger into me, feeling how wet I am for him. He's teasing me now, but it's so good I don't care, even as it makes me hungrier. I practically drool as he drops his pants and slides his hard cock between my legs. He rubs it against my folds, getting it nice and slick, while he stares into my eyes. "I've got what you need right here."

I grab his cock and slide it into me before I go mad. I hadn't realized how much I needed to feed before Marcus showed up at my door, and nothing will stop this until I'm sated. I'm not sure he could leave now if he tried.

But he doesn't want to leave. He wants to sink his cock into me over and over again, in long deep strokes that make me wonder how I possibly went without sex with Marcus for so long. What was I thinking, when it's this amazing to feel him buried inside me? I grab his ass and pull him even deeper, urging him to move faster, needing us to both get off right now. My nails dig into his skin, and his little grunts in my ear are the best sound I've heard in months. Harder and faster our bodies move together, skin against skin, until we're both right there on the edge. Then Marcus kisses me hard and I'm over it, climaxing around his cock, moaning in his mouth, totally lost in the pleasure. He comes inside me at the same time, and his power fills me to the brim instantly. I don't want it to end, and I know Marcus doesn't either because he keeps kissing me, even as our bodies calm and our hearts slow.

Eventually, I roll away from him and sit up. Shit, I just slept with Marcus in a succubus lust haze. I used him for quick and dirty sex, like I did with Bastien. Except Marcus actually cares about me, unlike Bastien, which makes this much more complicated. I have to make sure he knows this isn't something more than sex for sustenance.

"This doesn't mean I forgive you," I tell him.

"Uh huh," he says with a smirk. He slowly stands and pulls on his pants. It's hard to resist pulling him back into bed with me, so I look away.

"I'm serious."

"It's fine. I know about your deal with Bastien, but you can't survive off of him alone. Make the same deal with me, that's all I ask."

I hesitate, but I can't say no. I'm too desperate, and Marcus is too good in bed. His power rushes through my veins, making me feel like I can light up the entire building with magic. "Okay. But it's just sex. You have to remember that."

He leans over, touches my chin, and then gives me a kiss that's somehow both tender and dirty all at once. "Sure it is."

He's so damn cocky, so sure that all is forgiven between us just because we had sex. It makes me want to lash out at him, but he walks out of my room before I can do anything but seethe.

When he's gone, I pull myself together. This is a

dangerous game I'm playing. I have to remind myself that the Princes and I are not friends, not after what they did to me last year. That includes Marcus.

It's time for stage two of my revenge plan.

————

*O*n Saturday, Araceli and I head into Redding, the largest nearby city, to hit up the department stores. We take my car and fill it with stuff that makes us cackle in delight, especially when we imagine the Princes' faces. Then we head back to campus, and we wait.

Araceli lets out a huge groan when I wake her up at 2 AM, but she manages to rouse herself after a few minutes. Thanks to my Ishim classes, I know how to make her invisible now too, as long as I'm touching her. Together we grab some department store bags and fly over to the bell tower, which is dark and empty. The Princes are all in bed, leaving their lair unattended. They claimed this space as their own, another symbol of their authority over the rest of the students, and it's time to mess with it—just like they messed with my room last year.

It takes a few clandestine trips back and forth to bring everything over, and then we begin. Their masculine leather couches are decorated with sparkly pink blankets and pillows. Their dark wood tables get new tablecloths with shiny pink unicorns. Their little mini-kitchen gets pink heart stickers all over it—on the counters, on the microwave, on the fridge—until you can barely see anything underneath them. Sparkly pink streamers hang from the ceiling, while pink shimmering curtains cover the windows. For the final touches, we spray a ton of cheap floral body spray around the room, and cover everything with a heavy dusting of glitter.

"Wait, we almost forgot the best part," Araceli says, as she grabs the last bag. She pulls out tons of little stuffed animals, all super cute and very pink, ranging from unicorns to kittens to bunnies. There's even a pink sparkly llama with a nanny cam in it, which I place in the perfect spot to capture the Princes' reactions when they arrive. We scatter the rest of the stuffed animals liberally around the room, and then stand back to admire our work with a grin.

The Princes' mancave has been completely transformed into a pretty pink princess room, with three sparkly plastic tiaras on the table waiting to be crowned. It's totally over the top and ridiculous, and I love it.

I can't wait to see their faces when they walk in.

I fly into the bell tower, with Marcus and Bastien just a few wingspans behind me. The first thing that hits me is the smell as I set down on the alcove. My nose is assaulted by a strong fake floral scent that permeates the space, and I recoil as it hits me hard in the face. Then my eyes catch up to my nose, and my jaw drops as I scan the room, taking in all the pink sparkles, stuffed animals, and glitter. Fuck, there's so much glitter. We'll be finding that stuff in weird cracks for the rest of our lives.

Bastien lands beside me and covers his nose, then scans the room with disgust. When Marcus lands, he bursts out laughing, doubling over both from the smell and his amusement.

"Open all the windows and doors," I command. We can't do anything else until we air this place out. My eyes are watering just from being in here for a few seconds.

We cover our faces with our shirts and open everything up, then use our wings to create a draft that blows some fresh air through the place. But the smell is only the beginning. Our lounge has been twisted into some kind of pink monstrosity.

I stare at the room for a few minutes, and all I can finally manage to say is, "What the fuck?"

"It's so petty," Bastien says, shaking his head.

"We trashed her room, and now she trashed ours," Marcus says with a shrug. "It's nothing more than we deserve." He plops down on the couch, falling into the pile of pink stuffed animals. "Besides, I think it's pretty awesome."

"How long is this revenge bullshit going to continue?" I ask.

Bastien plucks a unicorn off his armchair and tosses it aside. "So far she's gotten back at you for her car, and this is obviously retaliation for what we did to her room. Assuming she ignores the smaller offenses like vandalizing her door and leaving her threatening notes, she should only have one more act of revenge left." He gives me a hard look. "Exposing a secret to the entire school."

"We have to stop her before it gets to that point," I growl.

"Stop her how?" Marcus asks with a snort. "That sort of thing is what got us into this mess."

I scowl at him. "I did what I had to do."

"Did you?" Marcus throws a stuffed dog at my head, which I catch. "Did you really have to threaten her?" He throws a stuffed llama next. "Or fuck up her car? Or betray her?" His words are laced with anger, and he keeps throwing things at me until there's nothing else within reach.

"Are you done?" I ask, knocking the last of the animals aside. "I did what I thought was right at the time. I didn't know she was Jonah's sister, only that I made a promise to him, a promise to keep Olivia away from this school."

"Some of it *was* particularly harsh," Bastien says, rubbing his chin.

I glare at him. I thought he was on my side. Guess I'm alone here. "Maybe it was harsh, but it was a necessary evil."

Marcus stretches his legs out on the couch and puts on a little plastic tiara, like he's totally cool with all this. "We should've been honest with her from the beginning. It would have saved us all a lot of trouble."

"We didn't know if we could trust her," I reply.

"No, but we knew she was connected to Jonah somehow," Bastien says. "We should have made her tell us how from the start."

Marcus nods. "Yes, and once we knew she was his sister, we should have told her that Jonah went to Faerie on a mission for the Order. We could have worked together to find him, instead of trying to get her to leave the school."

I roll my eyes. "And if we'd known Jonah would go missing, we never would have let him go to Faerie in the first place. There's no point wishing the past could be different. We already made the choices we did, and we have to stand by them. Even if we might regret them now."

"The only way to get this to end is to apologize to her," Marcus says. "Convince her to forgive you. That's what I'm doing, and it seems to be working. Very well, if the other night was any indication." A slow grin spreads across his face, and I want to punch it off. He's fucking her again, no doubt. Him and Bastien. She's got them both under her spell.

"Never." I hate all demons, including Olivia, and I hate that every time I look at her, I want her anyway. She must be using her succubus powers on me. There's no other explanation. She doesn't belong here, and even her brother knew it.

Her half-demon blood puts her at risk and makes her a threat at the same time. But I'm not going to try to get her kicked out again. I've accepted she's not going anywhere, even though I don't like it. Considering demons destroyed my family, I think that's pretty fucking big of me.

"I'll send someone to clean this place up," I say, as I pick up the llama on the floor. Something in it catches my attention, and I examine it more closely. A hidden camera. She's been recording all this, and now she has the perfect video to show the entire school.

I can't let her do that.

I track Olivia down an hour later, as she's leaving her yoga class. I land right in front of her in a rush, making her jump back.

"Callan," she says, her voice breathy and sexy as hell. "Having a good morning?"

I throw one of the plastic sparkly tiaras at her chest. "Thanks for redecorating our lounge. Pink's not my color though."

She catches it with a wicked smile. "Too bad. I thought it was perfect for such a pretty princess."

I grit my teeth at the reminder of my car. "What are you planning next?"

She starts walking back to the dorm, like she doesn't have time for me. "I'm sure you'd like to know that."

I match her stride easily. "I know you were watching us on that camera. You recorded us, didn't you?"

"I don't have any idea what you mean."

I grab her arm to make her stop and face me. "You need to quit this shit. Now."

Her eyes narrow. "Maybe you should listen to Marcus. This could all end if you just apologize."

"I can't apologize if I'm not sorry."

"Then I guess you deserve everything that's coming to you."

Fury rises up in me as I face her, and I imagine pushing her down on her knees and shoving my cock in that pretty mouth to shut her up. As soon as I have the thought, she smiles, like she knows what I'm thinking. She can feel how much I want her.

I release her arm in disgust and step back. "Quit using your succubus magic on me."

"I'm not doing anything. This is all you." She steps closer and runs a hand down my chest. "It must kill you, how much you want me. I see the way you look at me in class. The same way you're looking at me now." She licks her red lips, and I can't help but stare at them. "Your lust is tinged with hate, but somehow that only makes it more delicious."

She drives me mad, but for a second I'm tempted to kiss her anyway, and it takes everything in me to hold myself back. Maybe because she's forbidden fruit. Maybe because she's the sexiest thing I've ever laid eyes on. Maybe because she's the only woman who's ever challenged me.

Either way, it's not going to happen.

I knock her hand away. "You fucked up my car. You messed with my lounge. I accept your punishment as justice— an eye for an eye. But I'm warning you now...stop this before it goes any further. You don't want to push me."

"You're wrong. That's exactly what I want to do." She steps back with a cruel smile. "I'm going to push you until you break."

When I get back to my room, I sit at my desk and watch the recording again with a wicked grin on my face. I originally planned to show the video of their reactions to the entire school, thinking it would humiliate them, but then they started talking about Jonah and Faerie, giving me concrete evidence they've known all along where he is and that they're part of the Order. A video like this could ruin them. Just like they tried to ruin me. All I have to do is share it, when the time comes.

Even though I acted brave in the face of Callan's anger, I still dread going to Combat Training the next morning. We're still trying out different weapons to see which one we want to focus on, and today we're working with throwing knives.

I ignore Callan as best I can, while Hilda barks instructions at us and has us spread around the room to face targets. But then she sends Callan over to help each student with positioning, starting with me.

"Try not to kill me," I mutter, as he moves beside me.

"I think it's more likely you'll kill me." He grabs my hand and adjusts the knife quickly. "Hold it like this."

"Wow, that's some great teaching there."

"Would you rather I spend a long time with you?"

"No, on second thought, let's get this over quickly."

He crosses his arms. "Show me what you got."

I can feel the steady stream of his hate-lust, and it makes my head spin. Hate is a lot like desire, I've discovered. It makes you all hot and sweaty, and unable to focus on anyone else but that person. You think about them constantly. You imagine all the things you can do to them. You want to do whatever you can to get them out of your system.

Callan's hateful eyes are intense as they stare at me. I wonder if he's thinking about fucking me or strangling me right now. Probably both.

I roll my shoulders and focus on the target in front of me, but then Callan's eyes lower to my ass and his lust flares. I drop the knife instead of throwing it, and he laughs.

It's not a nice laugh.

"Don't mock me," I snap at him.

"Sorry," he says, with a haughty smirk. "Do you need me to show you how to hold the knife again?"

I glare at him as I pick up the knife. "No, I need you to stop thinking about fucking me. Your lust is very distracting."

His smirk falls and his eyes go hard again. "Just throw the damn knives already."

I throw one and it hits the side of the target and then clatters to the ground. I grab another, with even worse results. I bet I could do this if Callan wasn't hate-banging me with his eyes. And every time I fail, his cruel smile gets bigger and bigger.

"This is your fault," I say, after picking up the knives off the floor.

"Your inability to throw the knifes correctly has nothing to do with me."

"I thought you were supposed to be teaching me."

He shrugs callously. "I can only do so much for someone so innately bad at combat."

I'm tempted to bury one of these knives in his arm next, but before I can, he leaves to go work with the next student. Finally.

But even once he's gone, his desire hovers around me like a thick cloud, making it hard for me to breathe, or think about anything else other than how much I hate him. I picture his face on the target and throw, and this time, I don't miss.

———

*I*n Fae Studies, Raziel is discussing time in Faerie, which moves differently than on Earth, and he's wearing a bowtie with stars all over it.

"The early hours of the morning are spring. The temperature warms somewhat, the flowers bloom, the animals wake and frolic. In the middle of the day, it shifts to summer. The air gets hot, the sun beats down, and sometimes there will be summer showers. Late afternoon is autumn. As the sun sets, the trees lose their leaves, the air grows cooler, and the animals get ready to sleep. And finally, full dark is winter. It's very cold, the animals are snug in their burrows, and the trees are bare. However, this does change a bit depending on where you are in Faerie. For example, in the Winter Court, that season will be the longest."

He continues on about the layout of Faerie for some time, and then asks if we have any questions.

I raise my hand to ask the question that's been on my mind for months. "What do the fae do with prisoners caught in Faerie?"

Raziel looks taken aback by my question. "I imagine they either imprison them or execute them, but it's so rare, I'm not sure. No one gets into Faerie these days without their permission."

Not helpful at all.

In the last few weeks I haven't learned anything I didn't already know. The fae are reclusive and rarely leave Faerie. A few of them have wings, and all of them have unusual, colorful hair, unless it's jet black or pure white. They have extraordinary amounts of magic and can glamour people, although that doesn't work on Ofanim. Some powerful fae can make magical objects like my necklace. But nothing is getting me any closer to rescuing Jonah, and I'm starting to get frustrated.

"You should go to Faerie and find out," Jeremy says in a low voice behind me. "Maybe they'll execute you like the abomination you are."

My mouth falls open and I spin in my seat to face him, but I'm shocked into temporary silence by his words. I know many people here hate and fear me, but it's rare for anyone to say something as horrible as that.

Bastien speaks before I can, his voice filled with cold menace. "How dare you speak to her like that."

"She's a demon," Jeremy practically spits out.

"And you think you're so much better? You, whose father abandoned his post during the Great War, letting his entire squad die? Whose mother left her family to marry a human?"

Jeremy's face flushes with murderous rage. I'm impressed Bastien knows so much about him. Then again, he probably knows the dirty secrets of every student at this school.

"Jeremy, please leave this classroom until you can compose yourself," Raziel says with a disapproving tone.

The jerk stands up slowly and gathers his things while glaring at me the entire time. When he leaves the room, I relax and sneak a glance at Bastien, but he's back to ignoring me. Everyone else in class stares at us with wide eyes for the rest of the lecture, and I doubt any of us hears what Raziel's saying at all.

As soon as class ends, I hurry after Bastien to catch him outside. "Thanks for sticking up for me."

"It was nothing." His voice is still cold. He's always cold and emotionless. Or so it seems. But he must have felt something for him to snap at Jeremy that way, and I know from watching the video that he does seem to regret his involvement in what the Princes did last year, at least a little. But he still hasn't apologized either, so he's not off the hook.

Chapter Seventeen

OLIVIA

A rare thunderstorm sends everyone into the cafeteria for dinner one Thursday night, and it takes me forever to get food from the buffet. I plop my tray down beside Grace's plate and sit across from Araceli, then nearly faceplant into my food because I'm just that exhausted. It's been a month since I got my second revenge on the Princes, and my classes are kicking my ass. I probably need to feed again too, and not just on food. I had to lay off the sex dreams a little when I overheard two people laughing about how they'd both had a bunch of them recently. I don't want anyone to start connecting the dots. On the other hand, people on campus seem to be hooking up left and right, so they should really be thanking me. Love is in the air—or at the very least, a heavy dose of lust.

At least I know why Tanwen is over Callan. After the sex dreams started, she began dating one of the other Valkyries, a broad-shouldered girl named Marila. They sit together on the other side of the cafeteria with their identical blond hair, and I wait for some petty thoughts to come into my head, but they don't. I guess I'm fine with Tanwen these days. How strange.

"Is that a burn on your arm?" Araceli asks me, as I dig in to my burrito.

I glance down, surprised. "Oh yeah. I got it in Light Control today. One of the Valkyries zapped me. I think it was an accident, but who knows."

"Ugh, of course they did." Araceli rolls her eyes and covers the burn with her hand. Within seconds it's healed, thanks to her Malakim blood. "There you go, all fixed up."

"Thanks." It would have healed within a day or two anyway, but it's nice to have a healer on your side.

Cyrus sits at the end of our table, with his new boyfriend Isaiah across from him. Isaiah is like a ginger version of Cyrus, with his nearly identical hipster jeans and robin blue polo shirt. They're even about the same height. They're another of the new couples that spawned after I started turning up the heat in people's dreams, and there's always an invisible cloud of lust swirling around them. I have a feeling it won't last, but they give me a nice snack whenever they're around, at least.

Cyrus immediately jumps into his favorite pastime— gossip. "Did you hear about the attack in Angel Peak?"

"What?" Araceli drops her spoon in surprise. "No?"

He leans forward and lowers his voice. "Two angels were killed right outside the coffee shop. Their heads were severed... along with their wings."

The others gasp. Wings are a big deal among angels, I've learned. Touching someone else's wings without permission is taboo. Mutilation of someone's wings is a truly horrific punishment, only reserved for the most serious of offenders. And cutting them off? It's a rare, ghastly crime, and it makes the others shudder to even consider such a thing.

"Was it demons?" I ask, my stomach sinking. I don't need anyone to have even more reason to hate me for my demon blood.

"That's what they thought at first, but now there's a rumor going around it was humans instead," Cyrus says.

Grace's eyes widen. "Humans? How could they get into Angel Peak?"

"Yeah, I thought the place was warded so humans couldn't even find it," Araceli says.

Cyrus spreads his hands. "No one knows."

Grace pokes at her food with a frown. "That can't be right. How could humans manage to take out two angels? It must be a demon attack. They're the only ones who would be so heartless." She quickly glances at me. "Sorry, Liv. I didn't mean—"

"It's okay," I say, although it does sting a little.

"They're increasing security around the town to make sure nothing like this happens again," Isaiah says. I almost forgot he was here, since he's so quiet. I guess if Cyrus is your boyfriend, you let him do most of the talking.

The next day, the attack in Angel Peak is all anyone can talk about, and the campus is buzzing with fear. No one knows if demons or humans were behind it, and speculations are running wild. I get more dirty looks than usual, like somehow it's my fault.

It's Friday, which means another after-school lesson with Kassiel. Last week he talked a little about what the Great War was like from the demons' perspective. Kassiel lost his mother during it, and he spoke with passion about the horrors he witnessed when he fought. I was hoping to hear more stories about his time as a soldier, but today I have a more pressing question.

"Do you know anything about the attack in Angel Peak?" I ask, after closing the door behind me. "Was it demons who did it?"

One of his eyebrows arches up. "I see the attack has been weighing on your mind. Come. Sit."

I take my usual chair, and he sits behind his desk, a safe distance away from me. Every session with him is a lesson in restraint and self-control. I'm already thinking about banging him right there on his desk, which isn't a good sign.

"As far as I know, it wasn't demons who did it," he says.

"So it's true?" I ask. "Humans killed two angels?"

"It does seem that way."

I lean back. "Wow. I knew there were human hunters, but I didn't think they were a real threat to us."

"Most of the time, they're not. However, I've heard some stirrings about a group of humans that is growing in numbers called the Duskhunters. They're fanatical and cult-like, but worst of all, they're organized and well-funded. They believe all supernaturals should be wiped off of Earth completely, and will do whatever it takes to achieve that goal. It's possible they're behind this attack, although I'm not sure how they could have gotten into Angel Peak."

I knead my hands as I consider his words. "I spent most of my life afraid of angels and demons, worried about what they would do to me if they found me. Then my worry shifted to the fae, and what they might have done to Jonah. I never thought of humans as a threat at all...until now."

"As long as you stay on campus, you'll be fine," Kassiel says. "The Archangels have sent extra guards to Angel Peak, so the town should be safe too. You don't need to worry. Honestly, angels and demons are still a much bigger threat to you. And the fae, if you manage to make it to Faerie."

"Have you ever dealt with human hunters before?"

"I infiltrated a group of them once." He picks up a pen and idly plays with it as he speaks. "When my time as a soldier came to an end, I began working as a spy for Lucifer here on Earth. During the early 2000s, I was sent to deal with a group of humans in London who worshipped demons. They were Satanists with a murderous side, except they weren't very good at tracking down angels and kept killing humans instead. Lucifer didn't want the angels finding out and blaming us for it, since the Earth Accords were still in the early days back then. And frankly, he's tired of all the bad press too. I joined their group pretending to be a human, and discovered it was their leader who was behind the killings...the others were simply too scared to act against him. I convinced them one by one that demons weren't real, and that they should go back to their normal lives."

I could listen to Kassiel talk about his long life forever. He always has the best stories. "What about the leader?"

A sinful grin crosses his lips. "I convinced him I was Lucifer himself, and that I was displeased with his actions. He was so upset, he ended up jumping off a bridge and drowning."

"A fitting punishment."

"I thought so."

We chat a bit longer about his time with the humans, and then our hour is up. It always goes too quickly, and I'm both sad and relieved when it's over.

He gets up and walks me to the door. "It's been a pleasure, Olivia."

I hesitate, and then find myself blurting out, "Do you want to get dinner tonight? I'm free, and we could keep talking about the humans."

His face looks pained. "I wish I could. More than you know. But it's not a good idea."

I shouldn't feel rejected, but I do anyway. "You're right. I'm sorry. It was a dumb idea."

"It wasn't." He reaches for me, but then pulls his hand back with a regretful shake of his head. "Being alone with you during these lessons is hard enough. I can't handle any further temptation."

"I understand." I hover there at the door, knowing I should go, but delaying the moment as long as possible. Finally I step through the doorway and say, "I'll see you in class."

My throat tightens with emotion as I walk out of the professors' building. I'm not sure how long I can keep doing these lessons—because the more time I spend with Kassiel, the more it breaks my heart that I can't be with him.

Chapter Eighteen

OLIVIA

*N*ext Wednesday, I'm summoned to another meeting with Delilah in Uriel's house. Bastien lets me in, and there's no sign of his father this time.

"He's at an Archangel meeting," Bastien explains, even though I didn't ask.

"Are you reading my thoughts now?" I ask, raising an eyebrow.

"No, I don't possess that power, but it's obvious you were wondering where he was."

"And you're holding down the fort for him, as usual."

He leads me through the house. "Indeed."

"I guess you already know what you'll do when you graduate this year." I study him closely. It's hard to read anything on his face, but he seems troubled. "Does it bother you, that your path has always been laid out for you? Do you ever wish you could do something else?"

His brow furrows. "No. This is where I belong. Why do you care?"

I shrug, honestly not sure of the answer myself. I'm saved from having to reply when we reach the door to the parlor, which Bastien opens for me. He shuts it immediately after I step inside.

Delilah is already siting in one of the old-fashioned armchairs and sipping her tea, today wearing a deep purple that makes her eyes pop. She gives me a dazzling smile as I sit across from her.

"I don't have long today, but I wanted to check in on you. I'm sorry I couldn't do it sooner, but some other matters called me away."

"It's all right," I say, as I pour myself some tea.

"I can see you're feeding better, at least. There's more color in your cheeks, your eyes are brighter, and your hair is shinier."

"Is it that obvious?" I ask, self-consciously touching my hair.

"To anyone else, probably not, but I know what to look for, after years of training Lilim."

"I've been influencing everyone's dreams, as you told me, and that helped." I hesitate and think of my quick and dirty encounter with Marcus. "I also took another lover."

"Good." She takes a small sip of tea. "You do know that two lovers won't be enough though, don't you? Especially as your powers grow."

"Grow?"

She nods. "You're still young and are just now coming into your powers. As you grow stronger, you'll need to feed more. Your hunger will increase until it's all-consuming. Don't risk the lives of the people around you by getting to that point."

"I understand." I pause, staring into my tea. "What if my lovers are the sons of Archangels? Would that help?"

She arches a perfect eyebrow and smiles at me over her tea. "I did feel the lust from Uriel's son when he led you here. Yes, that would make it easier for you, because their life force is so strong. With Archangel blood you would only need three lovers, perhaps four to be safe. But that is the bare minimum."

"How do you know?"

"I've fed on Archangels before, and Archdemons too. Oh, and a few fae royalty now and then." She waves a hand. "When you've lived as long as I have, you get bored and want to sample a little of everything."

"Can I ask how old you are?" I'm not sure if this is an offensive question to an immortal.

"You've heard of Samson and Delilah?"

My eyes widen. "That was you?"

She gives me a conspiratorial smile as she stands. "I'm sorry for the short meeting this week, but there have been rumors of attacks on angels nearby, and Baal wishes me to find out more. I'll try to visit more often from now on though."

"It was good to see you again," I say.

"No, it was my pleasure." She leans forward and gives me a quick kiss on my forehead, surprising me. I look up at her in wonder, and then she gathers her purse and is out the door.

Once she's gone, I sit and go over her words, from the thought of taking another lover, to the news that the demons are investigating the recent attacks also. They're probably trying to determine if it was one of their people or if it was humans, like some suspect.

Bastien opens the door and finds me still sitting there, wrapped up in my thoughts. "Come," he says.

I obediently follow him out of the room and up the old, rickety stairs with an elaborate wooden handrail. He leads me down a hall and opens a door at the end. We step into a room that seems completely out of place in the old house—everything is black, modern, and very minimalistic, all clean lines and hard angles. It's like someone dropped an Ikea showroom in the middle of this Victorian house. The room is sparse too, except for the large bookshelf along the wall, which is so full of books it's a wonder it doesn't topple over.

It takes me a second to realize this must be Bastien's room. He lives in the dorms with Callan while he's a student, but this is where he grew up, and where he'll likely return after he graduates at the end of the year.

"Why did you bring me here?" I ask, spinning around to take it all in.

"I wanted to speak to you privately."

"About what?" I sit on the edge of his charcoal gray bed.

His brow furrows, and he almost looks...nervous? That can't be. "I've thought a lot about the events of the previous school year, and I regret my involvement in many of them. I was not truthful with you, and I did things I am not proud of. I should not have spied on you, or put a tracker on you, or helped Callan obtain that video—even though I am pleased with the results of those actions."

I tilt my head at him. "What do you mean, you're pleased with the results?"

"As an Ofanim, it is my nature to seek the truth, and you are especially good at concealing it. Though I regret my methods, I do not regret that your truth was revealed. Once knew you were part succubus, we were able to help you with your feeding problem and could protect you better. Once we knew you were Jonah's sister, we understood your actions. Once Callan exposed you, it allowed Gabriel to acknowledge you and for you to be your true self. The truth has a way of setting us free."

He isn't wrong, but I'm still confused. "I don't understand why you're telling me all this."

He scowls at me, like it should be obvious. "I'm trying to ask your forgiveness, though such a thing does not come easily to me."

My eyebrows jump. "This is your version of an apology?"

He shifts on his feet. "Something like that, yes. As I said, I regret that I acted in a way that may have caused you emotional or physical harm."

Wow. I did not expect this when I arrived today. Bastien, apologizing? In his own way, at least? I can't believe it.

I try to imagine everything that happened from his perspective. I arrived at Seraphim Academy as a mystery he was ordered by his father to solve, but I thwarted him at every turn. He thought I was a half-human, but discovered that was a lie. He had no reason to trust me or help me, when everything I did went against his own personal code of honor—but he did.

And he kept helping me, even after everything went south. He was there for me, every time I needed him, without question. He always made sure I was satisfied, even though that wasn't required. He never asked me for anything in return. Our "deal" feels a lot more one-sided when I consider it from his standpoint, but he's never complained.

That's when it hits me. Bastien, cold, unfeeling Bastien, actually cares about me.

I stand up and take his hand. "I forgive you."

"Truly?" he asks, searching my eyes.

I reach back and unclasp my necklace, the one thing

blocking his powers. He sucks in a breath as it's removed. "Yes, Bastien. I forgive you."

He slides his hand around my waist and pulls me toward him, then kisses me hard. It's been a long time since we kissed. During all our sexual encounters, we avoided kissing as part of an unspoken agreement that it would be too intimate an act. But now his fingers dig into my hip as he kisses me with all the emotion he never shows on his face.

Then he pulls back, and his eyes scan me from head to toe, like he's seeing me for the first time. "Your aura. I've never seen anything like it."

"What does it look like?"

"A perfect mix of light and dark, demon and angel, night and day. With a heavy streak of red, carnal desire." His hands slide down my hips. "You're hungry, aren't you?"

"For you, always," I admit, though it makes me feel vulnerable to say it.

He begins unbuttoning his shirt, drawing my eyes to his smooth chest. "You should have come to me sooner."

"I didn't want to hurt you."

He lowers his head, his eyes gleaming with his own dark hunger. "I'm stronger than you think."

Chapter Nineteen

BASTIEN

I've had sex with four women: two angels, one human, and Olivia.

The books say that coitus with a succubus is the most intense sexual experience a person can ever have. My sample size is small, but from my own research, I have to agree.

Then again, it could just be Olivia. She seems to have a strong effect on me, no matter how much I try to resist it. At this point, I've given up trying.

I remove her clothing slowly, savoring the reveal of her smooth, olive skin and feminine curves. Every inch of her seems to be perfectly sculpted to heighten arousal, even in someone as emotionless as me.

Once we're both undressed, we move onto my bed and resume kissing. I rarely sleep here at the moment, since during the school year I share a dorm with Callan. Perhaps it's wrong to do this in my childhood bedroom, but I find I don't much care.

I spread Olivia's legs and move my fingers to her clit. She

strokes my cock at the same time, while our tongues dart in and out of each other's mouths. We don't normally do any of this. We always skipped the foreplay before. I never thought I cared about any of that, but it's actually nice to move a little slower this time.

We continue on like this, until neither of us can resist any longer. With both of us on our sides, I hook her leg over my hips and adjust our bodies until we're lined up and my cock can slide into her. We stare into each other's eyes as we move together as one, and it's the most intimate moment of my life.

I take note of every moan, gasp, or sigh she makes, filing it away for future reference, becoming an expert on Olivia and what brings her the most pleasure. I previously thought she preferred things hard and fast, but it seems she also responds well when it's slow and tender. Very interesting.

More experiments are definitely required. Lots more.

She digs her nails into my shoulder and kisses me harder, and I sense she wants me to bring her to completion. That's the best way to feed her as well, I've found. When both of us come almost simultaneously, she seems the most sated. And above all else, I aim for her complete satisfaction.

I reach down to play with her clit in the way I know she likes, while my cock strokes in and out of her. Her eyes close and she breathes heavier, letting out a soft moan. I sense her orgasm approaching, and it makes me more aroused as well. We rock together faster, and I keep up the pressure on her clit, until she climaxes and tightens around my cock, which sets me off too. We keep moving as the waves of pleasure roll through us, until we can only hold each other and try to get our breathing under control.

I stroke her hair when it's over, marveling at the way it

shines and curls around my finger. She idly rubs a hand along my arm instead of jumping up and running away. Hmm, I could get used to this.

"What was it like, growing up here?" Olivia asks.

I prop my head under my arm and stare at the ceiling. "I don't know how to compare it to any other childhood, but it was fine, I suppose. I grew up with a big lawn to run around on, a large lake to swim in, and a library with all the books I could want."

"Were there any other kids around? Anyone your age?"

"No."

"That sounds lonely."

"There were plenty of students on campus to interact with, along with professors. Hilda and Raziel were especially kind, and would spend time with me when my father was busy. Which was often."

Olivia runs her nails up and down my chest. "What about your mother?"

"She has never been in the picture."

"No?" Olivia bites her lip. "Can I ask what happened?"

"Nothing happened. My parents had an arrangement, and she fulfilled her part of the deal and moved on." There's a bitter taste in my mouth as I say the words. I dislike talking about such things. It's easier to go about my day without thinking about any of this and keeping it locked away in the back of my mind.

Olivia sits up a little and looks at me with interest. "What was the arrangement?"

"I'm sure they covered this in Angelic History, but as immortal beings, supernaturals do not reproduce easily or often, at least in Heaven, Hell, and Faerie. It could take a hundred years, or even a thousand, for a couple to have a child. But that isn't the case on Earth."

"Yes, Kassiel told us about it in class. He said it's one of the main reasons angels and demons started migrating here."

I sit up too and fix the pillows behind us as I talk. "Indeed. Angels tried to regulate the migration, to keep us from moving too quickly into this world and revealing our kind to humans, but demons shared none of those concerns. Eventually none of that mattered though, once the Earth Accords were signed. Michael and Lucifer used the Staff of Eternity, and all angels and demons were sent to Earth, with Heaven and Hell being abandoned and sealed off. Once all of our people were here on Earth, they began to procreate a lot more frequently. Our population swelled with new angels for the first time, and the Archangels became worried."

"Worried?" she asks.

"Worried they would lose power without any heirs of their own. Together the Archangels made a pact to all have at least one child. Raphael, of course, had already had multiple children at that point, but was happy to sire another. My father reluctantly agreed, and chose another Ofanim named Dina, who was a prophet. They had me, and then she gave me up to be raised by Uriel as part of the deal. I've only met her a few times."

Olivia touches her neck reflexively, but she's not wearing her necklace still. "How awful. I'm sure she misses you."

"I don't know if she does."

She leans back on the pillows, totally comfortable with her nudity. "I always wondered why you Princes were born around the same time. I guess this explains it."

"Yes. Five male children, all sired from Archangels. Ekariel was the first by a few years. He was Azrael and Jophiel's son."

"And Callan's half-brother," she adds quietly.

"Yes. He was killed when he was a child, presumably by demons, but there's no evidence of that. Or that he's dead, as a matter of fact. Anyway, Marcus and I were born next, followed by Callan and Jonah." I raise an eyebrow at her. "And then you were next."

"Except I was an accident."

"A lucky one," I say, as I pull her into my arms again. Yes, I could definitely get used to this.

Chapter Twenty

OLIVIA

When I return to my room, I pull out my laptop and play the video again. As I watch the guys admit they've known all along where Jonah is, I mull over the idea of exposing them. Telling the world they knew my brother was going to sneak into Faerie. Revealing they're all in the Order. It would be the perfect revenge for them exposing me as a succubus.

The problem is...I'm not sure I want to do that anymore.

Callan was the true person behind that betrayal, but this video would incriminate Marcus and Bastien too. More than that, it would reveal my brother was in the Order with them.

Is it worth hurting so many people just to get back at Callan? I'm starting to think the answer is no. I'll have to find some other way to get revenge on him. He must have other secrets, and I'm good at sneaking around. I'll find something.

There's still so much I don't know too. Like why they let Jonah go to Faerie. That part infuriates me. I know the Order wanted him to get the staff, and my brother was uniquely qual-ified to find it because of his special ability to change the way he looks, but still, it was risky. What did they think was going to happen? The fae would just hand over the Staff and Jonah would walk out of there with a smile on his face? Even I know better than that.

Pausing the video, I study Marcus's expression and body language, then rewind and watch again, smirking as he throws stuffed animals at Callan. He really was pissed at them for getting him so far into this mess, but I've seen them together since then, so he must have forgiven them.

Now that I've forgiven Bastien, who did much worse things than Marcus, I should probably forgive Marcus too. I know he's sorry for what he did, and he's apologized many times, but somehow his betrayal stings more. He and I grew close last year, and he made me think there might be some-thing real to our relationship—and then I learned he was involved in all their bullying. Even though it was mostly Callan's plan, Marcus could've stepped up and been the one to put a stop to it, but he didn't.

A noise outside my room draws my attention to the sliding door that leads to the balcony. I look back at my laptop, trying to ignore it, but then I hear the noise again. It's like a strange gust of wind, and just when I think it's stopped, some music starts. Someone's playing a guitar, and it sounds like it's right outside my room. Probably one of the other students on their balcony. I listen to the words, about walking through fire or some such, and the voice sounds really familiar. My curiosity piqued, I hop off my bed and head to the balcony.

As I open the sliding door, my mouth falls open. Marcus is

flying outside, his glorious wings flapping slowly to keep him hovering a short distance from my balcony. There's a guitar in his hand, and he's belting out the lyrics to that song by Harry Styles, "Adore You." It's incredibly corny, especially when he grins and points at me during the chorus, but he has a sexy voice and I find myself captivated anyway.

When the song ends, I hear applause and cheers from some of the other balconies, and realize we have an audience. My face flushes, and I gesture at Marcus to come toward me. "Get in here, you're causing a scene."

Our onlookers hoot, and Marcus gives them all a wave and a charming smile before tucking his wings and shooting toward me.

"I didn't know you played guitar," I say. "Or sang."

He lands gracefully on my balcony and his wings vanish as he sets the guitar down. "I stopped after Jonah disappeared, but you inspire me."

I roll my eyes, but I'm smiling too. "You're so cheesy."

"It's true." He steps forward and holds out his hand. This time, I take it. "No other girl has ever made me feel the way you do. For the first time in years, I want to make music again." He brings my hand to his lips. "I'm so sorry for everything that happened last year, and I want to make it up to you. Let me take you to dinner."

"Okay."

His eyes brighten. "Okay?"

"I think you earned a meal after that performance, if nothing else."

He lets out a whoop, and then picks me up like I weigh nothing and spins me around. He sets me down and steps back with a grin. "Come on. I know a good place that's only a fifteen-minute flight from here."

I throw on a sweater and grab my purse, and then we launch ourselves off the balcony. My wings are jet black and blend into the night sky, while Marcus's are bronze and white, his feathers glinting like metal under the bright moonlight. True to his word, it takes about fifteen minutes of leisurely flying before he starts to veer down, and then we land behind a little diner called Angela's. The logo has a hamburger and milkshake with wings.

I raise my eyebrows at Marcus as we set down. "This seems very on-the-nose."

He winks. "You'll love it. Best food for miles."

I glance around. I've been to this little town once before to feed off a trucker at a bar, but otherwise have never had a reason to come out here.

When we step inside, a short, round woman with curly hair rushes over to us. "Marcus, dear! It's been too long!"

"I've been busy at school," he says, with a sheepish grin.

"Who's your girlfriend?" she asks, smiling at me.

Marcus doesn't bother to correct her. "This is Olivia."

"Is she..." She wiggles her eyebrows. "Like you?"

"Close enough," he says with a wink.

"Come, come." She leads us to a booth in the corner. The place looks like something out of the 1950's, with sparkly laminate tables edged in metal and plastic booth seats in neon blue. There's even a mini jukebox below the window.

We slide into the booth, and Marcus immediately leans over and queues up something. "Elvis," he says with a grin. "My mom's favorite."

I raise my eyebrows, but say nothing.

Angela hands us some menus and tells us to order anything, before heading behind the counter. "On the house, of course."

"What's that all about?" I ask when she's gone.

"I'm a very loveable guy," Marcus says.

"She knows about...our kind."

"Jonah and I used to come here during our first year at Seraphim Academy in the middle of the night to get waffles and chicken. They're the best, you have to order them." He doesn't even glance at the plastic menu in front of him. "Angela was always kind to us. Treated us like a mom. Made us feel a little less homesick, you know? Anyway, one night, she had a heart attack right there behind the counter. A bad one. Jonah called 911, but I knew no one would arrive in time, not out here in the boonies. So I healed her, even though we're not supposed to do things like that. Jonah used his Ishim invisibility to keep anyone else from seeing what was happening, but there was no hiding the healing glow from Angela. She was already a believer in angels and a devout Christian, and she swears she saw my wings. After that, it was impossible to convince her we weren't angels. So I just gave up, and let her feed me."

"A good deed," I admit. "But you could have gotten in a lot of trouble for that."

He spreads his hands. "What's the point in having these powers if not to help people? And not just angels, but everyone here on Earth?"

"That sounds odd coming from someone in the Order."

He looks out the window with a frown. "I was invited to join the Order, and it seemed like a cool clique that all my friends were joining. Once I realized what they were really about, it was too late to back out."

Angela comes and takes our order, and I let Marcus talk me into trying these infamous chicken and waffles.

Once we're alone again, I sigh. "I'm still upset with you."

Marcus shakes his head with a smile. "You said you forgive me. You're not allowed to take that back."

"I forgive you for your part in how the three of you treated me last year. I don't forgive you for letting Jonah go to Faerie."

Marcus's face darkens. "I didn't want him to go."

"Then why did you let him?" I throw my hands up. "All three of you knew where he was going. Even Grace knew. Did not one of you stop and think, hmm, this might be a bad idea?"

"Of course we did. I tried to talk him out of it, but he wouldn't listen."

"What about Callan and Bastien?"

He hesitates. "Callan hates demons, as you know. His half-brother Ekariel was killed by them as a kid, and then there was Michael's murder... Plus Jonah kept talking about duty and honor, and you know Callan is all about that shit."

I nod. "I get why Callan would be on board with getting the Staff, but what about Bastien? I've never gotten the sense that he hates demons."

"No, he doesn't, or no more than he hates people in general, anyway," Marcus says with a snort. "But Bastien is a scholar at heart, and the thought of retrieving the Staff and being able to study it proved irresistible. He warned Jonah of the dangers, but ultimately encouraged him to go."

I shake my head. "This is bullshit. The three of you should have stopped him."

Marcus sighs and slumps his shoulders. "Even if we wanted to, we couldn't have stopped him. The Order found out somehow that Jonah could change his appearance, and then they were determined to use him. And he agreed, all too easily."

Angela brings us some sodas, and then I ask, "So you are all members of the Order?"

"Yeah, we are. Jonah was too."

I already knew all that, but it's good to hear it from Marcus's mouth. "How did they find out about his power?"

Marcus shrugs. "I don't know. He wasn't exactly careful about hiding it. Maybe someone saw him. Maybe he told someone."

I believe it. He was so proud when he showed off his new skill to me, and then he went missing not long after.

"But why would Jonah want to get the Staff anyway? He doesn't want to send the demons back to Hell." Not the Jonah I knew, anyway.

He pokes at his soda with a straw. "At the time, I thought he did. He was dating Grace, who is a true believer in the Order and their purpose, and he kept talking about duty and honor and how it was the right thing to do. He said he had to do this, and that it had to be him."

That doesn't sound like Jonah at all. And then there's Grace... I'll have to talk to her at some point to get her side of the story.

Our food arrives, and it's just as delicious as Marcus said it would be. I can see now why he and Jonah came here all the time. My chest clenches as I think of Jonah, and how he's been gone for so long now.

"Letting Jonah go to Faerie is one of many things I regret when it comes to your brother," Marcus says. "I want to do whatever I can to make things right. With you, and with him. So if you have a plan for rescuing Jonah, I want in on it."

I push around a piece of waffle on my plate. "What makes you think I have a plan?"

He grins at me. "Because I know you, Liv. You always have a plan."

True that.

Chapter Twenty-One

OLIVIA

*A*fter my dinner with Marcus, I invited him back to my room, but he gave me a chaste kiss and declined. When he saw my surprised look, he stroked my cheek and said, "I want to show you what we have isn't just about sex."

Naturally, that only made me want him more.

A few days later, we had dinner again, this time in my dorm, and then we slept together. Now we've fallen back into our old groove, and with both him and Bastien giving me regular sex, I have more energy than ever before.

Somehow it's already the beginning of June. This school year is flying by, and I'm no closer to finding my brother. It's frustrating, to say the least. But when Family Day arrives, I jump out of bed with hope for the first time in weeks—hope that Araceli's dad will show up and provide the answers I need about how to get into Faerie and rescue Jonah.

I quickly shower and throw on a cute outfit, one that's not too sexy in case Father comes today, and something I can fight in, in case the Order makes a move against Araceli's dad. I need to be prepared for anything today.

When I head into our little kitchen to grab my coffee, Araceli is already there looking miserable as she eats a banana.

"What's wrong?" I ask, as I pour coffee into my mug, the one Marcus got me after the Princes broke my mug from Jonah. This mug has a little cartoon devil on it with the words, "Coffee fiend," and even though it doesn't replace what I lost, it still makes me smile.

"It's Family Day," Araceli says with a groan. "I'm worried my dad will show up, and I'm worried he won't. I can't decide what's worse."

"Everything is going to be fine," I try to assure her. "If he shows up, then it will give you a chance to reconnect. If he doesn't, then we don't have to worry about him getting kidnapped or anything. Either way, just try to enjoy it, and spend some time with your mom too. I know she's proud of you."

Araceli smiles at me and tugs on her purple streak. "Yeah, she is. It'll be good to see her. But what about you? Are you excited to have Gabriel follow you around all day?"

"Not really." I lean back on the counter and sigh. "I'm afraid it will become a spectacle. I'm one of a kind, and if Gabriel shows up, people will whisper. If he doesn't, they'll whisper even more. Either way, I'll be the center of attention, which isn't my favorite place to be."

She grins. "If it gets to be too much, we can ditch class and hide in our room."

I raise my mug to her in a salute. "Good plan."

There's a knock on our door, and Araceli runs over and opens it. "Mom!" she squeals, and then throws her arms around a woman who looks like a slightly older version of her, but without the purple streak. A pang of jealousy hits me as I watch them hug and smile and catch up. I've never had that kind of relationship with my mother, and in fact, I haven't heard from her in years. Even if I wanted her to come today, she wouldn't be welcome at Seraphim Academy.

I thought that once I was no longer hiding what I was, she would feel comfortable reaching out to me, but I guess that's not the case. She taught me to be a succubus when I was eighteen, and then she just...vanished. I miss her. A lot.

"Hello, dear." Araceli's mom, Muriel, holds her hand out. "I'm glad to meet you again. Araceli has told me so much about you."

With a nervous grin, I shake her hand, hoping Araceli hasn't told her *too* much. "It's nice to see you again also."

Araceli grabs her bag. "Ready to show off our weapons training?"

"Definitely." I get my things and hold open the door for them. "Araceli is a natural with a sword."

"Is she? I was never very good at fighting, so she must get that from her father's side." Muriel puffs up with pride, and that annoying jealous pang is back. I'm not sure Mother's ever been proud of me.

We chit-chat all the way to the gym, and Muriel tells me about how she's recently opened a wildlife rescue in Arizona, where she heals animals and rehabilitates them before re-releasing them in the wild. It's a great use of her angelic powers, since it doesn't attract too much human attention either.

"That sounds amazing," I tell her.

"I got to help out over the break, and it was really great,"

Araceli says. "Archangel Ariel came by too at one point. I'd never met her before, but she was sweet, although a little odd."

She quickly glances at me, probably because Ariel is Jonah's mother. I've never met her, but from what I heard from Jonah and Gabriel, she's very quirky and flighty. She's a Malakim, like Araceli and Muriel, but spends most of her time in nature, healing plants and animals. She has always given Jonah tons of love, but tends to flit in and out of his life like a colorful butterfly. Much of his childhood was spent either traveling with her on various wildlife excursions, or living in her little cottage in the middle of a forest. The rest of it was spent with Gabriel living in an angel community, growing up among his peers. Pretty much the opposite of my childhood spent in human foster care, with no real family or friends, but I try not to let that bother me.

"Yes, Archangel Ariel has been a great supporter of my work," Muriel says, as we reach the gym. "She actually gave me the funding to get started in the first place. She's a good soul, although she's been miserable ever since her son disappeared." Muriel shoots me a quick frown, as though she's just realized I'm connected to Jonah also. "Oh dear, I'm sorry, that must be tough for you also."

"It's fine," I say quickly as I open the door to the gym, hoping we can drop the subject. And then I freeze.

Gabriel stands against the wall in his perfectly tailored suit, radiating power and authority without even trying. But like Jonah, he also looks approachable, like a friendly neighbor who always waves at you from his front lawn.

His eyes light up when I walk in. "Olivia," he calls out, and my heart leaps a little as I notice how happy he looks to see me. I split off from Muriel and Araceli and go to him.

Father hesitates a moment, before giving me a quick hug. "Surprised to see me?"

It must have shown on my face. "A little. I thought you might be too busy."

He clasps a hand on my shoulder. "No, you're my priority now."

I'm saved from replying by Hilda clapping her hands. "Let's get started, class. Pair up, and show your parents what we've been working on."

"I've decided to choose daggers as my weapon to focus on," I tell Gabriel, as we walk to the table with all the weapons on it. I pick up the knife I like to practice with, a small one with a black hilt that fits nicely in my hand.

"You're focusing on daggers?" He sounds so surprised that I glance over at him, worried I've chosen wrong somehow.

"Yeah, why?"

"It's your mother's favorite weapon, too." He rubs his arm absently with a distant smile. "She got me one time. I teleported behind her in her bedroom once, and she was so startled she reacted by stabbing me in the arm with a dark-infused blade. Hurt like the devil, but what did I expect? I learned after that to never sneak up on her."

I stare at my father with my jaw slack. He's rarely mentioned his time with my mother, and never with any kind of fondness. I always thought I was the lucky—or unlucky— result of a one-night stand or a short affair, but maybe there was more to it than that. "Wow. What was your preferred weapon?"

"I prefer to avoid combat when I can, but in the old days I used a spear. You don't see too many of those around now though." He chuckles softly as he picks up a spear from the table.

As the leader of the Ishim, Father commands a large number of messengers, spies, scouts, and assassins. He also oversees the guardian angel program, which is used to protect important people around the world. He's definitely not a warrior, but more of a hide-in-the-shadows type, only fighting when absolutely necessary. Jonah was—no, *is*—the same.

I'm distracted by Callan sparring with Araceli, both of them wielding swords, although his is much larger. He's putting her through her paces, but she grits her teeth and fights back with everything she's got, trying to make her mom proud. She manages to disarm Callan, and ends with her sword at his neck and a big grin on her face. It seems a little too easy, and I wonder if Callan let her win. Araceli is a good fighter, but she's not *that* good. But I have a hard time believing Callan would lose on purpose either—his ego is way too big for that.

When they're done, Muriel claps, and Gabriel and I join in also. "Good show," Father calls out.

Callan pauses, and then walks over to us and bows his head to Gabriel. I've never seen him look so humble before. "Sir."

Father shakes Callan's hand. "It's been far too long. Is your mother here today?"

"No, she couldn't make it," Callan says. "Something came up at Aerie Industries."

Like Jonah, Callan's got the blood of two Archangels flowing through his veins. His father was Michael, the former leader of the Archangels, who was murdered a few years ago. His mother is Jophiel, who took over as the CEO of Aerie

Industries when the former CEO, Azrael, stepped up to lead the Archangel Council after Michael's death.

If Callan is upset by being alone on Family Day, I can't tell. For a second I pity him a little, especially as I glance around the room and see all the other students with their family members, but then I remember I hate him and the pity vanishes.

"Callan's the one who exposed me as a succubus to the entire school," I tell Gabriel.

"Is that so?" Father asks, raising his eyebrows. I have a feeling he already knew, judging by his tone. "I get the sense my daughter is not a fan of yours."

Callan lifts his chin. "I stand by my actions. If I hadn't done it, you wouldn't be standing here with her now."

Ouch. He has a point there. Gabriel's only here as a result of Callan's betrayal, and the reminder stings a little.

"I can't deny that," Gabriel says. "What are you doing in the Second Year class?"

I note the quick subject change, but let it go. "Callan's working as Hilda's assistant for these classes."

"Excellent." Gabriel stands back and waves us on. "Let's see what you've learned so far."

I turn to face Callan, who grabs a short sword off the table, before getting into a fighting stance. He lunges for me and I dodge, twist, and thrust. He taught me some of those moves, which means he's expecting them too, and he quickly retaliates. If I thought he might go easy on me like he did with Araceli, I am sorely mistaken. He slashes at me and nearly gets my arm, but I manage to get away in time. He roundhouse kicks me and knocks me down on the mat, but I roll and slice him along the shin. He grunts and steps back, and I jump to my feet. He rushes me again, and I use a move he showed me last year to let his momentum carry him over my shoulder and to the ground. As his back hits the mat, he drops the sword, and I put my foot on his chest with a satisfied smile.

Father claps for me. "Very good."

Callan stands and checks his cut, which is shallow and already healing. "She's improved a lot since she started."

It sounds a lot like a backhanded compliment, so I shoot him a glare, which he ignores. Then I wonder if he meant it as an actual compliment. No. That's impossible.

G abriel sits in on some of my other classes, and then we head out to the lawn, where the school has prepared a big banquet in honor of our guests. Picnic tables are spread out across the grass, and the weather is absolutely perfect—sunny, without a cloud in the sky, warm, but with a nice breeze. Banners hang between tree branches, welcoming everyone to Family Day, and there's a cheerful atmosphere as everyone grabs food, chats with their parents, and soaks up the sunshine.

I walk onto the lawn beside my father with a bundle of dread in my stomach, worried all eyes will be on us—and they are. We head over to the big buffet tables, and people stop and stare at Gabriel in awe while we grab some corn, barbeque chicken, cole slaw, and potato salad. I knew he was a big deal, but I've never seen other angels around him before. The only good news is that no one is looking at me.

Then everyone forgets about Gabriel completely when Marcus walks into the area with his dad, Raphael. Marcus is gorgeous, but he pales next to his father. The guy is practically sex on a stick, which feels wrong to think about, when he's an ancient Archangel like my father. Raphael leads the Malakim and is considered to be the most powerful healer in the world. It's even rumored he can bring back the dead.

But what he's most known for? Being a total player.

I can totally see it too, as he flashes a suave grin at every lady he passes by, while the sun shoots highlights through his dark curly hair and illuminates his bronze skin. He stops at each table, kissing women's cheeks, greeting everyone with warmth and exuberance.

"What a flirt," I say, without really meaning to, just as Araceli and her mom walk over to us.

"Yeah, he's...quite charming," Father says diplomatically.

"He's probably looking for his next baby mama," Araceli says, and then looks at my father and covers her mouth, like she can't believe she just said that in front of him.

"Araceli!" Muriel says, horrified.

But my father just laughs. "No, she's probably right. I can't even remember how many sons Raphael has at this point. Eight, maybe?"

Poor Marcus. He's being dragged along in his father's shadow, and it seems like Raphael is ignoring him completely as he soaks up the attention. I wonder if that's what his childhood was like—and where's his mother?

Uriel and Bastien, meanwhile, stand on the edge of the festivities, speaking to one another in low voices as they watch over the crowd. Uriel didn't bother to join us in Fae Studies, but I suppose he doesn't really need Family Day to see his son. I'm not surprised to see that Bastien's mother is missing either.

We move to an open table, and I wave Araceli and her

mom over to join us. They sit down, even though Muriel looks a little star-struck to be eating with Gabriel.

"Aren't you proud of these girls?" Father asks Muriel, as if we're in kindergarten and have just completed a finger painting.

"Bursting," Muriel says with lowered lashes. "Couldn't be happier."

"Any sign of your dad?" I ask Araceli quietly, while Gabriel talks to Muriel about her wildlife center.

"No. I wrote him a long email, and left him a voicemail too, so I really hoped he would show up." She sighs. "At least we don't have to worry about an ambush from the Order. Although I'm sorry you couldn't complete your task. I'll keep trying."

"Don't worry about that. I just want to make sure you're okay."

"I'm fine." She does not sound fine.

"I'm sorry, friend." I take her hand and squeeze it under the picnic table.

Raphael appears at my elbow, with his son behind him. "May we join you?"

"Of course," Gabriel says. Muriel's eyes get even bigger as she takes in the second Archangel at our table.

"This must be Olivia." Raphael holds his hand out and gives me a million-dollar smile. "I can see why Marcus is so taken with you."

I shake his hand and feel a little star-struck myself. He's so charming and attractive, it's hard not to get lost in his warm brown eyes. "Hello."

"Where's your mother, Marcus?" Muriel asks. "I haven't seen her in some time and would love to catch up with her."

"She's at home," Marcus says. "She says she's too pregnant to travel."

Raphael holds up his hands in surrender. "This one's not mine, I swear!"

The table all laughs, and everyone relaxes a little. I had no idea Marcus's mother was pregnant, and I wonder who the father is. Combined with all of Raphael's other sons, Marcus is the only angel I know with a big family.

I glance around at the other tables, and spot Grace eating lunch with a pretty redhead who I assume is her mother, plus a boy with the same fiery hair who must be her little brother. Nariel sits with them too, but there's no sign of Grace's father.

Behind them, I notice Tanwen sitting with a muscular man with very light, shiny blond hair. Like Gabriel and Raphael, he radiates power, although not as strongly. That must be Zadkiel, Tanwen's father, and Michael's replacement on the Archangel council. Beside him is a woman with the same glossy hair tied back in a tight ponytail. She looks even taller and fiercer than Tanwen, which is saying a lot. Her sister, I guess. I look around for their mother, and then remember Araceli telling me that Tanwen's mom was killed by human hunters.

Seems like most of us have a missing parent. I guess there are not many functional relationships among immortals.

Lunch passes quickly, and both Archangels are especially warm and friendly with Muriel and Araceli. I'm pretty sure they're trying to make an effort to show inclusion, supporting me and Araceli even though other angels consider us outcasts, and I want to hug them both for it. By the time lunch is over, I'm pretty sure Muriel wants to be next in line for making a baby with Raphael.

We get through the rest of my classes, and even though I

find it awkward to sit beside my dad while Kassiel lectures us on history, neither of them seems bothered.

When my last class is over, I think Gabriel will probably be more than ready to get out of here, but instead he asks, "May we go somewhere and talk? Privately?"

This is unexpected. "Is my dorm private enough?"

He nods, and I spread my wings and head that way. When we land on the balcony, he chuckles. "I could've teleported us here in half that time."

I roll my eyes. All Archangels have an extra power that's unique to them, and my dad's is teleporting. That's also how Jonah can change his appearance, since he has the blood of an Archangel. I wonder if I'll develop bonus powers too, or if being a half-breed makes that impossible.

We head into the dorm, and I'm relieved to see Araceli isn't back yet. Gabriel sits stiffly on the couch, and I sit beside him and grab a pillow to hug against my chest. I have a feeling something is weighing heavily on him. "What did you want to talk about?"

Father studies me for a long moment, and then he says. "I'm worried about Azrael."

"What do you mean?" Azrael is the leader of the Archangel Council, and I've heard he's pretty scary—he's known as the Angel of Death for a reason.

"As you know, angels and demons are forbidden from having relations, and a hybrid child is unheard of. Your very existence puts you in danger. It's the reason your mother and I kept you hidden for as long as we could."

"I know."

"The secret is out now, and there's nothing we can do about it. In a way, it's a relief. I no longer have to deny your existence and can openly be your father in public. But I am also going to be punished for the crime of siring you."

"Punished?" My eyes widen. "How?"

"I don't know yet. The Archangel Council will vote on my sentence at an upcoming meeting. I doubt they'll do anything too severe, but I wanted you to be aware of it anyway. That's why I wanted to speak with you. They might send me away for a while, possibly to Penumbra Prison, and then I won't be able to look after you. As such, I want you to know about the risks."

"Okay." I clutch the pillow tighter to my chest. I don't want anything bad to happen to Gabriel, especially now that we're getting to know each other. "Will you be all right?"

"I'll be fine. You don't need to worry about that." He reaches across the couch and pats my leg. "But I want to make sure you're especially careful over the next few months. If they send me away, no one will stand between you and Azrael. He hates demons, and if it were up to him, we'd restart the war tomorrow. Now that he's the leader of the Archangel Council, I worry he'll want to use you, or possibly kill you to make an example."

"I'll try to be careful. I think I'm safe here. Uriel won't let anything happen to me."

"I hope so." He sighs and drops his head. I've never seen him look so defeated before. "Things would be a lot easier now if I'd taken the leadership position when it was offered to me. Having Azrael in charge can only lead angels down a dark path."

"Why did you turn it down? You seem like the obvious choice to lead the Archangels."

"I turned it down to protect you." He looks up at me with pain in his bright blue eyes. "I couldn't risk having that level or attention or scrutiny on me at all times, not without it leading people back to you. If I'd taken the job, it would have put you in danger."

He gave up the highest position an angel can have. Turned down the leadership of the Archangels. For me.

"Do you regret that decision?" I ask.

He reaches over and takes my hand. "Never. I know it doesn't seem like it, but everything I've done has always been to protect you and Jonah. I just wish my decision didn't put you in greater danger now."

"Wow. Um, thank you." I stammer through the words, fighting the wave of emotion his confession brings up. He might have been an absent dad, but all along he was doing what he thought was best for me.

He nods and slowly rises to his feet. "Don't worry. I'm going to make sure you're well protected." He bends down and presses a kiss to the top of my hair. "I'll see you again as soon as I can."

I stand up, hating that he has to go, and fearing for his future. "Thanks for coming today. Goodbye, Father."

He gives me one last warm smile, and then disappears in the blink of an eye.

*G*abriel appears in front of me, and I nearly deck the guy. I've seen him teleport many times before, but I doubt I'll ever stop wanting to reach for a sword when it happens.

"Thank you for meeting with me," the Archangel says, as he glances around the lounge in the bell tower. "Interesting décor."

"Courtesy of your daughter." We removed most of the pink sparkly stuff, but Marcus insisted we keep some of the stuffed animals, and we'll never be able to get all the glitter off the floor.

Gabriel laughs. "She's full of surprises."

"Would you like something to drink?" I ask, trying to remember my mother's lessons in politeness. It still hurts that she cancelled on Family Day at the last minute. I get that her new job at Aerie Industries is important, but I never see her anymore. Not that we've ever been super close, but it'd be nice to know she is proud of me, like the other parents were with their kids today.

"No, thank you." Gabriel sits in Bastien's armchair like it's a throne. "I've got a very important task for you."

I sit on the couch, my back stiff and straight. "Yes, sir?"

"Your father and I had our differences, as you know. But the one thing we both agreed was that we wanted peace and unity between demons and angels. Nothing has changed in that regard, even after his death."

I nod. As much as I hate demons, I don't want the war to begin again. That's why I wanted to help the Order get the Staff of Eternity, and why I encouraged Jonah to go to Faerie to get it. If they send the demons back to Hell, another war can be averted. That was my hope, anyway.

Now I'm not so sure I want that anymore. As much as Olivia drives me mad, the thought of sending her to Hell feels wrong. Maybe I'm starting to think she belongs here too, as much as the rest of us.

Damn that woman, I wish she'd get out of my head.

Gabriel leans back in the chair as he continues. "Olivia is a sign that things could change between angels and demons, now that both races are living here on Earth. That also puts her in grave danger at all times. I've tried to watch over her as best I can, but I need your help."

"My help?"

"You are a fearsome warrior, are you not?"

I sit up a little straighter. "I am."

"I would expect no less from Michael's son. And as the son of Jophiel, you must be honorable as well. That's why I've chosen you for the most important thing I could ask of you—the protection of my daughter."

Fuck.

"Are you certain you want to choose me? Olivia and I... We don't get along on the best of days."

"I don't care about that. I only care about her safety, and I know you're the person who can protect her the best."

I glance down at my hands. I've been trying to avoid Olivia as much as possible, and this is going to make that a lot harder. But I can't exactly say no to an Archangel.

"Please, Callan," Gabriel says, with more emotion in his voice than I've ever heard. "I've already lost my son. Please make sure I don't lose my daughter too."

I glance away, my jaw tightening at the reminder of Jonah. I made promises to him too about Olivia. Promises that I couldn't keep. Surely he would want his sister to be safe now that she's staying at Seraphim Academy. If I agree to this, I'm not just doing it for Gabriel, but for Jonah too.

"All right," I say. "On my honor, I'll protect her with my life."

"Thank you." He stands and offers his hand, and I shake it firmly. "I feel better knowing her safety is in your hands."

I swallow hard and nod. What the fuck have I gotten myself into?

He clasps me on the shoulder. "I should've been around more for you after Michael died. And while he was alive too, perhaps."

I stare at him in surprise. It was well-known that Gabriel and Michael didn't get along. As the leader of the angelic spies, Gabriel works in the shadows, trying to get information before making a decision. When he acts, he prefers a knife in the back to an outright confrontation. My father, on the other hand, often acted first, usually with violence, and then thought later.

I should know—I often got the brunt of his violence, a secret I'll probably keep to my grave, since there's no way I could tarnish the image of the beloved Archangel Michael. Everyone admired him, and no one knew what a total dick he could be in private. But I think maybe Gabriel knows, from the look on his face now.

"One more thing." His fingers on my shoulder tighten, digging into my skin painfully. "If you ever betray or hurt my daughter again, you'll have to answer to me, and Michael's legacy won't be able to protect you. Do you understand?"

I swallow. "Yes, sir."

"I'm glad we understand each other," the Archangel says.

He vanishes, and I let out a long breath. I better call Bastien and Marcus and get them over here. I'll need their help to protect Olivia, since she won't let me near her. What was Gabriel thinking, putting me in charge of her protection? The woman hates my guts, and the feeling is mutual. Plus she's still plotting some kind of horrible payback for me.

This is going to be a disaster.

Chapter Twenty-Four

OLIVIA

*E*very year the three supernatural schools—Seraphim Academy, Hellspawn Academy, and Ethereal Academy—choose a sport to focus on, and this year it's soccer. It's well-known that the fae always kick everyone's asses at soccer, so our team has been training non-stop, which means I don't see Marcus as often as either of us would like.

Tonight is the first game, and it's against the fae. It's another chance for Araceli's dad to visit her, and another chance for me to complete my task for the Order.

The bleachers are packed as Araceli and I fly over to them. On one side, angels fill the stands, and the other side has a much smaller number of fae. Very few of them like to leave Faerie at all, so these are probably all family members of the players, here to show their support.

As we set down on the angel side, I notice Araceli looks a little paler than usual. "You don't have to be here," I tell her.

Last year, Araceli's boyfriend Darel was killed at one of these games. The Order made it look like it was a demon attack, but we know it was them. She's avoided the games ever since, and as she glances over at the fae side of the field, I think it's not just because of Darel that she's nervous. Araceli has never tried to hide her fae side, but she hasn't exactly embraced it either. I don't blame her, since they totally rejected her.

She straightens up and tucks her purple streak behind a pointed ear. "I need to do this. For me."

I nod. "Do you think your dad will show?"

"Probably not, but I did leave him another voicemail letting him know about the game." She offers me a weak smile. "I am trying."

She looks so sad while trying to put on a brave face, that I throw my arms around her and give her a big hug. "You're doing great."

She gives me a squeeze and then steps back with resolve in her eyes. "Besides, we need to make sure the Order doesn't try anything tonight. Even if my dad's not here, they might try and kidnap one of the other fae."

"We won't let that happen."

We scan the bleachers, but don't see Araceli's dad anywhere. I think she's probably right that he won't bother coming. It's frustrating, and not because of the Order—after reconnecting with my father, I want Araceli to be able to do the same with hers.

"May we sit with you?" Bastien asks, as he comes up behind me. He rests a light hand on my lower back almost possessively, and it sends a little thrill through me.

Callan's beside him, and he scowls as he notices Bastien's hand, but says nothing. I don't really want him anywhere near me, but I guess he's a package deal with Bastien. Ugh.

"We're not really planning to sit," I tell them slowly, then glance at Araceli. Can we trust the Princes? They're in the Order too, and there's no telling what task they've been given. For all we know, they're supposed to steal one of the fae away.

"You don't plan to cheer for Marcus?" Callan asks, making it sound like an insult.

"Of course we do," I snap back at him.

"We want to check out the fae," Araceli says. "Me, mostly. I'm so curious about them, with my heritage and all."

Bastien narrows his eyes at me. "And no doubt Olivia is interested because of Jonah."

"Fine, but we're going with you," Callan says, his voice leaving no room for argument. For anyone but me, anyway.

I shoot him a glare. "No one's inviting you along."

He stares me down. "Too bad. It's not safe for you over there."

"Since when do you care?"

"Since your father put me in charge of your protection."

"What?" I can't keep the horror off my face. "You?"

He raises his chin and gives me a cocky smirk. "Looks that way. So wherever you go, I'll be there, making sure no one tries anything."

I want to wipe that arrogant look off his face so bad. "That's really not necessary. I'm not the one in danger here."

"You're obviously worried about the fae being kidnapped by the Order," Bastien says in a matter-of-fact tone. "We can help you."

"We don't know if we can trust you," Araceli says, and I'm proud of her for standing up to them. Last year, they scared the crap out of her.

"I swear on the light of truth that I have no intention of

harming the fae," Bastien says, and a white glow surrounds him. He makes Callan do the same, and even though he repeats the words with an eyeroll, the light surrounds him too. "There. Now you know we speak the truth."

I glance at Araceli, since I'm not familiar with this, and she nods. "Fine," I say. "Come with us. We're going to patrol the area during the game and look for anything suspicious."

We take a quick walk through the angel side of the bleachers as the game begins. Marcus and the rest of the team run out onto the field to massive cheers. I notice that asshole Jeremy is also on the team, along with Cyrus's boyfriend Isaiah, but don't know the rest of the players.

The fae team runs out next, moving with otherworldly grace across the field. The fae side claps enthusiastically, but don't cheer or yell, like the angels did. Nope, they're way too refined for that. I study them closely, taking my first look at full-blooded fae. Most of the players are men, but there are a few women too. They're all tall and willowy, with pointed ears, sharp, beautiful features, and hair that looks dyed, ranging from sunflower yellow to lime green to snow white.

"How do we know they're not using glamour?" I ask. We learned a little about glamour in the last Fae Studies class, and how the fae can use it to create illusions, change their appearance, or trick people. Only Ofanim like Bastien are completely immune.

"Look up," Bastien says, pointing at hundreds of tiny hovering balls of light scattered above us, which cast a bright glow over the field and the bleachers. "Uriel and I spent hours filling the sky with those. The light of truth prevents fae glamour, along with Ishim invisibility and imp illusions. If anyone plans to make a move today, they will do it without any of those powers."

We stop and grab some hot dogs and beer, while the game continues. I take a minute to watch Marcus run across the field in his sexy little shorts, showing off his sculpted calves, and then cheer with everyone else when he scores. The game is tied so far, which is better than anyone thought we would do, and the crowd is buzzing with excitement.

Then we make our way along the outside of the field to the other side, where the fae are sitting. As we approach, we see two guards at the entrance to the bleachers, who seriously look like extras in the Lord of the Rings. They both hold spears and wear elaborate, shining armor, although the one on the left has bronze leaves on his chest, while the one on the right has copper flowers. They must be from the Autumn and Spring Courts, respectively.

"Halt," the spring fae says, blocking our path with her spear. "What is your business here?"

I hesitate, trying to come up with a quick lie, but Bastien steps forward and offers them the truth, of all things. "I am Bastien, son of Archangel Uriel, and his personal assistant. We come to ensure your people's safety, and to offer our assistance."

The autumn fae looks offended by this very suggestion. "As you can see, we have security well under control."

"Is there anything we can get you?" Araceli asks.

Both fae study her intently for a long pause, before the female guard says, "That won't be necessary."

Their spears continue to block our path, so we turn around and head back. Not much else to do. We're obviously not wanted there, and even though we could fly over them, that seems especially rude, and likely to cause problems between the two schools.

"Whatever happened to fae hospitality?" I mumble, as we make it back to the angel side.

"They're our guests," Bastien says. "If they'd invited us, things would be different."

Araceli asks, "Is there nothing we can do?"

"Not without sneaking over there," Callan says.

"My necklace!" I say, grabbing it. "It should let me go invisible, even with your little light of truth bubbles floating around us. I can fly over the fae side for the rest of the game, just to make sure nothing bad happens to them."

"That could work," Bastien says.

Callan grabs my arm. "I'm coming with you."

I shake him off and step back. "No way."

"I made a promise to your father. Trust me, I don't like this any more than you do, but I must keep you safe. And I know you can make me invisible too."

I pinch my brow, trying to decide if I'm more annoyed with Callan or Father at this moment. "Fine. Callan and I will fly over to the fae side and keep watch. You two make sure everything stays calm over here on the angel side."

Araceli and Bastien nod, and head off to sit with the rest of the crowd. I watch them squeeze next to Grace and Cyrus, and then Callan and I head behind the bathrooms so we're out of sight.

I hold out my hand to him. "We need to be touching for this to work. Don't let go of me."

He nods, but instead of taking my hand, he slides his arm around my waist and pulls me close. He's warm and strong and

I get a taste of his hateful desire again as our bodies press together.

"We don't need to be *this* close," I say, although I don't move away.

He looks down at me with inscrutable eyes. "It will make it easier for you. We don't want to accidentally break contact."

I suck in a breath and try to block out my own flaring lust. Then I gather light around us, taking it from the glowing baubles floating above us, the moonlight, and the lamps around the field. I bend it around Callan and me until we're invisible. "It worked. Let's go."

Callan holds me against him and launches into the sky before I can even extract my wings. He carries me like I weigh nothing as we dart over the field, while I make sure to keep us hidden.

"I can fly, you know," I say, digging my nails into his arms. His really strong, masculine arms.

"This is safer."

I huff, but there's little point in arguing with him when we're already there. I'm reminded of the other time he carried me, when I was attacked by demons and hit with a light-infused blade. His wings are pure white and edged in gold, and I have the strongest desire to run my fingers along them.

We do a few passes overhead, but don't see anything unusual, and then we land behind their bleachers in a spot of grass. Callan sets me down and takes my hand, before stepping back, then wipes his other hand on his jeans like he's got to brush my cooties off him. I roll my eyes and sit on the grass to wait, tugging him down with me.

We wait there for the entire game in silence, and though I worry it will be awkward holding his hand the entire time, it's surprisingly not. Turns out, as long as I'm not talking to Callan, or looking at his stupid handsome face, he's somewhat tolerable. Even as he runs his calloused fingers over the back of my hand idly, as though he doesn't realize he's doing it.

The most action we get is when two fae sneak under the bleachers to make out, before being shooed away by one of the guards. They run off with their shirts half-on, and I cover my mouth to suppress a giggle. Out of the corner of my eye I see Callan smile a little too.

The angels lose the game, despite Marcus's best efforts, and then the fae gather outside the field to depart. I stand up, dragging Callan with me, but can't see what they're doing. We move closer as a large portal opens up, shimmering and circling while the fae walk though it and vanish. The guards huddle closely around the portal with their spears raised to prevent anyone else from entering. One by one the fae head back to Faerie, and I think about my brother, and how Jonah must have disguised himself as one of them to join their group, then followed them inside. What I don't know is what happened after that. How long could he pass for one of the fae before being discovered? Did he find the Staff? And most of all, is he still alive?

Chapter Twenty-Five

OLIVIA

I have a shadow, and his name is Callan.

He follows me between classes with a glower on his face, like he hates me for existing, and hates himself for having to protect me. At one point I ask him, "What is this, the fifties? Want to carry my books for me too?"

He gives me a scathing look. "I'd rather impale myself on my sword."

I'm so over it.

During Ishim class, we're learning how to conceal larger groups of people by making a chain of hands. We each practice turning the rest of the class invisible, but only Grace and I can do it with ease. Nariel promises everyone will get there eventually, but his eyes linger on the two of us. Not with lust though, but something else. Pride, maybe? I can't tell.

This trick will come in handy when I go to Faerie, because I'm starting to realize I won't be able to go by myself. I'll need other people to help me, and I'll need to conceal them. Plans form in my head. The trick is opening one of those portals somehow.

As class ends, Grace walks out with me. "You did great in there. You're very powerful, which I guess is no surprise, with Archangel blood in your veins. Jonah was strong too."

"Yeah." I corner her in the hallway and lower my voice. "Is that why you let him go to Faerie?"

Shock registers across her face, and then it twists with sorrow. "Let him? I begged Jonah not to go. I did everything I could to stop him. I even tried to go with him, in the end. But he wouldn't listen to me. He was determined to go, and to go alone." Her eyes water with tears she tries to blink back. "Every day I wish I'd tried harder. It kills me wondering if I could have done something more."

Her grief is so sincere, I feel bad for even questioning her. "I'm sorry. I had to know."

She dabs at her eyes with her knuckles. "I understand. I would want to know too, if it was my brother."

I spot Callan hovering out of the corner of my eye and grab Grace's arm, leading her in the other direction. "Is there anything else you can tell me, like why he went?"

"To get the Staff for the Order, so that we can return to Heaven and begin to rebuild," she says, as though it's obvious.

"And to send demons back to Hell?"

"That too."

"That doesn't sound like my brother."

She gives me a kind smile. "I'm sure he didn't think it would work on you. Your angel blood probably protects you."

"Probably?" Seems like kind of a big risk to take on a *probably*. One I seriously doubt Jonah would take, unless he changed a lot in the year he was at Seraphim Academy. What did the Order do to him?

Grace loops her arm with mine as we walk. "You seem so stressed these days, Liv. Let's ditch our next classes and go to Angel Peak for some shopping therapy."

Getting away from campus does sound good, especially if I can ditch Callan in the process. "Is it safe there?"

"Definitely. The coffee shop attack was weeks ago, and security has been beefed up since then. No human is getting in that town now."

"All right, I'm in, but we have to go invisible before we fly off. I need to ditch my tail."

She follows my gaze to Callan. "Not a problem."

We head outside and agree on a place to meet, since we can't see each other while invisible, and then set off for Angel Peak, leaving Callan behind.

You probably think we're going to get attacked there, but it doesn't happen. We spend the next couple hours buying new clothes for summer, before heading back to campus. It's exactly what I needed to unwind after a stressful couple weeks, and I'm so glad Grace suggested it. I'm still wary about her involvement with the Order, but I know she's a real friend.

I open the door to my dorm, but then a large hand slams into it and closes it in my face. I spin around to face Callan, because who else could it be?

"Don't ever do that again," he growls. His hand is still on the door above me, causing him to lean in close.

I glare up at him. "You can't protect me 24/7."

The hatred in his eyes burns with an inner light. If I'm not careful, he'll set us both on fire. "What if something happened to you? How would I explain that to your father? You know it's not safe out there, not for any of us, but especially not for you."

"Nothing happened. I was fine."

"This time." He grabs my shoulders like he wants to shake some sense into me. "Do I need to put a tracker on you again?"

"No!"

"Then don't be so fucking difficult!"

His mouth crashes down on me, and that pent-up lust and hate and rage all mix into a kiss that scorches me in the best way. I claw at his broad shoulders, his blond hair, his strong jaw, kissing him back hard, until I'm gasping for air.

When we pull back, we both look shocked and dazed by what we just did. Callan steps back, and the menacing glow around him dies down a little.

"I gave my word to your father, and I intend to keep it," he says. "He cares about you and wants to make sure you're safe. Do you know how lucky you are to have that? Instead of throwing it in his face, accept it and try to let him take care of you, however he can."

I jerk back at his unexpected words. I'm not used to people caring about me, especially not my father. For so long I was on my own, with only Jonah looking out for me, and even he wasn't around much. Now I have family who want to keep me safe. And friends. And...Callan. Whatever he is.

Callan's voice sounds tough, but I sense something beneath it, some hidden pain. I remember how he was alone at Family Day, and I swallow my pride. "All right. I'll try to be less difficult about you protecting me, if you agree to be less of a dick about it too. Give me a little space, or I'll lose my mind."

"I'll do whatever I feel is necessary to keep you safe. Trust me, I don't like it either. I'd rather be as far away from you as possible."

"That kiss just now proves otherwise." I can't help but taunt him. "Or were you recording this one too? Was this another trick?"

"You're the one with the recording. What are you planning to do with that?"

"Nothing. I'm not going to use it. I don't want to hurt the other guys." I run my hand slowly down his chest and speak to him like a lover. "I only want to hurt you. I want to hurt you so bad."

"Then do it already." There's hunger in his eyes, and we both know we're not talking about getting payback. "I'm waiting."

"Oh, it's coming." A new plan is forming. One that involves the two of us and that nanny cam. Seducing him won't be too hard. Not with the amount of lust coming off him, and the pent-up desire in that kiss. He wanted the school to believe that he only kissed me because I used my succubus powers on him, but soon everyone will know he wants me, the half-demon, all on his own.

"And it's going to be good," I say, before stepping inside my dorm. "Real good."

I slam the door in his face.

Chapter Twenty-Six

OLIVIA

I have a hard time sleeping that night as Callan's words replay in my head. They remind me of a time when I was seven years old and playing on the swing at the park.

I wasn't scared as I flew through the air. Not until I saw the ground rushing at my face, anyway. It all passed in slow motion, like in a movie. The sounds around me faded, the other kids' voices disappeared as I watched the wood chips under the swings get closer and closer.

But at the last second, arms wrapped around my chest and legs, and I was flying up again, in a circle. Silver wings flashed around me, flapping through the air. My fear turned to delight as a male voice said, "It's all right, I've got you. You're safe."

Something about the voice sounded familiar, though I couldn't place it. The man set me on the ground and stepped back. For a second I saw the outline of his silver wings, but then they were gone, and I wondered if I only imagined it. "That was a close one."

"Thank you." I tucked my dark, wild hair behind my ear. The counselors at school said not to talk to strangers, but something about this man made me instantly trust him. He had brown hair that looked soft, and his eyes crinkled as he smiled at me. Sunlight seemed to shine down on him, highlighting his profile, and I felt a sense of awe when I looked at him.

"You're very welcome, Olivia."

I flinched when I heard my name, and a small stab of fear hit my heart. I looked around the playground, but nobody was paying any attention to us. Almost like they couldn't see us at all. Weird. "Are you a social worker?"

"No, I'm not." He backed up to show me he wouldn't hurt me. "I just didn't want you to fall."

"Who are you?" I asked.

"My name is Gabriel."

"Are you an angel?"

He gave me a warm smile. "I'm someone that cares about you very much, and will always make sure you're safe."

Those weren't words I'd heard very often in my young life. The family I lived with at the time was pretty good. They fed me regularly, and I was never cold or neglected or beaten. But they didn't love me. I didn't know if anyone ever had.

"Like a guardian angel?" I asked.

Another smile lit up his face. "Yes, a lot like that. Please don't jump off of the swings anymore, okay?"

Oh, yeah. I'd been trying to fly. I'd always wanted to fly. I turned to look at the swings so I could explain why I'd jumped out, but when I looked back at my new friend, he was gone. I glanced around the park, but didn't see him anywhere.

"Olivia!" My foster mother ran up to me. "There you are."

Uh-oh. She looked mad. "I've been right here the whole time," I tried to explain.

She grabbed my hand and dragged me out of the park toward our house. "Come on. You can't play at the park if you're going to disappear on me."

I forgot about that moment until tonight. That was the first time Gabriel visited me. Now I realize he was protecting me from the time I was a child, and that maybe he always did care for me after all.

———

The next morning, Uriel cancels all classes and calls an emergency assembly.

"What's this about?" I ask Marcus, as Araceli and I sit beside him in the auditorium.

He shakes his head. "No one knows, but it can't be good."

A nervous buzz moves through the crowd, and the place fills up quickly. I spot Callan moving down the aisles, but he takes a seat a few rows behind me. Bastien stands to the side of the stage, his hands clasped behind his back. Kassiel and the other teachers form lines along the walls, almost like guards.

Cyrus and Isaiah grab the seats next to Araceli. "There's been another attack," Cyrus says, leaning over Araceli to make sure we all hear him. "It has to be."

Uriel comes out onto the auditorium stage, looking every inch the powerful, immortal being he is. His eyes scan the audience, which quickly falls into silence, and then he speaks. "I've called you here today with some grave news. Three of our students, Gwen Svava, Favelyn Kyrja, and Marila Thruth were killed last night in a pattern consistent with the previous attack in Angel Peak."

My jaw drops at the names, and a shocked murmur goes through the crowd. All three of those names belong to Valkyries, and everyone knows they were fierce warriors. I didn't know any of them well, although I watched Marcus heal Gwen once, Favelyn was in a few of my classes, and Marila was dating Tanwen for a short while, although rumor had it they broke up last week.

Cyrus leans over again and whispers, "Told you."

We all shoot him a sharp look, and he shrugs and sits back, taking Isaiah's hand.

Uriel clasps his hand together on the podium and continues. "All of them were on their way back from having dinner in Angel Peak, when they were shot down between the campus and the town."

Oh shit. That wasn't long after Grace and I went to Angel Peak. I feel like the biggest idiot ever for ditching Callan now, especially after all my big words about not needing protection. If I glance over at him, I'm sure his face will convey his grim smugness at being right. Instead, I look over at Tanwen, who sits with the other Valkyries. Her eyes shine with unshed tears, but her jaw is clenched and her face is hard. She and the other Valkyries look like they're ready to go out and avenge their fallen sisters as soon as this announcement is over.

"Rest assured, we are doing everything we can to both investigate these attacks and prevent them from happening again," Uriel says. "However, until we are certain it is safe, we are locking the campus down. No one is allowed in or out without my permission until the threat is over, not even to visit Angel Peak. We also encourage you to wear a weapon on your person at all time. Hilda can assist in providing you one, if needed. Remain vigilant, and we will get through this threat without losing any more lives." He nods to the audience. "You are dismissed."

Panic grips the crowd as everyone stands and rushes out of the auditorium. A few more people shoot me angry or fearful looks, and I realize Uriel never mentioned who they suspected might be behind the attacks. Do some people actually think I could do this, or are they just looking to me because of my demon blood? We don't even know if demons were behind these attacks, but then again, how could humans take down three Valkyries?

I spot Grace talking with her uncle Nariel outside the building, and I'm relieved to see she's safe, even though she came back with me last night. People rush across the lawn, some carrying weapons, while others huddle in groups with heads together as they talk. The worry in the air is infectious, and I have a feeling it's only going to get worse, especially as people go stir-crazy after being cooped up on campus for weeks.

Classes start up again the next morning, but it's hard for anyone to focus when three of our peers were just killed. Combat Training is especially tense, with Hilda reminding us to carry a weapon on us at all times. I have a dagger in my bag, but probably need to come up with a better solution at some point. Tanwen spars with Callan, and the rest of the class stops what they're doing to watch, especially as she grits her teeth and goes at him with everything she's got. They're both so skilled in combat it's like watching a performance, but then Tanwen begins to glow with an angry light and Hilda barks out an order for her to go outside and calm down. Tanwen drops her sword and stomps outside, giving me a glare as she goes.

In Fae Studies, Raziel tries to teach us about the Faerie Wars, which we're also covering in Angelic History from the angel side, but no one is really listening, including me. During Light Control, our professor Eileen bites her nails and keeps glancing at me, like I might attack her at any moment. A fight breaks out in the cafeteria between two Erelim during dinner, while the dorm's common room is packed with people sitting in little groups, gossiping over the latest rumor.

And the week just keeps getting worse and worse. My mug from Marcus goes missing, and I can't find it anywhere in the dorm. Kassiel cancels our lesson with a note that he has to leave campus for the weekend, which shouldn't bother me, but I find such comfort in our extra hour together. I wonder if he is investigating the attacks, or if he has some other demon-related business.

Then I receive an invitation to the next Order meeting, and remember the task they've given me. I'm still no closer to getting Araceli's dad to come visit her. Still no closer to getting to Faerie. And still no closer to rescuing Jonah, dammit.

Chapter Twenty-Seven

KASSIEL

It's a short airplane flight to Los Angeles, and then I'm in the glass elevator heading up to my father's penthouse condo, staring out over the sprawling city below me. I'm reminded of my last time visiting this city, when I met a gorgeous bartender and took her back to my hotel room, something I'd never done before. I recognized Olivia as a succubus and she ran from me in a panic. Only later, when I met her at Seraphim Academy, did I understand why.

To keep up my disguise, Lucifer and I always meet in Los Angeles, instead of his domain in Las Vegas. This city is a hotly contested zone between angels and demons, although our two kinds battle it out in business instead of war these days. Lucifer has been opening nightclubs across the city as part of a new venture to gain control of it, and he's looking at a blueprint when I enter.

"Kassiel," he says, with his charming smile. He raises a glass in my direction. "Drink?"

"No, thank you."

"Nonsense, you look like you need one." He heads behind the gleaming bar counter and pours me a whiskey on the rocks from his collection of expensive alcohol on the silver shelves. He doesn't ask what I want, and I know he won't let me refuse it.

I sigh, but take the drink. Dealing with Lucifer is always a challenge. "I've been making progress on the assignment you gave me."

"Is that so?" The King of Hell leans against the counter and swirls his drink. "Tell me."

"I've completely infiltrated the Order of the Golden Throne. They trust me and accept me as one of their own. I don't think anyone suspects what I truly am."

"Of course not. There's a reason I chose you." His green eyes shine with pride. "You never fail me."

I bow my head in response to his praise. "As you suspected, they're after the Staff of Eternity. They know it's in Faerie, and they sent a kid to get it last year, but he never came back. Now they're doubling their efforts to get it."

"Those idiots." He takes an angry sip of his drink. "Michael and I worked hard to end the war and stop the extinction of our races, and yet everyone wants to go back to the old ways of hatred and violence. And with Michael gone and Gabriel in disfavor, there's no one to reign the angels in anymore."

I take a sip of my whiskey. It's damn good, and probably as old as I am, knowing Lucifer. Maybe I did need a drink after all. "They still think you killed Michael."

"Obviously." His smile is downright evil. "Who else, but their favorite villain?"

My fingers tighten around my glass. "When I finish this mission, I'm going to clear your name."

He waves a dismissive hand. "I'm not worried about that. Your current task is more important. We can't let the Order get the Staff. Or any of our people either, for that matter. Best it stays in Faerie, but if it does somehow end up on Earth, I want it brought to me for safety."

"I'll do my best." I finish my drink and set it down on the counter. "The Order have given their members tasks this year, and mine is to compile a list of people on Earth with fae blood. I've already included the obvious and well-known ones, but wanted to check with you before adding a few of the more obscure and hidden people, especially on our side."

He strokes his beard as he considers. "Yes, we must make sure you give the Order something they don't already know to prove your value to them as a member. I'll have my assistant get you the information by tomorrow."

"Thank you."

He pours both of us another drink. "What of the half-angel hybrid girl? I understand you've been giving her private lessons."

I hesitate. "Yes, and I've been keeping an eye on her, as you requested."

"And? What is she like?"

I consider my words carefully. "She has a hard time trusting others, which is understandable given her history, but she's level-headed and clever. She doesn't seem biased against demons either."

"Good. She could be a strong ally. The first true hybrid of angels and demons." He stares off into the distance for a beat, perhaps remembering something from his past. "For now, continue your lessons and keep her safe."

"I shall. I assume you heard about the recent attacks in Angel Peak."

"Yes, and I've already sent someone to look into it. The humans are growing bolder every day."

"Have there been any attacks near Hellspawn Academy?"

"So far, no, but Baal has increased the security there as a precaution." He swirls the cubes in his drink. "Do you have anything else to report?"

"Not at this time."

He moves around the bar and faces me, then dusts off the shoulder of my suit. "You look good, Kassiel. Your mother would be proud."

"Thank you."

"Come, now that business is over, we should catch up. There's this amazing Chinese restaurant we could go to nearby. Or we could order in. They have apps for everything now, you know. I do so love this era."

"I should really get back to Seraphim Academy. The campus has been in lockdown after the last attack." Not that it was difficult for me to sneak out. Being able to control darkness in a school of light-users has its perks.

"Already? You've only just arrived." He rests a light hand on my arm. "Stay for a meal at least. I rarely see you anymore."

My resolve falters. "All right. I'll stay for dinner."

It's almost impossible to say no to the devil.

Especially when he's your father.

Chapter Twenty-Eight

OLIVIA

I don my golden robes and mask, then make myself invisible and fly to the cavern's hidden entrance. It's empty out here and there's a layer of fog throughout the forest, giving the place an eerie vibe. I glance around me, worried someone might attack me, even though I know the campus gates are warded from intruders.

The boulder opens for me, and I head down the dark stone tunnel to the Order's hidden lair. Most of the benches are empty still, and I grab a spot on one of them and wait. The leader walks in and stands in front of the empty throne, and one by one, the room fills up with other members in golden robes.

"Welcome," the leader says. "These are troubling times. We have lost one of our own, and we need to remain vigilant now more than ever."

I glance around the benches and notice an empty spot. One of the murdered Valkyries must have been in the Order.

"With such senseless violence, it only proves how much

we need the Staff of Eternity," he continues. "As I mentioned before, you will all be given a special task this year to further our goal of obtaining the Staff. Some of you have already gotten your task, while others will receive it later this year. Has anyone completed their task who hasn't reported it yet?"

"I've compiled a list of all the people I could find on Earth with fae blood," another member says, stepping forward and pulling an envelope out of their robe.

"I've done the same for my task," someone else says.

"Good work." The leader gestures, and another member walks over and collects the two documents. "We shall compare both lists, and see what you have found. Does anyone have anything to report?"

Someone else raises their hand. "I've made small strides toward getting closer to the half-fae here on campus. We might still be able to use her to get to Faerie."

They must mean Araceli. White-hot rage fills my veins, as I wrack my brain trying to figure out who has been hanging around her more lately, but I can't think of anyone.

"Good," the leader says. "Another member is working on getting her father to visit the campus also. Has there been any progress on that?"

Shit, that's me. I step forward hesitantly. "He has been invited to campus twice, but doesn't seem interested."

"Keep trying. Push a little harder. Do whatever it takes to get him here." The leader glances around the room. "Remember, we do not tolerate failure from our members."

I nod and step back, swallowing hard. A few other people talk about the things they've been trying, but no one else has made any real progress, and I'm distracted with thoughts of

Araceli being in danger. I'll have to warn her as soon as I get back.

"That concludes our business for the evening. Let's join the initiates in the forest and see who has completed the first trial. It's always one of my favorites."

The leader strides regally out of the underground chamber, and the golden-robed figures follow in single file. We're ordered to join hands, and someone makes us all invisible. Grace maybe? She's definitely strong enough to do it. Nariel could also. Hmm.

We spread out around the clearing where the white-robed initiates wait, nervously shifting their feet in the dirt. Our leader gives his normal spiel, and then he and some other members step forward to collect the items the initiates have stolen from the professors.

The first person has stolen a pair of Kassiel's briefs from his laundry basket, and a member to my left sighs softly, so I assume it's him. The same thing happened last year, and I wonder if this is some new tradition, or if everyone on campus is just a little bit in love with Kassiel. At least I'm not the only one.

The second person claims to have a necklace from Eileen, but when one of our members checks it with the light of truth, they shake their head. Two golden-robed figures grab the initiate by the arms and drag them out of the circle, while the rest of us stand there, doing nothing. I feel dirty for being one of them.

The third initiate holds up a mug proudly. "This is the half-demon's coffee mug."

Wait, what? I nearly jump forward and snatch it from the initiate's hand, but manage to hold myself back. I thought I was losing my mind, looking for it all over the dorm, but someone actually stole it from me. What the fuck!

"The half-demon is not a professor," the leader says.

"No, but she's the most dangerous person on campus," the initiate argues. "That should count for something."

I can't help but snort, and then glance around hoping no one heard me. Then again, if I find out who snuck in my room and stole my mug, I will become very dangerous where they're concerned.

The leader takes it and examines it. "This is acceptable."

The hell it is! I clench my fists inside my robe. I know the mug will be returned, but it still pisses me off, especially since it means a stranger was in my dorm. I'll have to increase our security somehow to make sure it never happens again. Once again, I feel bad for sneaking into Uriel's office and taking his book last year. It's not quite the same, but it was still a violation, even if I had to do it in to get into the Order.

Do good intentions make up for bad crimes? I'm not sure.

Damn the Order. They force people to steal, cheat, and manipulate. They threaten the people we care about if we don't do what they say. They murder their own kind to get what they want.

I've got to stop them.

───────

*A*s soon as I get back to the dorm, I wake Araceli. "Hey, it's important."

She rubs the sleep out of her eyes. "What's wrong?"

"I just got back from an Order meeting."

That gets her attention. She sits up in bed. "Any news about Jonah? Or their plans?"

I climb into bed beside her. "They're trying to find more people with fae blood on Earth. They want me to keep trying to reach your dad. And one of them said he or she has been successful in getting closer to you."

Realization dawns across her face. "Cyrus."

I look at her in the moonlight streaming through her balcony windows. "What has he done?"

She shakes her head. "Nothing too bad. He's been extra nice to me in class, hanging out with me a lot during meals in the cafeteria, and he and Isaiah took me shopping two weeks ago, before the last attack. You were at your meeting with Kassiel, or we would have invited you too."

"Damn it. I know he's in the Order, so it must be him." I didn't exactly trust Cyrus before, but now he's definitely on my shit list. "You can't let on like you know, or they'll realize I told you. Just humor him for a few days, then come up with reasons not to be around him."

Her face falls. "I thought he was just being my friend. I hoped it meant people were getting more comfortable with me, and accepting me for who I am. But it was all a lie."

I'm angry all over again. Araceli is the best person I know, but so many people are too close-minded to see that. Now she's going to be convinced that anyone being friendly to her is doing it with an ulterior motive. I should know...it's how I feel too.

She sighs. "Then again, they probably threatened to cut off Isaiah's hand or something if Cyrus didn't agree to do this, so I can't be too mad at him."

"Good point." It's just like her to have sympathy for

someone who did her wrong. I pat her on the leg over the blankets. "It just means we have to stick together to take the Order down."

"You should talk to the Princes about it. They're members, right?"

My mouth twists. "Yeah, they are."

"It might be time to get their help. You've forgiven them and given up on your revenge, haven't you?"

"I forgave two of them. I still have plans for Callan. He needs to pay for what he did."

She stares at me with concerned eyes. "Don't become a bully like them in your quest for revenge. You're better than that."

I'm not better though. I'm really not.

The next evening, I spread my wings and fly to the bell tower after dinner. I've finally admitted it's time to confront the Princes.

The three of them are reclining in their private lounge, and I'm sad to see it's no longer pink and sparkly—although there are a few stuffed animals still around. All three of them swing their heads when I land. I'm wearing a little black dress, and they all take a moment to admire how it hugs my curves, giving me a little taste of their lust.

"Olivia," Marcus says with a smile. "What are you doing here?"

Callan raises his eyebrows. "Come to redecorate again?"

I sit in one of the armchairs. "We need to talk."

"About what?" Bastien asks, from where he sits in the other armchair. He sounds tired, and I notice his eyes are bloodshot. Is he not getting enough sleep?

I face each guy in turn. "We need to talk about the Order. I know you're all members. Marcus confirmed it for me."

Callan shoots Marcus a glare, before turning back to me. "And?"

"And I'm a member too. I infiltrated them last year to find out what happened to my brother. Now I'm trying to do everything I can to bring him back from Faerie—but I also want to take down the Order."

"You want to *what*?" Callan's eyebrows are in danger of popping off the top of his head. "Please tell me I heard you wrong and you're not that suicidal."

I scowl at him. "I know it won't be easy. That's why I need your help."

"The Order is thousands of years old," Bastien says. "Its scope extends beyond this school, which is mainly used for recruitment purposes, and stretches to all levels of angel society. They're in every angel community, working in the highest ranks of Aerie Industries, and probably even in the Archangel Council too."

"All the more reason to destroy them," I say. "They're controlling things from the shadows, and most angels probably don't even realize it."

"But why do you want to take the Order down?" Callan asks.

I spread my hands. "Shouldn't it be obvious? They hate demons and they manipulate humans. That alone is enough for me to want to bring them down. But they also killed Darel last year—were any of you involved with that?"

"Of course not," Bastien says.

"Though we did suspect it was the Order," Marcus mutters.

I lean forward. "They sent Jonah to Faerie even though he was just a First Year student. They've asked us to do unethical tasks and have threatened our loved ones if we don't do them. And they want to get the Staff to send all demons back to Hell. What will happen to me if they get it? Will it send me to Hell too? Will it kill me?"

Marcus rests a hand on my knee. "We won't let that happen."

"Good. So you'll help me?"

"Yes," Marcus answers immediately, but Callan and Bastien exchange uneasy glances.

"What?" They can't be uncertain, not after everything they've seen the Order is capable of, firsthand. "You're actually hesitating?"

"How exactly do you plan on defeating the Order?" Bastien asks.

"I haven't gotten that far," I admit. "Right now I'm trying to figure out who their members are and stop them from getting the Staff. Along with rescuing Jonah too."

Callan stands and walks away, rubbing his neck. "You make it sound so easy, but this is more dangerous than you know. They will kill you, without hesitation, if you cross them."

I meet his eyes with a challenge. "I'm not afraid. Are you?"

Marcus clears his throat. "How can we help?"

"Most importantly, we get Jonah back. I'm working on a plan to get to Faerie, and I think I can conceal all of us once we're there—"

"Wait." Bastien holds up a hand to interrupt me. "You plan to go to Faerie?"

"It's the only way to rescue him. I don't trust the Order to rescue him, do you? All they care about is the Staff."

Callan crosses his arms. "If you find a way into Faerie, we'll go with you."

"Thank you." I suck in a breath. "Otherwise, we need to start working together and share what we know. I've uncovered a few other members—Cyrus and Grace, for example—and I can tell you my task is to bring Araceli's father to the school."

"They told me to make sure we win the soccer game against Hellspawn Academy, no matter what," Marcus says, with a shrug. "We're way better than them at soccer, so it shouldn't be a problem."

"I haven't gotten my task yet," Bastien says. "And I know of two of the initiates this year, but that doesn't help us."

We glance at Callan, who frowns, before saying, "Tanwen is a member."

"Okay, that's good to know." I already suspected Tanwen might be a member, and this pretty much confirms it. I debate letting them know about Kassiel, but then decide that's not my secret to share. "Let's all meet here when we can and keep each other updated on anything new we uncover." I stand up and glance between the three of them. "Thank you."

Callan scowls and turns away, while Bastien sits back in his chair and closes his eyes, like he can barely keep them open.

"Are you okay, Bastien?" I ask him.

"Just tired." He waves a hand, but doesn't open his eyes. "It's nothing."

It's definitely not nothing. Delilah's words come back to me. *Eventually you will kill this person, just as you would a human.*

Bastien and I slept together a few days ago. I've had sex

with him for months now, using him for my own sustenance, and I must be draining him dry. Adding in Marcus wasn't enough. I was a fool to think I could survive off of two lovers. I need to add another one immediately, or risk losing both Bastien and Marcus.

Marcus puts his arm around me. "Want me to fly back to your dorm with you? Watch a movie?"

I want to. It sounds like a normal thing someone would do with their boyfriend. But it would probably lead to sex, and I don't know if Marcus can take it. What if I hurt him, like I did with Bastien?

"No, I can't tonight. Maybe some other time."

He leans close and kisses me softly. "Okay, some other time."

Bastien and Callan both watch the exchange—Bastien with interest, and Callan with disgust.

I fly back to my dorm, entering the living room through the balcony doors and closing them behind me. I need to visit the library tomorrow and check out that one good book on Lilim and see if there's anything I can do for Bastien. Does he just need time to recover? Or can I—

I'm interrupted from my thoughts by a banging on my balcony doors. I jump like ten feet and spin around, reaching for my dagger, but it's Callan.

I throw open the sliding door. "Are you trying to give me a heart attack?"

He practically pushes me out of the way as he steps inside. "You're hurting Bastien, aren't you? And probably Marcus too."

I tear my eyes away from him, the guilt punching me in the gut. "Yes, I am. Not on purpose though."

"I suppose I can't tell you to stay away from them."

"I would, if I could." I run a hand through my hair as I consider. "I could go back to sleeping with human strangers, but I'd have to leave campus."

"No. Not an option."

"All right, then I'll have to sleep with other people here. I've been trying to feed off of sex dreams and stuff like that, but it wasn't enough. But maybe I can find someone else—"

"How many angels do you need to survive?"

"Three I think. Maybe four. If they're strong."

He nods with a grim set to his mouth. "Then it has to be me."

I take a step back, my mouth open. "You?"

"I don't trust anyone else, and I'm the strongest person on campus, other than maybe Uriel."

"But—I hate you. And you hate me."

"I also swore to protect you. I can't have you running off and fucking some stranger."

"So you'll fuck me instead?" I let out a laugh that sounds a little crazed. How did I get into this mess?

"I'll do what I have to do." He grabs the front of my dress to yank me closer, and then his mouth slants down over mine. It's so forceful and sudden I bring my hands up to circle his neck, as if I might strangle him. I'm tempted, but then his kiss demands my full attention, and somehow my fingers have started caressing his throat instead of choking it.

His large hand slips down and cups my breast through my dress, then pinches my nipple hard, making me gasp. He groans a little at the sound and pushes me back against the edge of the couch.

I spin away from him and move to my bedroom door,

knowing he'll follow me. As I reach it, Callan claims me again with his hands and his mouth and his body, and I press myself against him, unable to resist. He reaches behind me and turns the door handle, and we practically fall inside. Someone slams the door shut, and I think it's me, but I barely notice anything except his mouth on mine.

Callan picks me up and slams me back against the door, hard. As hard as his cock, which grinds against me as he lifts me up and wraps my legs around his hips. We're devouring each other, hands and mouth and teeth, and all thoughts are gone as I pop open the buttons on his shirt and tear it off him. My dress is next, yanked up and tossed over my head, and then my bra's gone too. He unzips his jeans, I push my panties aside, and then he's inside me, hard and fast and huge. I can only gasp as I stretch around him, but he gives me no time to adjust.

He plunges into me, and each stroke feels like he's trying to conquer me, possess me, master me. But he's given himself up to me, a half-demon he claims he hates, and even though it looks like he's in control, I'm the one with all the power. Sex is my domain, and after one taste of this succubus, he'll only want more and more. Problem is, I'll want more of him too.

He bounces me up and down on him, pumping into me fast like he can't control himself. I wrap my arms around his neck and throw my head back, and his mouth finds my throat and claims me there too. We're both possessed by some kind of madness, and it has nothing to do with my succubus side. This is all us.

Harder and faster our bodies move, his hips thrusting me back against the door and making it rattle. It's intense and rough and so very good and exactly what I needed. Nothing relieves stress like a good round of hot, dirty sex, even with the guy you hate. Or maybe especially with the guy you hate.

Then he steps back, away from the door, our bodies joined as one in the middle of the room. He reaches down and grabs my ass, shifting me higher so he can get a better angle, and I cry out, but not in pain. Not exactly, anyway. I cling to his muscular body as he keeps pumping, and when the orgasm hits me like a freight train, I sink my teeth into his shoulder. He groans and digs his fingers into my ass as he keeps pounding me, before he fills me with his power. It's so strong I would fall over if he wasn't holding me up. Stronger than Marcus and Bastien. Maybe even stronger than Kassiel. It must be the result of his double Archangel blood.

Damn, a succubus could get used to this.

Of course, that would mean fucking Callan again. Because oh shit, I just fucked Callan. Or more accurately, he fucked me. Oh yeah, he fucked me good and hard.

But damn, it was worth it.

Chapter Thirty

OLIVIA

When it's over, Callan drops me on the bed and glares down at me, so I see we're back to our old ways again. He tugs on his shirt, then tosses me my dress, all without saying a word.

Finally I manage to say, "Thanks."

He frowns at me, like he's confused by the word. "How often do we need to do that?"

"Every couple weeks, I think."

"I can do that." Then he wipes his mouth with the back of his hand. "But don't think we're dating or anything. This is just fucking."

I stretch out on the bed, still naked and gleaming with sweat. His eyes can't help but devour me. "Fine with me. I don't want anything more from you. Not now. Not ever."

"One more thing. No one can know about this, or it's over." He grabs my ass hard, kneading the cheeks with his fingers. I wonder if he's an ass guy. Maybe he'd like to put his cock back there sometime. I'm wet again just thinking about it.

I gaze up at him. "What, you don't want anyone to know you're fucking the succubus? Or worse, that you liked it? That even now, you want more and can barely resist?"

He releases me and shakes his head, then stomps to the balcony door. He throws it open so hard the doorframe rattles, and then he launches himself through it with a flash of gold wings. Leaving me there with the door open.

I stand and close the door, then move to my desk, where I've set up the nanny cam that was once in a stuffed llama. After that initiate stole my mug, I made a point to record everything in my room when I'm not in it. Tonight I never turned it off once I got home.

I pull up the recording on my laptop. It got everything from the moment we stepped into the bedroom. Our frenzied fucking. Our conversation afterward. That look of angry desire as he left. It's all there, the perfect video to ruin him. I just have to decide when to strike.

———

A massive crash on my balcony jerks me from my sleep. My heart leaps through my throat as I sit up. Is Callan back? Or am I under attack? I quickly grab for my dagger off the nightstand and jump out of bed, glad Hilda told us to keep a weapon on us at all times.

I slip to the wall and turn on a small light on the balcony, then peer through the curtains. As soon as I can clearly see what's out there, I gasp and drop my dagger. Then I quickly throw open the balcony door.

"Father!" I ask, rushing to his side. He's collapsed on my balcony, completely naked and covered in blood. But the worst part are his wings—they've been butchered, the silver feathers missing and torn, the skin flayed and the bones broken. There's so much blood, I can barely look at the damage without wanting to throw up. "What happened?"

"Help me inside," he gets out through gritted teeth.

I bend down and help him up, and he leans heavily on me as we stumble into my bedroom. He can't retract his wings, and he lets out a small cry as they brush against the doorway. Tears roll down my cheeks at the sound. I may not have a perfect relationship with my father, but seeing him hurt like this is heartbreaking.

I help him onto the bed, not even caring that my sheets will be ruined. He can only lie on his side, with his wings hanging behind him, and every time he moves, fresh agony washes through him and makes his face tighten.

"I'm sorry," he gets out. "I tried to teleport to Angel Peak but I ended up here somehow."

"It's okay. I'm going to get help. Araceli is a Malakim, she can heal you."

"No. Must keep this quiet." He tries to shift a little and groans. "I'll heal...eventually."

"We can trust Araceli." I clasp his big hand and lean close. "I'll be right back."

Rushing out my bedroom door, I yell Araceli's name as I burst into her room. She jumps out of bed with a wild and scared look on her face. She's already got her hand on her sword. "What?"

"My dad. He's in my room and hurt."

It takes her a split second to process, but when she does, she places the sword back in its spot beside her bed, then grabs her robe, running ahead of me out of the room as she throws it on.

She pauses in the doorway of my bedroom and gasps when she sees the bruised and bloody naked angel on my bed. For a second she covers her mouth in horror, and then she gathers her inner strength and composes herself. She rushes into the room and touches Gabriel's arm, closing her eyes as a warm glow emanates from her hands. I've never been so glad to have a healer as my roommate.

As she works, I hover nearby, wringing my hands. "Were you attacked? Was it the human hunters?"

"No," he whispers between groans. "It was Azrael."

"Azrael? Why?"

Father's jaw is clenched tight, but he sucks in a deep breath and opens his mouth. I lean close to hear him. "Punishment. For you."

His words send a shard of ice into my heart. He warned me something like this would happen, but I never imagined *this*. How could they do this to one of their own?

Gabriel's eyes close, and his wings go slack. I rush forward, fearing the worst, but realize he's just sleeping.

Araceli removes her hands and shakes her head. "This is beyond me. I've put him in a healing sleep, but we'll need someone a lot stronger than me to heal him completely. Raphael might be the only angel who can."

"Raphael isn't an option." If this was punishment for me, then the entire Archangel Council must be in on it. "I'll call Marcus."

The phone rings and rings, but then finally Marcus answers with a groggy voice. "Liv? What is it?"

"I need your help in my apartment. Come quickly."

"Be right there."

He flies up to the balcony doors exactly three minutes later, wearing a worn Beatles t-shirt and loose pajama pants. "Oh shit," he says when I let him in, but he rushes forward immediately to my father's side.

"I put him in a healing sleep, but I wasn't sure what else to do," Araceli says.

"Good thinking." Marcus studies Gabriel's wings and touches them lightly, while his face takes on a look of determination. I've only seen Marcus work once before, but never on something as bad as this. "Dark-infused wounds. Whoever did this made sure it would take a long, painful time to heal. This is going to need intricate healing."

I remember when I was cut with a dark-infused blade last year, and how painful it was. I can't even imagine how much agony my father must have been in when he arrived, and I'm grateful to Araceli for knocking him out, and to Marcus for coming so quickly.

"What can I do?" I ask.

"We'll need some water. Both to drink and to clean his wounds."

I nod. "No problem."

I rush out of the room and gather supplies, including some towels from our bathroom. We'll need new ones after this, but whatever. When I get back, Marcus has begun the painstaking job of moving slowly over Dad's wings with his glowing hands. I stand in the doorway, feeling powerless. Callan left only a few hours ago, and his energy still bursts through me, making me feel invincible, but I'm no healer. All I can do is keep out of their way and hope my father gets through this without too much permanent damage.

Chapter Thirty-One

MARCUS

*H*ealing is a lot like playing the guitar, I've learned. Sure, any Malakim can do it, even without training, just like any idiot can pick up a guitar and strum it to make sounds come out. But to actually be a real healer, you need to study for years. You need to learn all the body parts and how they work together, just like a guitarist needs to learn the notes and chords and how to combine them into a song. You need to practice as often as possible. And to be really good, you need to have innate talent.

My father is the best healer in the world. I've personally seen him bring someone back from the dead. My healing is only a shadow of what he can do, and I'll have to use all of my strength and training to heal Gabriel. Even with Araceli here to assist.

"How can I help?" Araceli asks, at my side.

"The best thing you can do is keep him asleep the entire time. I'm going to try to heal what would take weeks or maybe months for his body to heal on its own." I walk around to the other side of the bed to get a better angle, while Araceli puts her hands on Gabriel's head. Olivia hovers at the edge of the bedroom, and I wish she didn't have to see this, but I know she won't leave either. I can't blame her. If it was my dad, I'd stay too.

Gabriel's wings have been shredded. There's no other word for it. I've never seen anything so horrible before, and when I feel the darkness in the wounds, it's obvious dark-infused weapons were used. Otherwise, Gabriel would be able to heal this himself in a few hours, as powerful as he is.

I use my light to heal his bones first, mending them and making them whole, while drawing out the darkness. As the muscles and tendons stitch back together, I grab some rags and wash away some of the blood. It's not just his wings that need healing, though. His collarbone was broken during the attack, and his shoulders also suffered damage. This is going to take hours to repair.

Some time later, I sit down on the carpeted floor with my back against the side of the bed and take a long sip of water. My hands are covered in blood, and I've done what I can for now, but I need a break or I won't be able to go on. There's still so much to do though.

"Are you all right?" Olivia asks, kneeling beside me.

"Just tired. I'm not sure I have the strength to do it all tonight, but I'll try."

Araceli places a hand on my head and frowns. "You're tapped out, Marcus. You need a break. I can try to heal while you recover."

"It won't be enough. Healing these kinds of wounds takes a lot of energy and life-force. Once the sun comes out it will be easier though. Especially if we bring in more healers to help."

"We can't do that," Liv says. "He didn't even want me to get Araceli involved."

"It's fine. Maybe you can get me something to eat. Or some coffee."

"That won't be enough," Araceli says.

"Can you give Marcus some energy?" Liv asks her.

"No, it doesn't really work like that. I'm sorry."

Liv bites her lip. "Maybe not, but... Hang on, I want to try something."

She sits on the carpet beside me and takes my hands, then leans close and kisses me softly. At first I'm surprised, but it's impossible to resist Liv's soft lips, and maybe we both need a little comforting after the rough night we've had.

A rush of power flows through me, and I realize it's coming from Olivia. From her kiss. Energy crackles in my veins like lightning, and it feels different from my own. Violent. Seductive. Powerful.

It's like chugging ten energy drinks at once. I sit up and look at Liv with awe. "What did you do?"

"I'm not really sure. I felt like I was overflowing with Callan's energy and had the strongest urge to try to pass some of it to you. I didn't know if it would work. Did it?"

"Yes." Then her words register and my jaw falls open. "Callan's energy?"

"Is that who was here earlier?" Araceli asks, her eyebrows shooting up. "Damn, girl. I thought you hated each other."

She grimaces. "We do, but you should have seen Bastien tonight. I'm hurting him by feeding on him so much, and Marcus was next, so Callan stepped in to save them. He's doing it for them more than me, I'm sure."

I don't believe that's true. Callan may pretend he doesn't

care about Olivia, but in his own, twisted way, he does. Otherwise he wouldn't go out of his way to torment her, or to make sure she's protected. Even when he bullied and betrayed her, in his mind he was doing it in her best interests.

"Are you upset because I slept with him?" Liv asks.

"No," I say, and wipe the frown off my face. "I was just surprised."

And jealous.

Shit.

Why am I jealous? I can't expect her to only sleep with me. She's a succubus, after all. I knew this would happen when I got involved with her, and she's never tried to hide it. I thought I would be fine with it, and I guess I was, for a while. But I've been struggling with this feeling ever since winter break, when she continued having sex with Bastien and not me. It felt like she chose him over me. Then she forgave him first, which made it hurt even more. Now she's sleeping with Callan, who she claims to hate. Does she care about me at all?

Growing up, I was always one of a dozen of Raphael's sons. He would come by and give me gifts now and then, and shower me with love and attention...but then he would leave again. He would always leave. Even so, I thought he was the greatest guy I'd ever met, and I would do anything to please him. When I got older, I realized he showered his many other sons with the same gifts and love and promises to visit more often. I wasn't special in any way. I was just another one of his many kids.

I'm starting to feel that way with Olivia too.

I offer her a weak smile. "I can't expect you to only have feelings for me."

"The only feeling I have for Callan is loathing. But he is

very powerful, so hopefully he can help you." She leans back on the side of the bed and closes her eyes.

"And now you're exhausted and need to feed again," Araceli says with a sigh.

Liv waves her away. "I'm fine. Just heal my dad. Please."

Right. The reason we're here. I stand up again and face my patient, who already looks a lot better, though there's still much work to be done. I rub my hands together, feeling Callan and Olivia's energy bursting out of my skin, plus maybe a little of Bastien's power in there too. I jump back into the healing with renewed vigor, fueled by Liv's gift.

She grabs a pillow and a blanket and dozes on the floor while Araceli and I work through the rest of the night, only taking breaks for snacks and water. Together we manage to heal Gabriel completely by the time sunlight is streaming through the sliding glass doors. I'm tempted to crawl over to a sunny patch of carpet and fall asleep in it, like a dog.

Araceli leans against the headboard with her eyes closed, but I know she's not asleep because her hands still glow against Gabriel's head.

"It's done," I say, and then collapse beside the bed.

A half-asleep Liv crawls to my side and wraps her arms around me. "Thank you for healing him."

I lean my head against hers and close my eyes. "Anything for you."

Chapter Thirty-Two

OLIVIA

A loud knock on the dorm room door makes me jerk upright.

I blink the sleep from my eyes. The three of us all passed out on the floor after the healing finished, and my dad is still on the bed, though his wings are gone and his naked body has been covered with a blanket. Through the glass doors, the sun is high in the sky, and I check the clock and gasp. We've slept half the day away. No wonder someone has come to look for us.

There's another loud knock on the front door. "Liv, are you in there?" a voice calls out.

"It's Callan," I whisper loudly to Araceli and Marcus, who are also waking up.

Father pushes himself up with a frown. "He can't know about this."

I'm so glad to see him awake that I rush to him and give him a big hug. He holds me close for a second, and then Callan bangs on the door again. I call out, "Be right there."

Father stands, wrapping the blanket around him like a toga, and glances between Marcus and Araceli. "Thank you. I owe you both a great debt."

"Are you okay?" I ask.

"Much better now, thanks to you and your friends. I'm going to the house to rest."

"I'll check on you tomorrow," Marcus says.

"I'd appreciate that," Gabriel replies. Then he vanishes.

"Stay in here and be quiet," I tell Araceli and Marcus. I grab a robe to cover up my blood-stained nightie, before shutting my bedroom door on my way out.

I throw open my door to a red-faced Callan. I think if I waited another few seconds, he would have used his Erelim powers to blast through the door.

"What's going on?" His eyes search behind me like there might be some hidden danger in my living room. "Have you been in here all day? You missed your morning classes."

"I forgot to set my alarm." I shrug and yawn. "I guess you wore me out last night."

His eyes narrow and I'm pretty sure he doesn't buy it. "Get dressed. You don't want to be late to your next classes."

"Yes, sir." I tell him, before placing a kiss on his cheek. "Thanks for checking on me. It's nice to know you care."

He steps back and looks surprised, but then his lip curls in disgust. "Don't get the wrong idea."

"Yeah, yeah." I roll my eyes, but my kiss worked in distracting him. "Now get out of here so I can shower."

I practically close the door on his face, before rushing back to my room. Marcus is gone, no doubt heading back to his room to get some rest, and Araceli is asleep on the floor again. Bless my sweet friend. She didn't hesitate to help my dad, even though he's never done much to warrant her kindness.

She stirs and gives me a weary grin. "Everything okay?"

"Yeah, although we're missing classes."

"It happens," she says with a shrug and a yawn.

I help her up and give her a hug. "Thank you. Now go take a nap."

"I will." She hesitates, her face concerned. She holds onto my hand a little longer than necessary, and I realize she's using her Malakim powers on me. "But what about you? I can feel how weak you are. You gave all your energy to Marcus for the healing. Now you need to feed again."

"I'll figure something out. Don't worry about me. Just get some rest, okay?"

"All right." She shuffles out of my room and back into her own, with another loud yawn.

I want to take a nap too, but I have an impatient angel outside waiting to walk me to my next class. Father doesn't want anyone to know what happened, which means going back to my normal routine. I take a quick shower to wash the blood out of my hair, and a wave of exhaustion and hunger hits me. Shit. I'm definitely going to have to feed soon. But on whom? I can't use Bastien again, not when he's so weak. Marcus is definitely in no shape to feed me either, not when he used all his energy healing my dad. I just slept with Callan last night. I'm going to have to come up with another option, fast.

I raid the kitchen and find a banana, which I devour, along with a bottle of Gatorade. Araceli likes it after a tough healing lesson. Now I know why.

I walk out and give Callan a nod as he falls in step beside me. Once outside, I pause for a minute and soak up the sunshine. It's the end of the summer, the day is scorching, and I instantly feel a little stronger. I should be able to make it through my classes, at least.

———

I get through Ishim class without jumping anyone, barely. The hunger is overwhelming, and I can't decide if I should go back to Callan for round two and hope he can handle it, or sneak off campus to make a quick trip to a human town, despite the danger.

For now, I have to get through my next two classes.

Unfortunately, my next one is Angelic History, and it's a serious lesson in self-control to last the entire hour without ripping Kassiel's clothes off. Not an easy task when I already want to rip pretty much everyone's clothes off and suck their sexual energy from them with a straw. As soon as class is over, I'm going to have to make a quick trip to a nearby trucker bar. I can't wait any longer.

I practically jump out of my seat the minute class is over, but then Kassiel calls out, "Olivia, can you chat for a minute? I'd like to talk to you about your last essay."

No, I really can't, I want to yell, but then the other students would know something is up, so I clench my fists and take a deep breath before heading over to him.

I move beside his desk, and he wipes his whiteboard down with a damp rag while the last of the other students file out. Once the door clicks shut, he whirls around. "You need to feed, don't you?"

"Is it that obvious?"

"Very, at least to someone who has met many Lilim before."

I give him a nervous laugh. "I'll be okay. I'm heading out to find someone to feed on right now."

"Who? A human stranger?" He moves toward me, his green eyes blazing with desire. "You know it's not safe for you to leave campus."

"Stop right there." I hold my hand up to keep him from getting any closer. Damn him and his English accent and sexy scruff and that perfect body in his tailored suit. We both know this can't happen, but it's taking everything in my power to resist him, especially when his lust hovers between both of us.

He takes another step closer. "Let me help you."

Without realizing it, I've backed away from him and pressed myself against the classroom door. The coldness in the wood seeps through my shirt, but it does nothing to calm my need. "You're my teacher. You'll lose your job if we're caught."

"We'll be careful." He offers his hand. All I have to do is reach out and take it, but still I hold myself back. "I'd rather you feed on me than some stranger, so I know you're safe."

"I'm so hungry, I might hurt you." The conviction in my voice is fading. I'm still pressing myself against the door, but my resolve is weakening. And I'm pretty sure Kassiel's resolve disappeared the moment I stepped in the room.

"I can handle it. Trust me."

I remember the power I got from him when we had sex before, and decide he's probably right. He's over a hundred years old, after all.

I rest my hand in his palm, and he closes his fingers around it. "And the risk?"

"Acceptable." His mouth descends to mine, but stops shy

of touching. "Besides, I don't think I can wait until you graduate. Can you?"

I answer by closing the distance between our lips. Waiting is not an option anymore.

Kassiel's lips press against mine, soft and pliant, but neither of us can take it slow. Our tongues meet in a sensual dance as his hands roam my body and his desire flows over me, the sexiest appetizer. He wants me as much as I want him, even though he's not being fueled by my need to feed. Moaning my appreciation for his ardor, I press myself against him, unable to keep my body still. The friction of our bodies together only increases my need.

He buries his fingers in my hair as he explores my mouth. When he pulls my head back with a hand tangled in my locks, I gasp, chest heaving as I wait for him to press his lips to my neck. He takes his time, licking and nipping along my jaw, then the lobe of my ear, before moving to my neck.

I'm not idle while he enjoys himself. My hands roam his body, pushing his jacket off of his shoulders. He shrugs out of it without lifting his lips from my neck.

Kassiel's toned body is one layer closer to my hands now. I lose some of the initial frantic energy as he lavishes my collarbone with attention. He wants to take his time, apparently, but I'm starving here. With frenzied fingers I remove his tie and yank it off his neck. Then I feel for the buttons of his shirt and unbutton them as quickly as I can with my head still held in his grip.

"I wish we didn't have to rush," he says against my neck.

"We'll go slowly next time," I say without thinking. But now it seems obvious there will be a next time. There has to be. This thing between us is too powerful to resist.

He wraps his arms around me and grips my ass, pulling me as close as we can be without being naked. I lift my legs and wrap them around his waist, using his shoulders for leverage. When I'm in his arms, Kassiel walks us across the room without looking. His lips are on mine again, and his tongue is in my mouth, tasting. Teasing.

"Please," I whisper in his mouth. "I need you."

He sets me on the edge of his desk, then sweeps everything off it and onto the floor. Books. Notepads. Pens. All of it.

I'd managed to undo all but one of his buttons. I reach for it. "Off."

His grin is mischievous as he looks down at himself. "What? You want to see my chest when yours is so woefully covered?"

I nod. "I do, *Professor,* if you please."

He steps back and takes care of the last button, then tosses his shirt onto the floor beside his jacket. I'm mesmerized by the sight of his taut abs and hard chest, along with the dark hair trailing into his pants.

I lick my lips. "I want to taste you."

When he hears that, his expression changes and I swear I see the devil in him. He reaches for his belt buckle. "How can I refuse my best student?"

For a succubus, a blow job is like eating dessert before dinner. Every act of sex has a flavor, and blow jobs are sweet, succulent. Rich. Humans can't survive on dessert alone, nor can I survive on blow jobs. But damn if I don't love to indulge.

Kassiel's belt hits the floor with a clank, and his black slacks fall a moment later, along with his boxer briefs. He's hard, as hard as it's possible for a man to be, and I forgot how perfectly sized he is. I suck him into my mouth, and he moans, his lust and attraction feeding my insatiable, gnawing hunger.

I could take my time and try to take him all in my mouth, down my throat. I could savor every lick, teasing, giving him big eyes and fluttering lashes. But I'm fucking hungry. His clenched hands in my hair spur me on to move faster, suck harder, and take him to the edge as fast as I can.

"Olivia, stop," he commands, pulling me off him.

I'm so hungry for more that it's hard not to latch onto him again, but I take a breath and calm down. That was just an appetizer. The real meal is coming soon. It better hurry though.

I open my blouse, revealing my pink lace bra. The weight of Kassiel's gaze feels like hands caressing my skin. I know exactly what he can do with his hands, and I can't wait to experience it again.

"Take off your bra," he says.

I unclasp my bra, and my breasts spill out of it. He grins, the devil in his eyes again, and then buries his face between them. With his hands on my ass again, he pulls me close and sits on the desk, then cups my breasts as he swirls his tongue around one nipple, then the other.

"I can't wait anymore," I said. "Please, Kassiel."

My pants fall around my ankles before I realize he's unbuttoned them. My core ignites, making my previous desire feel like a teenager's crush as Kassiel's fingers move between my legs and find my clit. He knows exactly what to do to make me writhe, moan, and cling to him as an orgasm builds inside me.

But then he pushes me back on the desk and climbs over me, wrapping my legs around him. His cock slips into me easily, filling me to the hilt. We both let out a sigh as we join together again after so long of waiting. With his hands flat on the desk on either side of my head, he begins a slow rhythm that tortures me in the best way, sliding all the way in and out of me so that I truly feel every second of it. I grip his ass and urge him on, craving more of him, feeling an intense desire to take everything he can possibly give me. I want it all.

And he gives it to me. Moving faster. Deeper. Harder.

He grinds me down against the desk as he hovers over me, his green eyes possessive, like a dark lord ravishing his lady. He gives me exactly what I need, and I give into it completely. Tiny explosions ricochet up my body and down my legs as the orgasm hits me. My low moan grows in pitch and volume while my inner muscles clench around his cock. When he comes, he says my name in a hoarse voice, holding me as tightly against him as he can.

"That was so much better than I remembered," he says, before giving me a long kiss. I can't help but agree with him as he stands up and reaches for his trousers.

"I'll get dressed and get out of here before someone comes in," I say, as I get up quickly. I'm not ashamed of what we did, but now that it's over and I'm in my right mind again, I'm worried about him getting caught. I couldn't stand if he left the school. Not now. Not while he's one of the few people I can trust.

"It's fine. I don't have any more classes today." He grabs his shirt and begins slowly buttoning it. "What happened? You didn't seem this hungry yesterday."

I pick up my clothes off the floor. "I had to give my energy to someone else. It's a long story."

"You gave someone your energy?" He arches an eyebrow. "How?"

"I'm not really sure. I figured it was a succubus power I hadn't learned yet."

"No, it's not. Or at least, I've never heard of it. But you're the daughter of an Archangel. Perhaps that's your unique power."

My eyes widen. For some reason, I never considered that. All Archangels—and Archdemons—have a unique power, as does anyone with their blood. That's how my father can teleport, and how Jonah could change his appearance. I just never realized I would have one too. I suppose it's because for the longest time I never felt like an Archangel's daughter. But now I do.

I'll have to ask Delilah about it next time I see her.

Chapter Thirty-Three

OLIVIA

That night, I go invisible and sneak off campus. I don't care if it's not allowed, or if it's dangerous, or if Uriel will find out and I'll get in trouble—I have to check on my father.

When I land at the house and step inside, Gabriel's on the couch. It doesn't look like he's moved at all since arriving earlier and collapsing. He's still wearing the same bloody blanket wrapped around him.

"Father?" I ask softly, as I approach.

He opens his eyes and gives me a weak smile. "Hello, daughter."

"How are you?"

"Better than when you last saw me," he says with a grimace, then manages to sit up on the couch. He glances down at himself, as if he's just realized he's butt naked and covered in dried blood.

I keep my eyes averted. "You should take a shower and get dressed. I'll make you something to eat."

"Probably a good idea." He manages to stand and takes a moment to check his balance, then heads off to his bedroom. I hear the sound of running water a minute later, and hope he's okay in there by himself.

After heading into the kitchen, I open the fridge and stare at the shelves in dismay. It's totally empty, except for some moldy cheese and wilted lettuce. Father must not come by much now that I've gone back to school.

I rummage through the drawer and find the menu for the pizza place in Angel Peak, and order a supreme pizza plus a BBQ chicken pizza. I have no idea what Gabriel likes, so I figure that covers all my options.

When Father returns, he looks a hundred times better, although there are bags under his eyes that weren't there before he was punished. Bonus, he's not naked anymore. No one wants to see their dad naked, even if he looks just a few years older than you.

"There was nothing in the fridge, so I ordered some pizza," I tell him, as we sit back down on the couch. "Hope that's all right."

"I'm grateful for anything at this point." He sinks into the cushions with a frown. "I'm sorry I arrived outside your room last night and in such a state. I was trying to come here, but teleporting works by picturing where you want to go, and I guess I couldn't stop thinking of you."

"I'm glad you came to me. If you hadn't, you'd still be injured and in pain." I shudder as I remember the state he was in last night. He really thought he could handle that on his own? Angels truly are the most prideful race out there. "Are you safe here? With the attacks nearby?"

"This property is warded so no one can get in without invitation from one of the three owners—you, me, and Jonah. That's why I came here to recover."

"What happened? How could Azrael hurt you like that?"

"The Archangel Council had a meeting to decide my punishment. I knew it was coming, which is why I warned you and asked Callan to protect you. I hope he's been doing a good job?"

"Yes, he's been annoyingly protective at all times."

"Good." Father closes his eyes and draws in a breath, before speaking again. "At least I know you're safe at that school. Especially now."

"What do you mean?"

"I'm no longer a member of the Archangel Council."

My stomach drops. "Because of me?"

"Because of what I did with your mother, and because I lied about it. They no longer feel I can be in a position of power."

"That's total bullshit. You didn't do anything wrong."

"They believe I did."

I swallow hard and ask the question that's haunted me my entire life. "Do you regret doing it?"

"Not for one second." He rests his hand over mine. "I would take a thousand of those punishments as long as it meant having you as my daughter."

I give his hand a squeeze as emotion makes my throat tight. I'm not used to feeling this way, and I try to shake it off before I start crying or something. Luckily the doorbell rings at that moment and saves me from an embarrassing moment.

I grab some plates and napkins, then head back to the couch. Father looks like he's become part of the cushions, so

I'm not sure he has the energy to move to the dining room table. Casual it is.

"Thanks for ordering this," he says, as he fills up his plate with some slices. "How did you know BBQ chicken pizza is my favorite?"

"I didn't—it's my favorite too."

He smiles at me, and I think how nice it is to sit on the couch and eat pizza with my dad, like a somewhat normal family. But the moment's ruined as he continues his story.

"As I was saying, the Archangel Council kicked me off, but they decided that wasn't enough. They want to make an example of me, to show that even an Archangel isn't above the law. Azrael claimed I should be sent to Penumbra Prison for twenty years, which is the normal punishment for my crime."

"Twenty years?" I ask, nearly choking on my pizza. "That's so long!"

"Yes, although Ariel argued I should get a reduced sentence because I'm an Archangel, and some of the others agreed."

"Good." More points for Jonah's mother. "What exactly is Penumbra Prison?"

"It's a prison for all supernaturals here on Earth who commit a crime, whether they are angels, demons, or even fae —although the fae are so rare on Earth that we don't have very many of their prisoners. In Faerie, they handle their own punishments as they see fit."

"Are they sending you to this prison?"

He grabs a glass of water and takes a sip before continuing. "No. Raphael argued that since I was the leader of the Ishim, I was too valuable an asset to imprison. The Council doesn't want a group of angry and rebellious spies and assassins on their hands. Azrael reluctantly agreed because he knows it's true, as an Ishim himself. He tried to take over as Ishim leader before actually, but our kind were loyal to me. When the Archangel Council offered me Michael's position, Azrael thought he would take over as Ishim leader finally. Instead, I refused the position and he became the leader of all angels. And he never forgets to remind me of it."

"He sounds like a real asshole," I mutter, which makes Father laugh. I give him a little smile. "Sorry, but it's true."

"Oh yes, he's definitely an asshole, it's just funny to hear someone say it out loud." He chuckles softly as he grabs another slice of pizza. "Anyway, Uriel suggested that instead of sending me away to prison, they invoke the old punishment of destroying someone's wings with dark-infused weapons. It hasn't been used in many years, since it's considered so barbaric, but the other Archangels agreed to it."

"*Uriel* suggested that?" I thought Bastien's father was a pretty decent guy. Scary, as all Archangels are, but he convinced both Jophiel and Baal to allow me to stay at Seraphim Academy. I can't believe he'd suggest something so horrible.

"It sounds harsh, I know, but if you think about it, he was actually doing me a favor. This punishment was incredibly painful, and they knew it would take me a long time to heal from it, but it's still better than a long prison sentence. At least this way, I can still see you. And Azrael definitely enjoyed giving the punishment to me, the sick bastard."

I've never met the guy, but I already hate him. And it's a different hate than what I feel for Callan. This is deep in my bones, because he hurt someone I love.

"They did strip all my powers as an Archangel though. I'm basically just a regular angel now."

I shake my head, my appetite gone. "I can't believe they did something so horrible to you."

"It was worth it. If they hadn't punished me, they might have gone after you instead. I couldn't let that happen." He lets out a long sigh. "All your life, your mother and I have worried that if anyone found out about you, you'd be put to death. That's why we hid you for so long, and why we will always do whatever it takes to protect you."

That emotion is back, making my eyes water. I cough a little into my napkin. "Have there ever been others like me?"

"No. Plenty of angels and demons have had relations before, of course, but all other pregnancies ended in miscarriage. You're the only one that's survived."

My eyes widen. "But...why?"

He shakes his head. "We have no idea. We always assumed it was because your mother and I are both very powerful, but I suspect it will always be a mystery. Just like some human couples can be infertile for years, and then suddenly become pregnant. Perhaps it's fate. Or luck. Who knows the will of the universe?"

I take a minute to absorb that, and then get mad all over again that my father was punished for having me. "Angels and demons are at peace now. Why keep the old rule that the two races can't be together? It needs to change."

"I agree. But with Azrael in charge, I fear it never will."

"I wish you'd taken the job." It's exasperating to think how much good he could be doing right now instead of hiding in this house.

"Sometimes I do too, but I never would have risked your safety like that."

"But now that I'm in the open, couldn't you challenge him?"

"Probably not. Azrael's powers have increased now that he's the leader of the Council, and he has many people who are loyal to him too, like Jophiel. Even if I was still a member of the Council, it would be extremely difficult to remove him."

Gabriel yawns, and I decide it's time to cut things short, even though it's been nice to talk to my dad so openly for a change. I grab our plates and take them to the kitchen, and make a mental note to do a grocery store run for him tomorrow. He walks into the kitchen behind me, but he's stiff. Is he still hurting?

I rest a hand on his shoulder. "I should get going so you can rest. Marcus will check on you tomorrow, and I'll be back as soon as I can. Please be safe."

Before I know it, I'm enveloped in his arms. Tears well behind my closed eyes. This is the most affectionate hug he's ever given me.

"I love you, Olivia."

My breath catches in my throat. "I love you too...Dad."

I've never called him that before. He was always Father, a formal name for our formal relationship, but maybe we're starting to move past formalities to become a real family. I know I'd like that.

Chapter Thirty-Four

OLIVIA

*A*s fall arrives, the trees begin to change, and the campus becomes beautiful in a different way. It's hard to believe the school year will be over in a few more months.

Our soccer team has a game at Hellspawn Academy, and I ask Uriel if I can go, but he denies my request and says it's too dangerous right now with the recent attacks. Our team wins, fulfilling Marcus's Order task, and I'm sad I don't get to see him play or check out the school. Someday I'll make a point to visit it, but not now. I have more important things to worry about anyway.

Father—Dad?—is completely recovered, but he's basically been placed on house arrest, and isn't allowed to leave Angel Peak. I sneak off to visit him when I can, and we have a few more relaxed family dinners. I consider talking to him about the Order and about my plan to rescue Jonah, but he's been through so much lately, I decide it's better to wait until I know something more concrete. Besides, it's not like he believed me last time I mentioned it.

In Fae Studies, Raziel finally starts talking about magical objects and relics, like my necklace. "Some of the fae have the ability to imbue objects with magic, and they're known as enchanters. It's a rare and powerful ability, usually used in conjunction with other magic, including that of angels and demons. For example, Raphael once worked with an enchanter to create a blanket that would heal anyone it was placed upon. Unfortunately such a relic was lost during the Great War."

He goes on to talk about some of the objects the Fae have made, and I twirl my pen as my mind wanders. I have my meeting with Delilah at the end of the day, and I want to ask her about what happened to me on the night my dad was injured.

"This is also how angels, demons, and fae moved between the worlds," Raziel says, drawing my attention again. "Fae enchanters created special keys that can open portals to the other worlds. Most open portals to two worlds, i.e. between Earth and Heaven. A few rare keys can open portals between any world. The most famous of these is the Staff of Eternity, of course."

He has my full attention now. It's been over a month since the guys promised to help me defeat the Order and find Jonah, and not one damn thing has happened, other than they asked me to start spending more time in the bell tower with them. The request came from Callan, oddly enough. He was a total jerk about it, but explained that he takes his promise to my father seriously, and he'd appreciate it if I helped him by staying close when I could.

"The Staff is one of the most powerful relics in existence."

Raziel rubs his hands together in excitement. He clearly loves talking about it. I wonder if he's in the Order. "It was created by an enchanter named Culann with the help of Michael and Lucifer, and it can work as a key between any world. But it also used their power as leaders to send both our races to Earth, and to close off Heaven and Hell from anyone who might try to open a portal to it."

"Can it work in reverse to send all the demons back to Hell?" Jeremy asks. He narrows his eyes at me as he says it. Prick.

"Yes, and it could also send all of us back to Heaven too. Not that anyone would want to go there. Both worlds were pretty much decimated by the time Michael and Lucifer signed the Earth Accords. Our only hope of long-term survival was moving to this world."

A girl I don't know raises her hand. "Couldn't we try to rebuild Heaven?"

Raziel gives her a sad smile. "Perhaps eventually we will. For now, we're focusing on replenishing our population while on Earth and finding a way to live in harmony with both demons and humans."

"Where is the Staff now?" someone else asks.

"No one knows. Michael and Lucifer hid it after the Earth Accords so that it wouldn't fall into the wrong hands. Of course, it requires both an Archangel and an Archdemon—or one of their children, perhaps—to unlock its full power, and it's unlikely anyone could find two of them to agree to such a thing."

He continues telling us about different Fae relics, but Bastien and I have already finished our paper on this topic and he's covering things I already know. I shift in my seat, impatient to meet with Delilah, and my pen rolls off the desk. When I bend over to get it, I realize it's rolled all the way under me and into the row to my right. I stretch my body and reach for the pen, and see something gold in Jeremy's bag. I snatch my pen and knock the bag at the same time, just enough to get a better look at the gold mask inside.

I quickly sit up straight, bumping my elbow in the process. Bastien gives me a quizzical look, but I just shake my head. I should've known Jeremy was in the Order. He's definitely a believer in their cause.

When class is over, Jeremy grabs his bag and purposefully kicks my chair on his way out. I can't wait to take the Order—and that asshole—down.

———

"*J*s your dad out of town again?" I ask Bastien with a wink, as he leads me to the parlor.

He smirks. "Alas, he is not. But I can come to your dorm tonight."

"I'd like that." We pause outside the doorway and I reach up to touch his sharp jaw. I gave him a few weeks off to recover, but he's back to his normal strength now, and I can't wait to spend some time alone with him tonight.

He takes my hand and kisses my fingers in a move that's surprisingly tender for him. Then he drops my hand and walks away, like it meant nothing to him. *Oh, Bastien, you'll never change.*

I step into the parlor and smile at Delilah, who's wearing a sleeveless black sheath dress that accentuates her shapely arms and legs. As always, I'm momentarily dazzled by her beauty for a split second, and then I recover and take my seat across from her.

"You look much better," Delilah says.

I pour myself some tea. "Thanks. At your advice, I took additional lovers and I'm feeding more regularly now."

"Good. You should be feeding once a week, at least. Remember that the more often you feed, the less you'll need to take at each meal."

"Just like if you skip a few meals, you'll be starving and stuff yourself until you can barely move?"

"Exactly. It's much better to have a steady diet, both for you and for your lovers." A naughty smile crosses her dark red lips. "And if you can convince two of your lovers to join you for one meal, it will be even better."

Two at once? That does sound amazing, but I'm not sure any of my guys would agree. I take a sip of my tea and stare off into space.

"Is there something on your mind?" Delilah asks. "You seem troubled."

"A few weeks ago I transferred some of my energy into one of my lovers. Is that a succubus power we haven't covered yet?"

She pauses while holding her tea mid-sip. "No, it isn't. In fact, that shouldn't even be possible. It must be your unique power due to your...special parentage."

"I thought that might be it."

She leans back with a proud smile. "Now that you're feeding more often your powers are growing, although I would guess something probably triggered this one's emergence."

"Someone I cared about was hurt, and this was the only way to help them."

"Yes, that explains it. Just be careful with such a power. Don't give too much of yourself, or you'll risk growing weak."

"I understand."

"Is there anything else you wish to discuss?" she asks.

I hesitate. "Have you ever been to Faerie?"

Her face changes, her lashes lowering as she stares into her tea cup. "Yes, though it's been many years. I used to have a lover there named Culann."

"The one who made the Staff of Eternity?"

"The very same. Alas, we had a falling out some time ago, and I haven't seen him in many years since it's so difficult to get to Faerie now."

I lean forward in my seat. "Do you know how to get to Faerie?"

"I do. You need a special relic called a key to open a portal to Faerie, but those keys have mostly been destroyed over the years, or are being held by the fae themselves. Some keys can only be used by fae too. Getting one now would be near impossible." She taps her fingers on her tea cup. "I used to have one, but it's long gone now. Probably for the best, since I have no interest in facing the High King again, and he would definitely notice if I stepped into his lands."

Sounds like we're not getting a fae key anytime soon, dammit. I remember Raziel telling us about the High King in class, and wonder how Delilah knows him. "Is it true the High King killed his wife?"

"Oh yes. Titania was a powerful fae queen, but could not bear him any children. Oberon desperately wanted a son and had many affairs in the hopes of having one, and because he has a hard time keeping his dick in his pants. In retaliation,

Titania cursed him to sire only daughters. When he discovered what she'd done, he killed her. Yet the curse remains."

"He sounds horrible." And speaking of horrible men... "What about Azrael? Do you know him?"

"You're full of interesting questions today." She sets her empty tea cup down. "Yes, I've met him, though you'd be wise to stay far away. Before he became the Archangel leader, he was their assassin. They call him the Angel of Death for good reason, and he has a personal vendetta against demons since he believes we killed his son. Not that there's any proof of that, mind you."

"He seems to have a vendetta against my father too," I mutter.

"They've always had something of a rivalry, or so I'm told." She rises to her feet, and reaches down to rest her hand upon the top of my head, lightly stroking my hair. "Be cautious. There are people on both sides watching you at all times."

"Including you?"

That makes her smile. "Especially me."

*E*very time I sleep with Olivia, I put everything at risk. My job. My mission. My heart.

But I can't stop myself from going back for more.

I tell myself I do it because she needs me. Or because Lucifer wants me to keep her safe, and making sure she's well-fed is part of that. I tell myself all sorts of excuses, anything to make it easier on my conscience when I meet her alone. In my classroom. In my office. In my room.

She sits up in my bed after our latest round, and I run my hand up and down her back. Even her back is beautiful, with soft, smooth olive skin. I roll on my side and press a kiss to the curve of her hip.

She smiles at me over her shoulder. "I should get going. We both have classes tomorrow."

"Don't remind me." I lean back and prop my head up on my pillow. "You could stay though. If you wanted."

She shakes her head. "I don't do that, and I don't allow anyone to stay over either. It's one of my rules."

Probably smart. I know she's sleeping with other men too, but it doesn't bother me since I grew up around Lilim. Her angel lovers, on the other hand, might get jealous to find another man in bed with her.

It wasn't hard to figure out who her other lovers are either. The Princes hang around her like they're her personal body-guards, even after what they did to her last year. But three angels aren't enough, even ones with Archangel blood. Olivia needs me too.

Besides, I have to be up way too early. Damn these angels and their love of mornings. I let out a yawn, and Olivia pauses while putting on her dress, then stares at me with a worried expression.

"Are you feeling all right? No weakness or exhaustion?"

I laugh softly and sit up. "You don't need to worry about me. I'm just struggling with this angelic schedule. I have a hard time sleeping at night still."

She searches my eyes. "Are you sure?"

"Liv, I'm not a young demon. I can handle feeding you."

"I know, but the others have Archangel blood, and they were still weakened by me. You don't."

"Ah, I see." I pause as I consider my next words. I haven't revealed this secret to anyone in a long time, but I trust Olivia and care about her more than any other woman in many years. "As I said, you don't need to worry. I have the demon equivalent of Archangel blood."

"Your father is an Archdemon?" she asks, but then frowns as she remembers our discussion. There is no Fallen Archdemon, not really.

"My father is Lucifer."

Her mouth opens and closes, opens and closes, before finally she asks, "Lucifer?" She stares at me. "Like, *the* Lucifer?"

"The very one." I scan her face, trying to read her. Is she going to panic? Run away? Scream? People tend to have pretty strong reactions to me being the son of the devil. "How does that make you feel?"

"Wow. I suppose I really don't need to worry about you then." She lets out a soft laugh. "No wonder you're so powerful and know so much inside information about him. I hope you can tell me more sometime."

My eyebrow arches up. "That's it? You learn my father is the most powerful demon in the world and the greatest villain of all time, and you just want to learn more about him?"

"How else would I feel? Your father could be Azrael, who I hate much more than Lucifer." She tilts her head as she considers. "I mean, I don't hate Lucifer at all. I don't have any feelings about him one way or another."

"Maybe I can change your mind about that." I take her hand and caress it softly. "Perhaps someday you can meet him."

"I'd like that." She pauses. "Maybe. The real question is, how does he feel about me?"

"He thinks you could be an ally, and has asked me to protect you."

"Does he want to punish my mother?"

"I don't believe so."

She blows out a breath. "That's a relief. After what they did to my father, I've been extra worried."

"Demons are much less strict about that stuff. We're all about personal freedom, after all."

She nods. "It's angels who are fixed on the old traditions.

We need to find a way to change things, so demons and angels can be together if they want."

"It's hard to overturn ancient laws and thousands of years of hatred. We've only been at peace for a little over thirty years. We'll get there eventually."

"I hope so." She bends down and gives me a kiss, before moving toward my balcony. "I'll see you in class tomorrow."

She goes invisible before flying back to her own dorm. I lean back in the bed and stare at the night sky through the open sliding door, soaking in the darkness that creeps inside. When I was born in Hell, angels and demons were at war, both intent on wiping the other race out. Now I'm teaching at an angel school, and sleeping with the first angel-demon hybrid. Change is coming, whether the angels or demons are ready for it—and I have a feeling Olivia will be leading the charge.

A week later, Araceli and I are heading to the cafeteria for dinner, when there's a loud boom and a tremble in the earth. We freeze, whirling around to find the source of the sound. It's not close, but it's definitely on campus.

"Was that an explosion?" Araceli asks.

I zip up my hoodie. "I think so. It came from the direction of the lake."

We both sprint toward the sound, heedless of the danger, and spot Hilda outside the gym.

"Gather to me, students!" she calls out to anyone nearby, and some other students run to her. She gestures for them to enter the gym, while she stands guard outside.

Another boom fills the air, closer this time, and I hear a few nervous screams. Wow am I glad that Hilda had us all start carrying weapons. My dagger's already in my hand, while Araceli's unsheathing her sword.

There's a flash of gold and white feathers, and then Callan

sets down beside me, wielding his huge barbarian sword. "You should be in the dorm," he snaps at me.

"If the school is under attack, we want to help."

"You want to get yourself killed, as far as I can tell," he grumbles, as he falls in step with us.

"Do you think it's the humans?" Araceli asks.

"Possibly," Callan says, before eyeing me. He's probably thinking it could be demons too.

Marcus and Bastien land beside us, and I'm relieved to see they're all right.

"I've done a quick sweep of the area, and it seems like they've moved away for now," Marcus says. "But it appears they can throw whatever is causing the explosions."

"That could explain how they're getting them past the gates," Bastien says. "They're warded against both humans and demons right now."

"We should take cover somewhere until it's over," Callan says.

"No way," I say. "Don't you want to defend the school?"

"Of course I do, but your protection is more important."

"And I'm going to fight," I say, stomping off toward the gates. "So you'll just have to stick with me."

"I wouldn't be anywhere but by your side," Marcus says and grabs my hand to give it a quick kiss. Callan grumbles, but he and the others move with me toward the forest.

A group of angels fly overhead, and I spot Kassiel's black and silver wings. The professors must be going to investigate. I wonder if Uriel's already there. What will we find when we reach the gates?

We creep through the woods, weapons ready, but it's pitch black and I'm the only one who can see much of anything, so it's slow going. There's no moon tonight either. A perfectly timed attack against angels.

"If they can't get onto the campus, why are we moving like they can?" Araceli whispers.

"Because what if they could?" Callan asks. "What if we're wrong? We must be prepared for anything."

We hear a rustling in the woods and ready our weapons, but then Tanwen emerges from behind a bush, her eyes bright and determined. She clutches a mace tightly in her hand, and her straw-colored ponytail whips behind her as she moves with purpose. She shoots us a quick glance, sizing us up, and then continues forward.

A black shape comes toward us in a hurry, just above the tree line. It's so dark, I'm probably the only one who can see it, with my demon vision. I squint, watching it fly, but it's too small to be an angel, and it moves in a way that seems almost familiar.

"Look out!" I scream, my heart clenching as I realize it's a drone—and it must be behind the explosions. I grab Tanwen's arm and yank her to the side, just as the drone drops an object. A bomb.

As everyone takes cover, Callan raises a hand and shoots a beam of burning light at the bomb. It explodes with a horrible sound and a bright flash, making dirt and leaves fly all around us. We all slowly stand up again, while Callan brushes dirt off his shirt. That brave idiot.

"They're using drones," Bastien says with a voice full of appreciation. "It's genius."

Callan gives him a chastising look. "You sound like you're on their side."

"Don't be ridiculous. But you have to admit it's smart. They can't get through the gates, so they're using drones. With cameras on them, almost certainly."

"Not too smart," Marcus says, as his wings snap out. "Or they'd know the sky is our domain."

I search the night sky but the drone is gone. "There must be more of them. Araceli, you should fly back and make sure everyone knows to take cover."

She hesitates, but then nods. "On it."

The rest of us take off and fly toward the gates. Up ahead, we see other angels flying with balls of light by them, helping them see in the dark. And also making them targets.

A burst of automatic gunfire pierces the night, and one of the angels goes down. My chest clenches, and I pray it's not Kassiel who's been hit. Marcus dives down after the angel, presumably to heal them. One of the angels up ahead blasts the drone with Erelim light, but more approach and begin firing at us. With a roar, Callan flares out his wings and faces the oncoming drones, his arms wide. There's a flash of white light that spreads all around him, both above and below, and the gunfire bounces off it. He's created a giant shield to protect us all.

His Archangel power, it must be. I've never heard of any other angel doing that.

The angels fly forward to attacks the drones, since there's no telling how long Callan can hold his shield. It quickly becomes total chaos, with wings flashing in the night, swords slashing into machinery, and bursts of light that make me blink back white spots. I've never fought in anything like this before —year three of Combat Training is where we learn things like aerial combat—and it's chaotic. I lunge for the nearest drone with my dagger, but then someone shoves me hard, and I miss.

I glance back and spot Jeremy, who hovers there with an evil grin.

"Two birds, one stone," he says, before darting away.

The drone unleashes a volley of gunfire as I spin to the side, and I scream as something hot and sharp hits me, sending excruciating pain through my arm. Then there's a blast of light and I'm yanked aside, before the drone explodes. Another drone appears at my side, but the person who saved me swings her mace and knocks it to the ground. Tanwen.

"That was close," she says, her white wings slowly flapping to hover at my side. All around us the battle is ending, with the drones either defeated or flying away. "Are you all right?"

I check my arm, which is bleeding quite a bit but doesn't seem to have a bullet stuck in it, at least. Marcus or Araceli can heal it when they get a chance. "I got hit, but I'm okay. Thanks for saving me."

"What kind of warrior would I be if I didn't protect the weakest of us?" Tanwen says with a haughty sniff. "Besides, I saw what that asshole Jeremy did. Not cool."

No. I'll have to deal with him at some point. Like I need more shit added to my To Do List.

Bastien flies over to us. "They're gone, but we've confirmed it was the Duskhunters. Their symbol is on the drones."

Tanwen grips her mace tight, her eyes glowing with angry light. "We need to go after them. They have to pay for what they did."

Bastien shakes his head. "The headmaster has ordered all students back to their dorms, while the professors finish up here."

"I'm not going back while they're still out there!"

"I know you want justice for your friends, but this isn't the time," I tell her.

"Not just my friends. Those bastards killed my mother too." With a great flap of her shining white wings, she takes off.

I sigh as I watch her go, then turn back to Bastien. "What were the Duskhunters trying to do?"

"They were testing our defenses, I believe." His brow furrows as he gazes across the forest. "I fear this is only the beginning."

Chapter Thirty-Seven

OLIVIA

$\mathcal{I}$n the aftermath of the Duskhunter attack, defenses are increased around the school, with regular patrols along the gates at night. My father personally takes over Angel Peak's security, and I feel a little better knowing he's got it handled.

Three angels were seriously injured in the attack, including Hilda, but thanks to Marcus and the other healers, they recovered quickly. Otherwise, there was no real damage done, luckily. Still, it seems like the wrong time to throw a birthday party, so I decide to just have a small gathering in the bell tower, with absolutely no gifts allowed. Instead, I set up a little jar to collect money for the families of people who were killed by the Duskhunters.

"What's she doing here?" Araceli whispers to me, as Tanwen steps inside the lounge.

"She helped me during the attack, so I invited her here," I say, with a shrug.

Tanwen stuffs a wad of bills into the donation jar, then heads over to me. "Happy birthday, Liv."

"I'm going to get a beer," Araceli says, and I get the impression she just wants to bolt. "Want one?"

"Sure," Tanwen replies.

I decide to just come out and ask. "You're being a lot nicer to me this year, and you protected me from Jeremy. What gives? I thought you hated me."

"No, I hate humans." Her nose wrinkles, and it's annoying how cute it is. "But I guess I realized I was a total bitch to you last year, and that wasn't cool. You got back at me too. So hopefully we're even now."

My jaw practically hits the floor as I process her words. "Yeah, we're cool. But if you don't hate demons, why are you in the Order?"

She glances around us quickly, her face worried. "Don't say that so loud! And how do you know?"

I drag her off to a corner where no one can hear us. "I'm in the Order too."

She blinks at me. "You? They let you stay in even after they found out you're part demon?"

"I was surprised also. Maybe they kept me because Gabriel's my dad?" I shrug. "Either way, I'm in it, but only to find my brother. What about you?"

She bites her lip, and for the first time ever, she actually looks a little worried. "I'm working against them."

"Why?"

She pauses, but then she must decide to trust me. "My sister is in love with a demon."

"Oh." Was not expecting that. "Wow."

"She's set to be the next leader of the Valkyries, but since her relationship with the shifter is forbidden, she keeps delaying taking on the job." Tanwen tugs on her ponytail. "At first I joined the Order because all the other Valkyries were doing it. Now I stay to try and thwart their plans against demons, for my sister. And because her boyfriend is a pretty good guy. His family is nice too. They've opened my eyes a lot to the fact that demons and angels are not all that different. Most of us want the same things."

"I know what you mean. My dad was punished for being with my mother. It was horrible."

"That's why I'm worried for my sister. Angels are strict about this, much more so than demons. The law needs to change if we ever want true peace between the two races."

I nod. "Totally agree."

"I'm guessing you don't believe in the Order's crap then either?" she asks.

"No." I hesitate, but decide to trust her, since she trusted me. "I joined at first to find my brother, which I'm still working on. Now I want to stop them from getting the Staff, and eventually find a way to take them down."

"Whatever you're planning, count me in." She offers her hand, and I take it. Tanwen, my ally? Maybe even...a friend? It's hard to believe, but she gives me a fierce smile, before heading off to talk to Callan.

My dad shows up with a bunch of pizzas like he's a delivery boy, and everyone laughs and cheers. He gives me a big hug and then goes to start serving, and I look around the room at the people I care most about, and smile. The only person missing is Kassiel, but he gave me a birthday orgasm earlier to make up for it. I couldn't exactly invite him to the party, after all. Not without a lot of questions.

As the party is winding down, Callan corners me outside the bathroom. "I got my Order task," he says quietly.

"What is it?"

He looks behind us, where Grace, Cyrus, and Isaiah are sitting on the couch, laughing about something. "They want me to beat up Isaiah to punish Cyrus for failing his mission."

My hand flies to my mouth to cover my gasp. Cyrus's mission was to get close to Araceli, but ever since I found out about it, she's been avoiding him. The Order must have noticed. "That's horrible. Are you going to do it?"

His face darkens. "Of course not. Do you really think I'm the kind of man who would?"

I consider this. He rules over the school and intimidates everyone. He bullied me, although he did it thinking it was in my best interests. He never actually hurt me or anything else though. "No, I know you're not like that." Then I have another thought, and it makes me grip his shirt. "But if you don't do it, they'll punish you next. Someone you love. Maybe your mom."

"They can try, but I won't be intimidated by them," he growls. "Besides, we're going to take them down anyway, right?"

He always seemed like he was on the fence before about going up against the Order, but not anymore. He's willing to do what's right, even if it's dangerous. The last little ice in my heart melts, and I give him a hug, resting my head on his chest. "Yes, we are."

He stiffens and awkwardly pats my back, probably worried about people seeing us. I don't care. I can finally admit that I don't hate Callan, not anymore. I don't think he hates me either. If he did, he wouldn't protect me so fiercely, and he wouldn't kiss me so hard. He cares about me, even if he won't admit it.

When I get home, I'm destroying that video of us having sex. I'm done with revenge.

Araceli's right—I'm better than that. Or at least, I want to be.

*W*hen I get to my bedroom, I find someone waiting for me. I grip my dagger tight as I hit the light switch.

"Lilith?" I ask, so shocked I drop my weapon.

She's been lounging on my bed like it's her own while playing on her phone in the dark. She looks up at me with a smile. "Hello, daughter."

How does one describe the Archdemon of the Lilim? She's so beautiful it nearly hurts to look at her, yet so alluring you can't do anything but stare. We share the same olive skin, dark brown curls, green eyes, and seductive curves. If someone were to look at us side by side, they'd probably think we were sisters, except she has this magnanimous power that is unique to her. And much like the Archangels, when you look into her eyes you can somehow sense the thousands of years she's lived.

"What are you doing here?" I awkwardly bend down and pick up the dagger, then close the door behind me.

"It's your birthday. I came to give you a gift."

"I haven't seen you in years!" My shock is starting to give way to anger. "Where have you been all this time?"

Lilith rises from the bed like a queen, and I'm reminded of the first time I met her, when I was six years old.

"Are you a princess?" I asked with awe in my voice.

She laughed. "More like a queen."

"An evil queen?"

A wicked smile touched her red lips. "Some would say so. But you have nothing to fear from me."

"I'm sorry for my absence, but it was unavoidable," she says now.

"I haven't seen you since I was eighteen." She vanished right after she finished my succubus training, and all I got after that were a few birthday cards and postcards from various places around the world. Even when I was revealed as a half-succubus to the world, she didn't come for me. Only Gabriel did.

"I didn't mean to stay away so long, but someone I care about dearly went missing. I've been searching for her ever since." Lilith moves to stand in front of me and brushes the back of her hand against my cheek. "But this past year I've come to visit you, many times. You simply didn't know it."

She takes something from her pocket and puts it on. A gold ring with rubies on it. As she does, her appearance melts into something else. Her hair and skin turn darker. Her nose and mouth shift slightly. The only thing that remains are her eyes. Even her presence and power are lessened a little. A perfect disguise.

"Delilah?" I step back, my stomach twisting. "You were her all along?"

"Yes, thanks to a fae relic from Culann." She gestures at

my neck. "Much like your necklace, it allows me to hide myself. He made that for me too, you know."

I can barely process what she's saying, because I have so many other questions. "Why would you hide? Is Delilah real?"

"I hid because I couldn't exactly show up on your campus as Lilith. Delilah is one of my disguises, like Laylah. She doesn't exist, but everything I said to you during our meetings was true otherwise."

Laylah's the name I was said to use whenever anyone asked about my mom. I was told demons might have heard the name, but wouldn't know exactly who she was—unlike the name Lilith, which everyone knows.

"But why hide from *me*?"

She looks down, her lashes lowered. "I worried you'd be mad, since I've been away so long. I wanted to get to know you as a friend or peer, not as your absent mother. I am sorry for that."

I sigh, but it's hard to stay mad with her. I think it's probably part of her magic. Or maybe I'm just so happy to see my mom again and to know she's been there for me over the past few months after all.

I open my arms to her. "I'm happy to see you, Mother."

She moves close and embraces me tightly, and I breathe in her rose-scented hair. Yes, she even smells amazing.

I pull back with a frown. "Why didn't you tell me about my brother?"

She waves a light hand. "Asmodeus is thousands of years old. He's your brother by blood, but his concerns are very different from yours. He used to rule for me in Hell, and he's had a hard time adjusting to Earth. I thought I would introduce you someday, when you were both ready. For now, he doesn't know you're related. I never told him about you for your own protection."

"Are there others?"

"Yes. Some living. Some not." Sadness crosses her face. "Some lost."

"Lost?"

She takes my face in her hands and kisses my forehead. "I'll reveal all in time, I promise. For now, I must continue my travels. After you open your present, of course." She picks up something off the bed that's wrapped in a dark silk shawl, then places it in my hands carefully. I remove the fabric and find two daggers, one glowing with pure white light, the other pulsing with inky black darkness.

"These daggers have served me well for many years, but I wish for you to have them now."

I hold one in each hand, feeling the weight of them, and how perfect they fit. Like they were made just for me. "I understand the dark-infused blade, but why do you have a light-infused blade too?"

"Sometimes the greatest threat to us comes from one of our own."

I nod, thinking of my father and Azrael. The daggers have a belt sheath, and Lilith helps me attach it, so the daggers rest on either side of my hips.

"Perfect." She claps her hands together. "I feel a lot better now, knowing you have those."

"Thank you."

"I'll try to visit more often. I promise." Her phone makes a noise and she checks it, then lets out a short laugh. "Sorry, I'm totally addicted to this Star Wars game and my energy is full."

"You...what? You like Star Wars?"

"Oh yeah. Saw the first movie in the theater, and I've loved it ever since." She winks at me. "I'm an original fangirl."

Wow. That is something I never knew about my mother... and totally unexpected.

We embrace again and she kisses me on the cheek, before she walks out my door and slips away into the night. Without wings, she has to find some other way off campus, but I have no doubt she'll manage.

That's my mom—ancient demon, leader of all Lilim, queen of lust...and a Star Wars geek. Who would have thought?

Chapter Thirty-Nine

BASTIEN

School is almost over, and it's time for our penultimate Order meeting. We go as a group this time—me, Callan, Marcus, and Olivia. After we put on the golden robes and masks in the bell tower, we link our hands in a chain, allowing Olivia to turn us all invisible. Flying is difficult and feels rather foolish, like we're holding hands and about to sing songs or something. Good thing no one can see us.

The woods are quiet and dark at this early hour of the morning, as we set down in the soft dirt. Olivia leads us forward, her hand tightly grasping mine. It feels small in my own, and I rub my thumb reassuringly along the back of it as we wait for the boulder to open. As I do, I realize this is not normal behavior for someone who cares nothing for her.

I can't deny it any longer. I've developed feelings for her.

How peculiar.

As I ponder this new development, we release each other's hands and lose our invisibility, then move down the corridor to the cavern at the bottom. We split up and join the other Order members, sitting beside them on the bench. Others continue to file in, until we're all present, and our leader steps from the shadows, wearing his crown.

He clasps his hands together. "You should all have been given tasks by now. Some of you have completed them. Some have not." His gaze scans the crowd, and even though we can't see his face or hear his voice, his displeasure is obvious from the tilt of his head. "Remember there will be consequences should you fail."

"I completed my task this week," I speak up.

"Excellent. Come forward."

I move closer and open a small, clear container. Inside is an inky black feather that emanates darkness, which once lived in my father's office. My task was to steal it, though I'm not sure what it does. Uriel told me it was one of Lucifer's feathers, and I can't imagine why the Order would want it.

I hold it out to the leader, who takes it carefully at the end and holds it up to the light. Shadows cling to it like mist, and the room seems a little darker.

"You have done well," he tells me with a nod. "This, my friends, is a feather from Lucifer's wings, stolen from Headmaster Uriel's office." A few people gasp, while some cringe backward, and others lean forward like they want to get a better look. "The feather has many interesting properties, but we're only interested in one of them. It can lead us to the Staff of Eternity."

Soft murmurs go around the room at this. "How does it work?" someone asks. I think it's Olivia.

"The feather will try to seek out its master. Here on Earth, it would fly to Lucifer. In Faerie, it will seek out the Staff, which contains a touch of Lucifer's essence."

"What about Jonah?" That's Marcus, I'm sure of it. "Can it find him too?"

"It is my hope he is with the Staff, but if not, we will do what we can to find him. However, we must stay focused on our purpose."

Another member nods. "Jonah knew the risks when he volunteered. He would want us to make finding the Staff the priority."

Callous, but practical. I would say the same thing, if I believed in this foolish mission. I still have a hard time understanding why Jonah went to get the Staff in the first place, especially after meeting Olivia. Why would he put his sister at risk?

"But how will we get to Faerie?" someone else asks. Callan maybe.

"Do we have a key?" the person I think is Olivia asks.

"We do not, but the fae coming to the championship game will have at least one, possibly more. There are also ways of getting to Faerie without keys, using fae blood."

I've heard rumors along those lines, and it explains why they want Araceli so badly, but it must be a highly guarded secret among the fae if it's true.

The Order's leader continues. "We will kidnap a few fae from the game tomorrow. The initiates will be tasked with torturing them into opening a portal to Faerie for us. If they don't succeed, I'm sure one of us can be very convincing. You'll receive your instructions after this meeting." He stops and looks around the circle, his gaze landing on each of us for a second. "If all goes well, we will have the Staff within a few days' time. It's taken us many years to get to this point, and soon our hard will work all pay off—and the demons will be returned to Hell."

A few of the Order members begin to clap, and more join in a moment later, so I add my applause so I don't stand out. Then we're all dismissed, and we exit the cavern and disperse into the woods. The four of us split up, and then meet back in the bell tower.

"How could you give them that feather?" Olivia asks, as soon as I land.

"I didn't know what it did." I scowl, angrier with myself than her. I should have made more of an effort to find out why they wanted it first.

She slumps down on the couch and rests her head in her hands. "Now they can find the Staff, and we're no closer to finding Jonah or getting to Faerie."

"We'll need to stop the kidnapping and then convince the fae to let us go with them to Faerie, in the hopes that Jonah is with the Staff," Marcus says. "Oh, and steal the feather from the Order."

Callan rolls his eyes. "You make it sound so easy."

"At the very least, we need to stop the kidnapping attempt," Olivia says. "We can try to get the feather too."

Suddenly there's a rush of wind and Tanwen lands on the balcony. "If you guys are planning something, I want in."

Marcus glances at us and then back at her awkwardly. "Uhh...I'm not sure..."

Olivia stands up. "It's okay. Tanwen is on our side. She's agreed to help us take down the Order."

Callan's jaw drops. "What?"

Tanwen tosses her blond hair. "It's true. I want to take the bastards down, and I have inside information that can help you —if you agree to help me fight the Duskhunters in return."

I nod as the rightness of her words makes my Ofanim senses tingle. "She's speaking the truth."

"Then we agree to that deal," Callan says, crossing his arms.

Tanwen gives a short nod in response. "When I got back to my room there were instructions waiting for me. I'm supposed to pack a light bag with supplies and food for a few days of travel, and then I'm supposed to join them in the Order's cavern during halftime. Someone else must be handling the kidnapping. Probably an Ishim."

"Maybe Grace or Nariel," I speculate. We know Grace is a member, and it makes logical sense that her uncle would be one as well. Plus the Order tends to favor using invisibility to hide its members, a trick only a few powerful Ishim can handle.

Callan rubs his chin. "Do everything they said, and keep us updated if anything changes. They obviously trust you more than us, since we weren't invited to go on this mission, so you'll be our inside woman."

"Got it," Tanwen says.

"Marcus can keep an eye on Jeremy, since they're both on the soccer team." Callan's eyes scan the group. "The rest of us will split up and follow the other members we know are in the Order, or have suspicions about. Grace. Cyrus. Nariel."

"And Professor Kassiel," Tanwen adds. "He's a member."

"How do you know?" I ask.

"During the final test last year, when the demon escaped, there was chaos and fighting, and his mask got dislodged slightly. I recognized him."

"Kassiel is working to take down the Order also," Olivia says. "We can trust him."

"How do you know?" Marcus asks.

She hesitates, considering her words. "He and I made a pact at the end of last year to stop the Order. He has his own reasons for doing so, which aren't mine to share. I was going to ask him to help us tomorrow."

"I don't like it," Callan says.

Marcus shrugs. "If Olivia says we can trust him, then we can."

I cross my arms. "You realize that if we do this we'll be going up against the Order, and they'll know it. There won't be any turning back."

"That's why we have to succeed," Olivia says, her eyes burning with determination. "This is our one chance to stop the Order from getting the Staff, and to rescue my brother at the same time. Failure is not an option."

It's the day of the final tournament game against the fae, and I step back and check myself in the mirror. I'm wearing a new pair of black jeans that happen to make my butt look amazing, with my mom's infused daggers on my hips. A long, flowy red shirt covers them up and hides my butt too, which is probably for the best. I don't need anyone's lust distracting me. Then I double-check my necklace and make sure it's secure. We're going to need it today.

There's a knock on our door and I head to answer it, thinking it must be one of the Princes, or maybe Tanwen. When I open it, there's a man with sharp features who is wearing a hood over his head, even though we're indoors.

"Oh, hello. Is Araceli here?"

Araceli walks out of her bedroom at that moment, and her face goes from confusion to disbelief to delight. "Dad?"

He gives her a hesitant smile. "I got your messages. I'm sorry I couldn't make it to Family Day, but I was halfway around the world at the time. I hope it's okay that I'm here now."

"It's great." She walks over and I see her eyes are wet. "Thank you for coming."

"I'm so happy to see you, my little plum." The two of them embrace, and as they do, his hood falls back and I see pointed ears and shiny purple hair, slightly darker than Araceli's.

"I'll give you two a few minutes to catch up," I tell them, before retreating to my room. I'm happy they're reconnecting, but also worried. I've now completed my Order task, of all the irony, but it puts Araceli's dad at risk.

As I shut the door, I hear Araceli's dad apologizing. Even with it closed, I can hear them talking through the walls, although it's muffled.

"I'm so sorry I haven't been around as much," he says. "I've been traveling a lot, working for the angels, but that's no excuse. I guess the real answer is that every time I saw you, it made me feel guilty."

"Guilty...why?" Araceli asks.

"Your mother never told you why we split up?"

I don't hear Araceli's answer, but I'm guessing the answer is no, because then her father continues talking.

"Muriel wanted to have another child, and I said no. After what my people did to me, and how hard it's been for you, I didn't think it was fair to put another child through that. I left your mom in the hopes she would find another man who could give her a pure angel child. One who wouldn't suffer for having fae blood, like you have."

"That's why you two split up?" Araceli asks loudly.

"Yes, and I've been wracked with guilt ever since. I love your mother, and I wanted her to be happy, even if it meant being with someone other than me. I hoped you might get a sibling out of it too."

"That's not going to happen. She doesn't want anyone else. And you don't need to worry about me. Sure, the other angels treated me like an outcast when I was a kid, but it just made me stronger." She pauses for a second. "A sibling would be cool though. Would you ever reconsider?"

"I don't know. It depends if Muriel would ever take me back."

"She would. You should talk to her."

"Maybe."

I feel like a jerk for invading their privacy, so I walk out onto the balcony to watch as the field is set up for the soccer game. A short while later, Araceli enters my room. "Liv? Can you come chat?"

"Sure."

As we head into the living room, she says, "Dad's given me some information that will help us get to Faerie."

"I'm Fintan," he says politely, offering his hand.

My heart races as I shake his hand. This is it. He's going to tell me how to find Jonah. "Do you have a key to Faerie, by any chance?"

"I do not, I'm sorry to say. I used to, but it was taken from me when I was excommunicated from Faerie. Most keys have been lost or destroyed, and the others are well-protected or hidden. But there are other ways to get there." He studies me with kind, intelligent eyes. "Araceli tells me you have a fae relic."

I lightly touch my gold necklace. "I do."

"May I see it?"

I hesitate, but then lean forward so he can look at it closer. I refuse to take it off, even for my friend's dad.

"Yes, this will work. It's very old and very powerful. Since it's not made for opening portals, it will require some blood from a fae to activate."

I stare at him open-mouthed. "That's all we need—Araceli's blood and my necklace?"

"Yes. Araceli will have to activate it with her fae magic, while picturing where she wants to visit. Since she's never been to Faerie before, it's best if I take her now for a few minutes. Then she'll have somewhere to envision."

"We're going to Faerie?" Araceli asks, her eyes dancing with excitement.

"If you'd like," he says with a smile. "Is there anywhere in particular you want to visit? The Summer Court, perhaps, to see your own kind?"

"Do you know where the Staff of Eternity is being kept?" I ask.

Fintan shakes his head. "No, I don't know anything about that."

I sigh. "Then I guess it doesn't matter. We won't know where to find the Staff or Jonah until we get that feather from the Order."

"Just take us somewhere safe," Araceli says.

"I shall." He clears his throat. "Trust me, I don't want to get caught. If they find out I took you to Faerie, they will kill me."

We clear some space in the middle of our living room and then Araceli grabs a knife and hands it to her dad. He cuts his hand, and then presses his bloody palm against my necklace. As he does, he mutters a few words in a language I've never heard before and holds out his other hand. After a few seconds, a portal opens up, a lot like the one we saw the fae make, but smaller.

Fintan drops his hand and wipes it off with a dishtowel. The wound is already closing up by the time he's done. "Let's go."

Fintan walks through the portal first, and Araceli gives me an excited, goofy thumbs up before following him. I take a deep breath and move through the portal, which makes my skin tingle, sort of like when your foot falls asleep. The world goes hazy, and then I'm standing in the middle of an overgrown forest. Everything is verdant green, and we're surrounded by the sounds of birds calling out and the wind rustling through the trees.

"Where are we?" Araceli asks.

"A forest in the Summer Court near my family's holdings. I figured if they caught us, they would probably be more merciful than other fae, though I could be wrong about that." He takes a few steps and touches the side of a thick, gnarled tree. "I carved my initials here when I was seven. It's an easy place for me to envision when I need to travel here, and few people venture into this forest anymore."

Araceli stares at the initials on the tree and nods. "I think I can envision it."

"Good. Now open a portal back to your dorm."

He instructs her in the phrase she should say, and then she cuts her hand, gives me an apologetic look, and touches my necklace. A portal opens up, and we return through it back into the dorm.

"I did it!" she says with a laugh.

"You've done well, little plum." Pride shines in his eyes. "Your fae magic is stronger than you know."

She shakes her head. "I don't have any fae magic."

"Of course you do." He smiles at her, but then it turns to a frown. "Speaking of magic, be careful using any angel magic in Faerie. Someone nearby might feel it." He turns to me. "Your necklace should protect you from being detected though, as long as you're wearing it."

I nod. "Thank you for helping us."

"It's the least I can do. Now, shall we head to the championship game? I haven't been to one of those in years, and I'd love to watch it with my daughter at my side."

I glance at Araceli. "Actually, it's not safe here for you. It's probably best if you leave."

"Leave?" he asks, blinking at us both.

Araceli nods sadly. "I'm sorry, dad. I would love to watch the game with you too. Maybe when school ends we can have a longer visit?"

"I'd like that." He kisses her on the cheek. "Be careful if you go to Faerie. I'd go with you, but I fear I'd only put you in more danger. Remember, the fae are powerful allies, but terrible enemies. Most importantly, don't get caught. I worry about what they would do to you."

"We'll be careful," she says.

She walks him out and I clutch my necklace tightly. We're so close. All we need to do now is get the feather. Oh, and stop the Order's nefarious plan along the way. Piece of cake.

Chapter Forty-One

OLIVIA

The crowd cheers as the Seraphim Academy soccer team runs onto the field, and I take a second to give Marcus an appreciative glance, before going back to scanning the crowd. Araceli and I are sitting with Grace and Cyrus in the bleachers, keeping an eye on them in case they run off. So far, they mostly seem excited to cheer for Isaiah, who stands next to Marcus on the field. Jeremy is on the team too, although I don't see him run out with the other players. Hmm.

"I'm going to get a soda, anyone need anything?" I ask, while giving Araceli a pointed look. She nods at me in response.

"No thanks," Grace says.

I head off to the closest food stand, and spot Callan leaning against a nearby wall. He meets up with me as I buy a soda.

"Jeremy's missing," I tell him quietly.

He gives a short nod as his eyes scan the field. "I'll have Bastien look into it. Have you seen anything else?"

"No, not yet."

"What about Nariel?" he asks.

I gesture to one side of the bleachers. "Kassiel is sitting with him and some of the other professors."

"I hope we can trust him."

"We can." We all met up briefly before the game started and went over the plan, then shared our new information on how we can get to Faerie. We're all ready for multiple scenarios. Now we just have to wait.

I grab my soda and head back toward my friends. The fae team is on the field now, and the game's about to start. We believe nothing will happen until half-time, but we want to be prepared when it does. Our plan is to try and prevent the kidnapping from happening at all, but if we fail, then we'll head to the forest with Tanwen and stop the Order there.

We watch the game, cheering for the angel team, who manage to hold their own against the fae. Still no sign of Jeremy though. Cyrus spends the entire time either cheering for Isaiah, talking about how hot he is, or sharing the latest rumors and gossip about the Duskhunter attack. Grace cheers along with him and nods at his newest story. They give no indication they're up to something.

As halftime approaches, Cyrus stands up. "I'm hitting the bathroom. Be right back."

Araceli gives me a quick look and then jumps up. "I need to pee too. I'll walk with you."

They head over to the bathrooms together, while I wait with Grace and watch the game. But Araceli and Cyrus take longer than I expect, and I can't help but glance back to look for them.

"Are you okay?" Grace asks.

"Yeah, fine." I shrug casually. "That bathroom line must be

long, eh?"

Just as I'm about to go look for them, there's a huge boom behind us and a drone flies overhead. People scream and duck and someone yells, "The drones are back!"

Professors and other angels assigned to security launch into the air immediately, while others run to take cover. Everyone in the bleachers stands up and tries to shuffle away, while the players on the field are whisked into safety, including the fae. It's total chaos.

Shit, a Duskhunter attack is the absolute last thing we need right now. Although it might stop the Order from kidnapping any of the fae, so there's that at least. I extend my wings and fly up into the air to do whatever I can to help. As I do, I see Hilda blast the drone with burning light, and it explodes in a flash. Other angels continue to fly around, searching for more, but after the initial panic, it seems there was only one drone.

As Kassiel flies past me, I grab his arm, my eyes wide. "It was a diversion!"

"I think you're right." He glances around. "I don't see Nariel anymore. I was following him, but he must have slipped off and gone invisible."

"Grace too. I lost her in the chaos as everyone panicked. Dammit!"

I scan the crowd, which is dispersing quickly, but still don't see Araceli or Cyrus. This has all gone to shit.

"Time for plan B," I tell Kassiel, who nods. We know where the Order is meeting thanks to Tanwen. We'll have to try to stop them there. I just hope everyone else realizes it, since I have no way of finding them in this chaos.

I go invisible, and when I look back for Kassiel, he's gone

too. He probably slipped into a shadow or something. I head toward the forest, and land near the boulder to throw on my golden robes and mask.

When I get to the cavern, there's a group already gathered there, some in gold, and some in white. Someone is already screaming from behind a closed door. It's just like when they wanted us to torture a demon last year. I messed that up for them, and now it's time to do the same this year.

As I walk in, the prison door opens and someone drags a shaking initiate out of the room. Behind them, three people are tied to chairs. Araceli. Her dad. And the female fae guard from the Spring Court that I met at the previous game.

My blood boils as I see my best friend's forehead covered in blood. Those fuckers are going to pay for this.

"Stop," I yell, but it sounds odd since the mask distorts my voice. I remove my dark-infused dagger, leaving the light one at my hip. It won't help here. "Let the prisoners go!"

"We can't do that," the leader says, standing near the prison door. He waves a hand, and some of the other golden masked people rush toward me to grab my arms. I slash at them and they dart back, but another one manages to knock off my mask—revealing my face.

Everyone stares at me, but I'm officially done with this cat and mouse game. I stand up to my full height and adjust the grip on my dagger. "Don't make me use my succubus powers."

A few people gasp, mostly the initiates. I figured focusing on my demon side would get a response.

"Put down your weapon," the leader says, as other members draw their weapons and surround me. "You're going to get hurt. You must realize this is the only way to get to Faerie...and to find your brother."

How dare that asshole use my brother to justify torture. I'm done playing nice. I haven't used my succubus powers like this in a long time, since I stopped seducing strangers, but now I reach out and incite lust in the leader. I used to need to touch someone to do it, but not anymore. I'm so angry that my power radiates out of me like a bomb, slamming into some of the other members too.

The ones holding weapons immediately drop them and step toward me. I can feel their desire, and how much they want me. How much they'll do anything to have me.

"You want me, don't you?" I ask in my most seductive voice. "I'll be yours...you just need to let the prisoners go."

"Do it," the leader stammers. "Anything."

That was too easy. He must already have wanted me a little.

"Don't listen to her!" someone calls out from the back. My power must not have extended that far. "She's using her dirty demon magic on you!"

I have a pretty good idea who that is. I slam some of my dirty demon magic into Jeremy in response, and he falls to his knees while reaching for me at the same time. "Be quiet, asshole."

The leader shakes his head and tries to resist my power, and others break free and rush toward me with their weapons. But then three people move in front of me, protecting me with their own swords. With everyone in masks, it's hard to tell who is who, but I'm guessing these are my friends. One of them is definitely Callan, judging by the size. Two others rush into the prison room and begin working to free the fae, starting with Araceli. The person who freed her hands her a sword, and she guards them as they free her dad and the fae woman.

"Remove your masks," I tell everyone under my power.

The kneeling scumbag removes his mask, and to no one's surprise, it's Jeremy. Cyrus removes his too, he's one of the ones who dropped his weapons. Which meant he was going to stab me, if he had to. That hurts. I knew he wasn't trustworthy, but I thought we were friends. A few others remove their masks too, but I don't see Grace among them, thankfully.

The leader rips his off last, and his crown hits the floor. Nariel stares up at me with a mixture of lust and hatred. "I should've killed you."

"I'd like to see you try," I snarl. "Give me the feather."

He snorts, and I raise my chin, then release more lust into him. He tries so hard to fight it, but in the end he crawls to me on his hands and knees, then removes a clear plastic container from his robe, which holds the feather. He offers it up to me with love-struck eyes, and I kick him in the chest to push him back.

Araceli and her dad stumble out of the other room, with the fae woman held between them. She's in the worst shape, and I cringe at the realization one of her ears was torn off. "We need to get this woman back to her people," Araceli says.

"Let's go." I hold my dagger out to the members and initiates who are either under my spell, or held back by my friends. "Don't even think of following us."

I lead the way out of the cavern, and draw in a deep breath of fresh air when we get outside. Araceli and the other fae are right behind me, followed by my golden-robed allies. They all rip off their masks, and my chest swells with pride to see Callan, Bastien, Marcus, Kassiel, and even Tanwen all on my side. Unlikely allies? Definitely. But it worked.

Chapter Forty-Two

OLIVIA

We move some distance away and hide in the forest, so Marcus can heal the fae woman with Araceli's help. Our group spreads out around them, keeping an eye out for anyone following.

"Have they taught you how to create a bubble of invisibility yet?" Fintan asks me.

"No, not yet."

"Let me show you."

He bends light around our group, bouncing it off the trees and the ground, creating a little dome around us. No one from the outside can see us, but we can see everything inside our little shell. It's definitely an advanced Ishim move, and one only someone very powerful could accomplish. No wonder Fintan was such a good messenger.

"I think I got it," I tell him. "Thanks, that will come in handy in Faerie."

"Will she be all right?" Callan asks, kneeling beside the fae woman.

"Yes, she's already recovering," Marcus says. "Araceli managed to grab the ear on the way out, so we re-attached it. She should heal completely within a few hours."

Araceli stands up and wipes blood on her pants, like it's no biggie. "We need to take her back to the fae before they realize she's missing and attack the school."

"I can take her," Fintan says.

"Are you sure?" I ask. The fae don't seem to like him much, from what I've heard.

"Yes. It has to be either me or Araceli, and you need her to get to Faerie." He gives Araceli a warm smile. "Don't worry about me."

"I'm sorry your visit turned into this," Araceli says, as she hugs her dad.

"It was worth it to spend time with you."

The fae woman stirs and looks up at us, then focuses on me. "Thank you. Your rescue will not be forgotten."

Fintan takes the fae guard's hand to help her stand, and then they go invisible as they walk into the woods.

As they leave, I turn to the others and hold up the container with the feather. "Now that we have this, we can go to Faerie. I vote we leave immediately, before the Order can regroup and come after us. Go back to your rooms and gather whatever supplies you need for a couple days in Faerie. Food, water, weapons, extra clothes, whatever. Then we'll meet in the bell tower in thirty minutes."

"Remember that the weather in Faerie fluctuates from very hot to very cold every day," Bastien says. "Dress accordingly. We won't want to have to use our magic unless absolutely necessary."

"Why not?" Callan asks.

"It might alert them to our presence," Araceli says.

"I'm going to stay behind and do what I can here," Tanwen says. "Things are crazy after the drone attack, and someone needs to keep an eye on the Order from this side. But I wish you the best of luck."

"Thanks for your help, Tanwen," I say. "This wouldn't have been possible without you."

"Just remember our deal." She gives me a little nod, before flying off with a beat of her bright white wings.

The rest of us split up and head back to our dorms. Araceli and I are already packed, so all we do is grab our bags, run around doing one final check to make sure we have everything, and go. We don't want to spend a second longer in our dorm, in case Nariel or Jeremy or even Cyrus comes after us there.

Back in the field, it looks like they're trying to get the championship game underway again, but it might be tough with two of their players missing, and half the audience hiding in fear of the Duskhunters.

"What happened at the game?" I ask Araceli, after we land at the bell tower.

"When I came out of the bathroom, Cyrus knocked me out and kidnapped me. He apologized and said he had to do it to fulfill his Order task. That snake." Her eyes harden. "When we got to the cavern, Jeremy was already there with my dad, and someone else brought the fae guard in after that."

My hands clench into fists. "They must have been watching our dorm or something, and grabbed your dad on his way out."

"Probably." She shudders a little. "Then they had the first two initiates torture us for info on getting to Faerie. They barely roughed me and my dad up, but you saw what they did to that poor woman."

I give her a warm hug. "I'm so sorry you had to go through all that."

"I'm going to make them pay for what they did," Araceli says, and I've never seen her look so bloodthirsty before. Not that I can blame her. First they killed her boyfriend, now they kidnapped and tortured her and her dad. I'd be out for blood too.

"We will," I say, as the Princes arrive carrying backpacks and weapons. They begin moving furniture to give Araceli space for the portal, and I move to help them, but then I'm distracted by a knock on the door.

I open it and find Grace outside. "What are you doing here?"

"You're going to Faerie, aren't you?" she asks. "That's why you took the feather. I'm coming with you."

"No way," Araceli says. "We can't trust her."

I shake my head at Grace. "Sorry, but she's right. Your uncle is the leader of the Order."

"Bastien will know I'm telling the truth," she says, looking at him for confirmation. "I want to help you find Jonah."

"True," he says.

"Were you involved in kidnapping or torturing Araceli, her dad, or the other fae?" I ask.

"No!" Grace looks horrified by the very idea. "I was there because Nariel made me go, but I had no part in any of that, I swear."

"Also true."

I stare at her for a long moment. I know Bastien can sense truth, but that doesn't mean I trust her.

She takes my hands and looks at me with pitiful eyes. "Please, Liv. I care about your brother, and I have to know what happened to him. Whether he's alive or dead. Whether he found the Staff or not. I need to know, or I'll never be able to find peace."

I glance at Bastien, who nods.

"All right." She does seem to really care about my brother, and I guess she can't help it if her uncle is the leader of the Order. "You can come, but we'll be watching you closely."

"Thank you," she says, with a relieved sigh.

Kassiel lands on the bell tower then, and everyone stares at him. I sense an awkward moment approaching.

"Kassiel is coming too," I tell them.

"Can we trust you?" Bastien asks.

"Yes," Kassiel says. "I want to stop the Order as much as you do, if not even more. They can't ever get ahold of the Staff."

Bastien crosses his arms and nods. "He's telling the truth."

"Let's hurry," Araceli says, as she cuts her hand. "Everyone stand back."

She presses her palm to my necklace and mutters the fae words, and I hold my breath in anticipation. We're actually going to Faerie to rescue my brother.

It's about damn time.

Chapter Forty-Three

MARCUS

In Faerie, everything is a little...*more*. It's like someone turned up the volume to max on the entire world. The plants are greener. The sky is brighter. The flowers smell sweeter. Even the birds sound better somehow.

Our group made it through Araceli's portal, and now we're just standing in the middle of a forest, taking it all in. It's different from the forest around Seraphim Academy. This one looks more like a rainforest, and the air is humid and hot.

"Where are we exactly?" Bastien asks.

"We're in the Summer Court," Araceli says. "This is where my dad's family lives."

"Does that mean you have Summer Court magic?" I ask her.

She spreads her hands. "I guess so? I don't really know. Once we get back, I should probably find out."

"Okay, I took Fae Studies two years ago, so I might be a little rusty, but time moves differently here right?" I ask.

"Yes, the season changes depending on what time of day it

is," Kassiel says. He's still acting like our professor, even here in Faerie. "Right now it's probably summer, which means it's mid-day. Since we're in the Summer Court, that season will last the longest. At night it will be winter."

"I knew Faerie experienced all four seasons over the course of a day, but not so drastically," Grace says with awe in her voice. "I figured the temperature changed a little."

"We need to hurry," Callan says. "We need to find shelter before it gets dark and becomes too cold."

Liv pulls out the black feather, which pulses with darkness, even here in Faerie. "Our best bet is to find the Staff, and hope Jonah is being held prisoner somewhere nearby. If not, maybe someone there will know where he is."

I notice she doesn't mention the possibility that Jonah's been killed. It must be too hard for her to consider when we've come this far, although it will probably be a relief when she knows his fate, one way or the other.

Liv holds the shadowy feather up in the air. "Return to your master."

She lets the feather go and it flitters and floats and twirls, like feathers do in the wind, before blowing on the breeze toward Kassiel. At first I think it's not working and we're screwed, but then it seems to hover around him for a second. He takes a step back with a frown, and the feather continues onward, flying higher into the sky with clear purpose.

Grace claps her hands together. "It's working!"

Liv creates an invisibility bubble around all of us and the feather, and then we take off after it. First we travel by foot through the forest, moving past clueless rabbits and deer, plus some weird glowing flowers I wish we had time to investigate, and some huge green insects I'm glad we don't. Then the feather gets too high, and we have to fly after it, careful not to move too far from Liv. As the day grows hotter, we soar over the dense canopy of trees, which stretch for miles, only to be broken up by a castle sitting on a hill in the distance.

"What is that?" Grace asks.

"No clue. I only know a few random things about Faerie." Araceli gives us an apologetic look. "Sorry."

"Don't apologize," Liv says. "It's your dad's fault."

"We should probably steer clear of it," Callan says.

We take a break in the forest, after plucking the feather from the air and putting it back in its case. The sun beats down on us as we eat some granola bars, but none of us mind the heat. When it gets cold, we'll have to bundle up because we can't use our magic to stay warm. I just hope we can find somewhere indoors to hide for the night.

We set off again down a dirt road, with no hint of concrete or asphalt. I feel like we've stepped a thousand years into the past. The sun heads lower in the sky and the air begins to cool, while the leaves begin to change color, turning red, yellow, and orange. It's hard not to stop and stare at the beauty all around us, but we put on some jackets and keep moving.

Then Araceli whispers, "Someone's coming!"

Callan grabs the feather, and Liv keeps her little invisibility bubble around us as we move off the road and onto the grass. We hide in the trees as a fae male comes down the road on a beautiful white horse. He has hair the color of lemons, and he looks like he's stepped out of a Tolkien novel in a floor-length silver tunic and a gold jacket. His shoes look like they're made of cloth.

We crane our necks as he walks by, and I breathe as quietly as possible without moving too much. When he's past us, we wait a while for him to go out of sight. Finally we can move back onto the road.

Liv starts to get the feather, but then more people appear on the road, probably a half-dozen of them, wearing similar clothes to the other fae we saw. After they pass, Callan says, "We don't have time to hide every time more people appear. We need to keep flying."

Liv nods, but her face is paler than normal and she moves a little slower. "I guess it's the only way."

"Are you all right?" I ask her. I press a hand to her forehead, and can feel how weak she is with my powers. She's going to need to feed soon. Sunlight alone isn't going to be enough to keep her going.

She waves off my hand. "I'm fine. It just takes a lot of energy to keep this bubble around us. Let's keep moving."

"We'll have to find somewhere to stop soon," Kassiel says, his brow pinched with concern.

"Keep an eye out as we fly," Callan says. "Otherwise we'll have to sleep outside, and I don't think any of us brought our camping gear."

We continue on as the sun sets, the air grows colder, and the leaves turn brown and begin to fall. A frigid rain soaks our clothes and sends a chill through my wings. We pass a town, but decide it's too risky to stop there. I don't see anything else for miles, while it gets darker and colder, and Liv grows weaker.

"There," Kassiel calls out, pointing down below. "A ruin of some kind."

I don't see anything in the darkness, but we all follow him anyway, just as snow begins to fall. He leads us to a group of old stone buildings that are clearly abandoned, with some missing walls or with holes in their roof, and vines growing up the side. There's one building that still looks mostly intact, and we land in front of it.

Callan tries to use a flashlight, but it doesn't work. Something about Faerie blocks technology, if I remember correctly. Bastien uses some matches with some shrubbery to create a makeshift torch. We head into the building, which looks like it was abandoned long ago. At least it's a little warmer inside.

Liv staggers as she steps inside, and I know I need to help her somehow. She needs all her strength for what's to come tomorrow.

Once everyone is settled in, I pull Bastien aside. "Liv needs us."

His eyebrows dart up. "Us?"

I swallow and push my lingering jealousy aside. "I read once that a succubus can feed off two men at once for an extra boost. Liv needs that tonight."

He nods slowly. "Yes, you're probably right. Do you think she'll be open to such a thing?"

"Definitely."

Chapter Forty-Four

OLIVIA

"I'll take first watch," Kassiel says. Probably a good idea, since he doesn't feel the cold like the angels do, and can see much better in the dark. It's how he found this place.

As everyone spreads out and tries to get comfortable while shivering, Araceli gathers some sticks and stones, building a little fire pit in the center of the room.

"What are you doing?" I ask.

"I'm not sure." She sits back on her heels and holds out her hands, then squints in concentration. A few seconds later, the little bundle of twigs catches fire, instantly bringing heat and light to the room.

I blink at the flames. "How did you do that?"

She grins as she warms her hands over the fire. "Ever since we arrived it's like my fae side has started waking up. Summer Court fae have fire magic, so I thought I would try it. I wasn't sure it would work though."

"That's incredible."

"When I get back, I think I'm going to learn more about my Summer magic. I've been trying to forget my fae side all my life, but I don't want to do that anymore. I'm not ashamed of my fae blood, and it's time to own it."

"I think that's a really good idea." I'm so proud of Araceli. She's grown so much this year, and it's a real honor to be her best friend.

"Nice fire," Callan says. "We should get more sticks to keep it going all night."

He heads outside with Grace and Araceli, and I'm about to follow, when Marcus grabs my hand and pulls me back. "Come with me," he says.

He leads me through the ruined building, down a long hallway, to another intact stone room. It's much colder in here without Araceli's fire, but Bastien is waiting next to a makeshift bed of blankets surrounded by candlelight.

"Sorry it's not more romantic," Marcus says. "But we did the best we could under the circumstances."

"It's really sweet," I say, smiling at him.

"You need to feed," Bastien says, getting straight to the point as usual. "On both of us."

Sex with two guys at once? It's like a Thanksgiving feast. I'm going to need to wear my stretchy leggings afterward. Too bad I left them at home.

I wonder where they got the blankets, but the whole thing is so sweet—and sexy—that I don't care. Plus, I'm starving and weak. I didn't realize how bad I felt until they mentioned feeding, but now I can't stop thinking about it.

Marcus puts his hand on my back and nudges me toward Bastien and the blankets. I taste their desire. They want to do this, together. It turns them on, the thought of sharing me.

It turns me on too.

"What are your intentions with me?" I ask with a coy smile.

Bastien looks at me with confusion on his face. "We thought you'd enjoy both of us together. Is that not the case?"

I shake my head quickly. "No, I do want it. Very much."

"Good." Bastien takes my hand and pulls on it, inviting me to join him on the makeshift bed. I step out of my shoes and drop to my knees, surprised to find the blankets rather comfortable.

"We found some furs," Marcus explains. "They're surprisingly plush and clean, once we shook out the dust."

He sits beside me and presses his lips to mine. His desire overwhelms my nerves and my body ignites. In all my time using men for food, I've never had a threesome, and my heart beats faster in anticipation.

The two of them take off my shirt, then make quick work of my bra. Marcus bends over me, pushing my back against Bastien's chest. Bastien slides his hands around my front and cups my breasts as he buries his face in my neck. I throw my head back, as Marcus moves my hair to the side so he can also press his lips on the nape of my neck. They kiss along my skin, both of them sending little sparks through my body with each soft touch.

From behind me, Bastien lifts one breast up, holding it for Marcus to lean down and wrap his lips around my nipple. He runs his tongue across the tip before sucking hard, then going soft again. I moan as he drives me mad with wanting.

My hands find their way up and into Bastien's hair as Marcus moves his lips to my other nipple, while his hands drift down my stomach to the curve of my hips. I push back on

Bastien and lift my hips up so Marcus can pull off the rest of my clothes.

While Marcus gets undressed, Bastien slips his hand down between my legs and begins stroking me there, preparing me for his friend. Then Bastien digs his fingers into my thighs and spreads my legs wide. Marcus moves in, and the hunger in his eyes matches my own. His cock pushes inside me, and I cry out in pleasure as I lean back against Bastien. Marcus starts off slow, rocking me back and forth between the two of them, and I've never felt more adored in my life than at this moment. Having both of their bodies pressed against me, with their mouths on my skin and their hands roaming my curves, it's the best feeling in the world. It hits me then how much I care about these two, so much more than I did even a year ago.

Lilim aren't supposed to love, but I'm starting to wonder if maybe I can. If I do already.

Marcus's pace increases and all thoughts flee my mind as he fills me over and over again with his amazing cock. I suck up all the sexual energy he has to offer, immediately feeling a lot better, while also wanting more. I turn my head and find Bastien's lips, as he reaches down to rub my clit. The combination of sensations sweeps an orgasm through me, and I tighten up around Marcus, but he's nowhere near done.

He pulls out and grabs my hips, rolling me over on the blankets. "Bastien could use some attention too, don't you think?"

"Definitely," I agree.

Bastien unbuckles his pants, and I reach in and pull his hard cock out. After giving him a few strokes, I lick him slowly, then take him into my mouth. He groans and his lust spikes, while his fingers tangle in my hair.

Marcus presses kisses to my back and shoulders, then slides inside me again from behind. With each stroke, he pushes me onto Bastien's cock, making me take him further in my mouth. I have two of my lovers inside me, giving me their sexual energy, and it's amazing.

Opening my mouth wider, I use Marcus's rhythm to push me up and down on Bastien's cock. The erotic feeling of his head sliding deeper and deeper down my throat combined with the stimulation of Marcus slamming into me helps me get close to another orgasm. I sense Marcus is close too, as he moves faster and harder, slamming into me from behind. He rubs my clit too at the same time, knowing exactly what to do to make me climax.

Moaning through it, I tense up and ride it, my voice getting louder and louder around Bastien. The jolts of pure pleasure keep me moving back against Marcus until he comes inside me too with a loud groan.

When we're both sated, Marcus pulls out of me and drags me onto the blankets, holding me close. We stare into each other's eyes, and I see how much he cares for me too. But I can't ignore Bastien. I pull away and turn back to my other lover.

"I hope you're not full," he says. "I've got plenty more to give you."

"I can take it."

He hums deep in his throat. "Come here."

He stretches out on the blankets beside Marcus, and holds his long, hard cock up in invitation. I straddle him and sink down onto it, with a delirious sigh. This is so much better than sex with strangers.

I begin to rock up and down on Bastien, getting into a good

rhythm. Marcus moves behind me, his hands roaming my body and caressing me, while Bastien's fingers dig into my hips. Each time Bastien fills me, tiny waves of pleasure shoot through me. He fits inside like he was molded just for me.

My third orgasm grows, making me move faster and faster. Bastien is growing close as well, and his sexual energy rolls into me in waves of delicious intensity.

"Yes," I cry. I can't say much more. I'm moving too fast and the pleasure is too high. "Harder."

Bastien thrusts up into me harder in response, while Marcus cups my breasts and begins working my nipples. They work together, focusing on my pleasure, and it's incredible.

I cry out and throw my head back as the orgasm crests. Bastien pulls me forward against his chest, almost into an embrace, then finds my lips. Flexing his hips, he rides out his orgasm inside me as we kiss. As he finishes, I soak up his pleasure, his lust, his passion. It feeds me, sates me, sustains me. I'm filled to the brim, possibly fuller than I've ever been before. And more than that, I'm happier than I've been before too.

With a sigh, I move to Bastien's side, cuddling up between him and Marcus, who pulls a thin, fresh-smelling quilt over the top of us. "I had this one rolled up in my backpack," he whispers.

None of us have any desire to get up and dress, and even though it's cold, we don't feel it at all. They wrap their arms and legs around me and we fall asleep, safe and comfortable in each other's embrace. Or as safe as we can be in an abandoned ruin in the middle of Faerie, anyway.

*I*n the morning we continue on, and the temperature is absolutely perfect as we set off, with bright blue skies and vibrant flowers blooming everywhere. Faerie is beautiful, but there's something about it that feels unusual too. It's like a deal that's too good to be true, and you're just waiting for the catch.

Thanks to the boost I got from Bastien and Marcus, I'm able to maintain the bubble of invisibility around us as we fly, which saves us a lot of time over walking. After a few hours, the feather starts moving faster and faster, and I think we must be getting close. It leads us toward a dark, imposing stone building with a wall around it, with armored guards perched in regular intervals and at the gates. Our only bit of luck is that they're not looking for an attack from the air, which gives us a chance to sneak inside.

"It's heavily guarded," Callan says. "The Staff must be in there."

And hopefully Jonah too. It definitely looks like a prison, with small windows and heavy defenses.

"Everyone stay close," I tell them as we approach.

We slowly fly over the gate and hover above the building, looking for a good place to land. I spot a small empty alley and gesture for everyone to follow me. The feather practically quivers with excitement, so we know we're close now.

We land next to some trash bins, and everyone takes a moment to collect themselves and look around for a way inside. Around the corner, two fae women stand on a small porch outside a closed door, one with rosy pink hair, and the other's snow white. They seem to be arguing, and they're both wearing plain green dresses with aprons, so I'm guessing they're servants or cooks or something.

"Fine. I'll do it," the one with white hair says. It's pulled back into a dozen or more intricate braids that fall way down her back. "But you owe me."

The pink-haired fae rolls her eyes. "I don't owe you anything. Now go."

The first one pushes the door open with a huff, and they both slip inside. Callan launches forward in a half-jump half-flight and manages to get his hand on the door just before it swings shut.

He waits, listening for the sound of the women to recede, and then opens the door and lets us inside. We enter the building in some sort of mudroom. There are benches, shelves, and hooks along the wall with a few coats hanging from them. The coats seem to be well-made, but not as nice as some of the clothes we saw other fae wearing. This is likely a servant's entrance.

It's crowded with all of us in here, and I glance among the

faces of my friends. We all look exhausted from the lack of sleep and the non-stop flying or walking. Not to mention, the time difference. But we're so close now, I can feel it. Soon we'll have the Staff and my brother too.

Bastien holds the feather by the end, and it twitches for us to go further into the building. We walk into a long, empty hallway made of whitewashed wood planks. Most of the doors leading off the hall are closed, but the feather keeps telling us to go forward.

Bastien stops at a closed door, and glances back at us. Callan moves to the front, back in over-protective mode, and turns the doorknob slowly. It's locked.

Luckily, I knew something like this might happen, and I brought my trusty lock picks. It takes me a few minutes because the lock is a harder one to crack, but then the door swings open.

One the other side is a stairwell with broken steps that disappear into darkness. If this was a movie, this is when people would yell, "Don't go down there, you idiots!" So naturally, we start going down.

It's narrow and twists into a tight spiral, and if we meet anyone going up it, we're in trouble. We try to make as little noise as possible while both staying close together and moving quickly, and I just hope no one is right there at the bottom of these stairs.

The stairs seem to go on forever. We pass some doors, but the feather wants us to keep going down. We've got to be several stories underground now.

"We're getting close," Bastien whispers, as he holds the feather back so it doesn't dash away.

We reach the bottom of the stairs, and discover a new problem. Ahead of us is a large stone door that's clearly bolted shut. Two guards in bronze armor stand beside it wielding spears.

How are we supposed to sneak past that?

We never get a chance to formulate a plan, because the second my feet hit the ground, the invisibility bubble vanishes. I quickly reach for light to bend it and hit something like a magical wall, but it's too late anyway.

The two guards start when they see a group of us suddenly appear, but they're obviously well-trained, because they lower their spears at us. "Halt!"

"Shit," Marcus mutters.

So much for not getting caught by the fae.

There's an open door to the right, and I wonder if we can dart through it and escape, but no, someone would get stabbed by one of those spears. The fae are as quick as we are, if not more so. We could try to overpower these guards, ideally without really hurting them, but there's no telling if there are more nearby. And we can't seem to use our magic here.

"State your business," one of the guards says.

The others glance at me, like I'm supposed to get us out of this mess. Crap.

I step forward and hold up my hands in surrender. "We're looking for the Staff of Eternity...and for an angel named Jonah."

The two guards glance at each other, and I have a feeling they're about to arrest us, when I hear a familiar voice ask, "Liv?"

I turn toward the open doorway and gape at the man standing there.

Jonah.

Chapter Forty-Six

OLIVIA

My brother is alive. He's *alive!*

I thought he would be a prisoner. I worried he might be dead. I spent two years trying to find him—and he's standing there, with a book tucked under one arm.

"Jonah!" I rush toward him, and he drops the book to embrace me. I hold him tightly with tears in my eyes, then pull back to look at him in disbelief. Is it really him? Is he really okay? He has a new beard, he's wearing fancy fae clothes, and there's a sword on his hip, but he looks good otherwise. Healthy. Unharmed. *Alive.*

I've envisioned this moment for so long. I pictured him lifting me off the ground and spinning me around, ecstatic to see his baby sister. But instead he frowns at me. "What are you doing here?"

This is definitely not the reunion I was expecting.

"I'm here to rescue you," I say. It sounds silly, since he obviously doesn't need rescuing.

"You shouldn't be here," Jonah says. The guards eye us warily, but he raises a hand to them. "It's fine. I know them."

I step back, wounded by his words, as the others rush forward.

Grace throws her arms around Jonah and gives him a kiss. "It's been two years," she says. "I could have moved on, but I didn't. I never gave up hope you were still alive."

"I'm sorry," Jonah says, as he holds her close. "I'll explain everything."

Marcus moves forward to give Jonah one of those quick man-hugs. "You better."

"We've been worried," Callan grumbles.

Bastien clasps Jonah's hand. "Well, some of us assumed you were dead."

Jonah lets out a short laugh at that. "It's really good to see all of you. But how are you all here together?"

"That's a long story," I say. "The short version is that I started attending Seraphim Academy in an attempt to find you. All of us worked together, including Araceli, my roommate, and Kassiel, one of our professors, and it led us here. To you, and to the Staff." I glance at the heavily guarded door. "Is it in there?"

"It is," Jonah says, but then he turns to Callan with hard eyes. "I thought I told you to keep Liv away from Seraphim Academy."

"I tried," Callan says. "Believe me, I did everything short of actually harming her, but none of it worked. She's very...stubborn."

"More like determined," I mutter.

"It's not safe for her at Seraphim Academy. Or here." Jonah shakes his head. "You should go back."

"We're not leaving without you," Callan says. I was about to say the same thing.

"Why did you even come here?" I ask. I'm feeling at my wit's end at this point. "Were you really trying to get the Staff for the Order?"

His eyebrows dart up. "I see you know a lot. No, I wasn't. I came here to protect you from the Staff—and that's why I stayed." He sighed. "C'mon, let's go inside, and I'll show you."

He gestures to the guards, who move aside, and then Jonah touches an unremarkable spot on the wall behind them. The bolts unlock, and the heavy stone door slowly opens. Inside is a large stone dais, and floating above it is a staff that glows with both darkness and light. It's made of twisted silver and gold metal, and at the top is an orb that shifts and swirls with a rainbow of colors, surrounded by two wings, one black and one white.

I step forward slowly. "Is this it? *The* Staff?"

Jonah walks beside me. "Yes. I've been guarding it all this time."

Our friends walk in behind us, and I hear Araceli gasp. The Staff radiates power and beauty, and it's hard not to stare at it in awe.

There's another guard inside, a beautiful fae woman with hunter green hair and matching eyes. She's wearing Autumn Court armor, and draws her sword as we approach. "Jonah? Who are these people?"

"Eveanna, this is my sister, Olivia," he says. "She came to rescue me."

"It's a pleasure to meet you," she says, with a slight bow. "Jonah has spoken of you many times."

"Eveanna is the current guardian of the staff," Jonah

explains. "Michael and Lucifer entrusted it with the fae, and it moves to a new Court every year to keep its location hidden."

She sheathes her sword. "It is my great honor to protect the Staff."

I turn to Jonah to demand some answers, when suddenly there's a loud bang and a flash of light on the floor near us, and then the air fills with white smoke. It smells horrible and burns the eyes, and we're all instantly coughing and trying to wave it away.

"What was that?" I ask, spinning around and trying to see in the darkness.

"We're under attack!" Eveanna yells. "Protect the Staff!"

I move toward it, and as the smoke clears, I see a portal like the one we came through. Grace is holding something long and using it to open the portal. The Staff of Eternity.

"Grace?" I ask. "What are you doing?"

It's a dumb question. She's obviously stealing the Staff. I'm just so shocked by what I'm seeing that I can't say what I really want to ask, which is *what the fuck, Grace?*

"Getting a present for my father," she says, with a devious grin I've never seen before. Her father? Who is he?

I'm gaping at her, trying to wrap my head around what she's doing, when Nariel, Cyrus, Jeremy, and five other Order members appear through the portal.

"Grace," Jonah whispers. "How could you?"

She glares at him. "It's our duty to retrieve the Staff. You failed in that task. I will not."

As she says it, she shoves the Staff into Jonah's chest, and there's a burst of light as he goes flying backward. Fury overtakes me and I grab my succubus magic, but nothing happens. It's still trapped inside, along with my angelic powers too. This room must block magic somehow. But I'm not defenseless, thanks to my mother. I draw my dark-infused dagger, and my friends grab their weapons too.

"Cover her," Nariel calls out, and all the Order members raise their weapons as they make a barrier between Grace and the portal.

The place interrupts into chaos as the Princes—including my brother—clash with the Order members. Kassiel and Araceli fight too, along with Eveanna. I dodge through the mayhem and try to get to Grace and the Staff, but she runs into the portal with it before I can reach her. Dammit!

Cyrus follows her, right at her heels. I try to go after them, but Nariel grabs my arm and yanks me back, hard.

"Die, demon spawn," he growls, as he raises a light-infused sword over me. There's no time for me to get away.

Before he can strike, Callan's huge sword slams through Nariel's chest from behind. My Ishim teacher lets out a gurgling gasp, before his body goes slack. He hits the floor, and I stare at the blood covering him in horror. How did it come to this? My own professor trying to kill me. Callan saving my life. Dead bodies on the floor. All because of the Staff.

"Are you okay?" Callan asks, touching my arm and shaking me from my thoughts.

"Yes. Thank you."

He gives me a brief nod, then spins around to stop another attack coming my way. As I do, I see Jeremy running toward the portal. No way, fucker. I grip my dark-infused blade and go after him, blocking his path to the portal.

He swings his short sword, his eyes wild, and I have the sense to duck and roll. Good thing I paid attention in combat classes. Jeremy turns, ready to attack again, but I raise my dark-infused dagger and block him, even though the blow is so strong it sends waves of pain through my wrist. But then I spin away and slash, cutting his arm with my dark-infused blade. The arm holding the sword, which hits the ground. Jeremy screams and stumbles back, as the darkness sinks into him. I remember how painful it was and can only smile.

"How does it feel?" I ask. "You're in a room devoid of magic, and you were taken down by a half-demon."

He sneers at me as he backs away, holding his arm against his chest. "It doesn't matter, because soon you'll be back in Hell...or you'll be dead."

He leaps into the portal, and I lunge after him, but it closes the split second he's inside.

"No!" I yell, as I stumble through the empty space that once had the portal. They got the Staff. *They got the Staff!*

All around me, the fighting has ended. Nariel lies dead, along with three other Order members whose names I don't know. All of my friends are alive, thank goodness, but they're staring at the spot where the portal was, and every single one of them looks defeated.

We failed.

Chapter Forty-Seven

CALLAN

"Arrest them," a voice commands behind us, and before I know what's happening, dozens of armored fae are swarming into the room and clamping us in chains. None of us fight back. We're too shocked by what just happened.

Jonah tries to explain things to a fae captain, who doesn't look impressed, as the rest of us are dragged out of the room. I glance back and spot Olivia just behind me, physically unhurt, though I've never seen her look so broken before. Grace's betrayal must have hit her hard.

My magic comes back the second my feet touch the stairs and we're no longer on this floor. We go up and up the swirling stairs, until a door in unlocked on a random floor, and we're brought into a prison cell. They shove us all in one and slam the metal door shut.

Jonah's not with us. He must be trying to explain to the fae what happened. I don't see his fae friend either.

I stare at the guards perched outside the prison cell, and

then turn around to look at my friends. Araceli wraps an arm around Olivia, and they lean against each other, both exhausted. In one corner of the cell, Bastien is bleeding from one arm, but Marcus is taking care of it. Kassiel stands alone, staring at nothing, his gaze haunted.

We wait there for at least an hour. None of us says much. What is there to say? We lost, and the Order won. Now Olivia's at risk. Fuck.

Food and drink are brought to us, and we all eat like we're starving. I guess it's been a long time since we ate, actually. I have no idea. Time is so odd in Faerie, and it's impossible to tell anything in this damp, dark cell.

I lean my head against the bars and close my eyes, trying to get a little rest so I'm alert in case we need to fight again. Olivia soft voice wakes me up, and I see she's speaking quietly with Kassiel in the corner of a cell. Everyone else seems to be asleep, except for the two of them. As I watch, Olivia's head drops, and Kassiel reaches up to touch her face. The moment looks so intimate, I glance away, feeling like I'm intruding.

Then it hits me—is Olivia sleeping with our Angelic History professor? Is that why he's really here? I'm not sure how I feel about that.

Before I can figure it out, guards arrive, and everyone in the cell stands up. "Come with us," one of the guards says.

They lead us up the stairs and onto the main floor, and then we're taken down a long hall with a dark green carpet decorated with red and orange leaves. All the guards wear bronze armor decorated in leaves as well. At some point we must have entered the Autumn Court lands, though none of us realized it.

Tall double doors open up, leading us into a grand room. A

long red and gold carpet leads us to a throne, upon which sits a man with long black hair and cruel eyes. He wears a large crown covered in gems and taps his long, sharp fingernails on the arm of the throne as he waits for us to be brought down to him.

"Kneel before High King Oberon," one of the guards orders.

I grit my teeth, but go along with it, dropping down to my knees. A son of Michael should never kneel, but I've also heard of the power and brutality of Oberon, and since this is his realm, it's best to play it safe.

Jonah is led in next, with Eveanna at his side. He gives us a worried glance, before facing the king and kneeling.

"Such interesting specimens we have found lurking in our basement," Oberon says, as his eyes move down the line. "A child with diluted fae blood who should never have come to this world."

Araceli's head lifts and she meets his look with hard eyes. She's grown a spine somewhere in the last two years. Good for her.

"A son of Uriel and a son of Raphael," the king continues, and then smirks. "Who shared the same bed last night."

My eyebrows lift at that. How does he know? Jonah's gaze jerks to Bastien and Marcus, clearly very confused.

He pauses on me and a chill runs down my spine. There's something very unnerving about him, and I'm not scared of anything. Then his gaze continues to Kassiel and Olivia.

"And finally, a son of Lucifer and a son of Michael, both consorting with the daughter of Lilith and Gabriel." He throws back his head and cackles. "How wickedly delightful."

My jaw practically hits the floor. Everyone's head turns to

Kassiel, whose brow is furrowed. Did Oberon just call him the son of Lucifer?

Things quickly snap into place from the last twenty-four hours. His desire to come on this mission. His excellent night vision. His resistance to the cold. He's not an angel, he's a Fallen who's tricked us all.

My hands tighten into fists. That asshole kneeling next to me is the son of my father's murderer. And he's sleeping with Olivia.

Olivia, who is the daughter of Lilith. The *Archdemon* Lilith.

I knew she was half demon, but I had no idea she was the daughter of the most powerful succubus in the world.

All of that goes through my mind while High King Oberon taps his fingers on the arm of his throne. He watches me like he senses my turmoil and delights in it. I want to burn this whole fucking room down.

"We've guarded the Staff of Eternity for over thirty years, as part of a deal struck with Michael and Lucifer," he says, finally ending the long silence. "Today the Staff was stolen, and shame has been brought upon our people. Needless to say, if any of you had different parentage, you'd be dead by now."

"Your majesty, I can explain—" Jonah starts.

Oberon holds up a hand. "Silence. I already know what happened. Your half-sister and her friends came to find you, but one of their own betrayed them and stole the Staff."

I heard Oberon is wise, and that his power comes from the land itself, but he seems to know everything. Way too much.

"All of you are responsible for this disturbance, and all of you must return to Earth and correct it. That includes you,

Eveanna of the Autumn Court. You are henceforth banished from Faerie until the Staff is returned or destroyed."

The green-haired fae's eyes are saucer-wide, but she lowers her head. "Yes, your majesty."

"Now go, I tire of looking at your faces," he says, waving his hand in dismissal. "I'd forgotten how much I loathe angels and demons and their drama."

We're escorted out of the throne room and into another room, where a fae in a bronze robe opens a portal. One by one we head through it, including the new member of our group, Eveanna.

We emerge in the bell tower, and it's pitch black. The sun is down. I wonder how long we've been gone.

I switch on the nearest light, and look around for Kassiel, but he's gone. Fine. Right now we have more pressing matters.

I'll deal with him later.

Chapter Forty-Eight

OLIVIA

We're all shell-shocked and exhausted, but we're back and Jonah is with us. It's not a total win, but it's something.

I throw my arms around him again, now that we're on Earth and the danger has passed. He hugs me back hard, and then I'm crying into his shirt. Crying because I'm so relieved he's alive. Crying for the two years we lost. Crying because Grace betrayed us.

"I missed you so much," I tell him, while wiping my eyes. "I never stopped looking for you."

"I should have known you'd find me, even in another world," Jonah says, with that crooked grin I've dreamed about seeing for so long. His eyes are wet too.

"Stubbornness runs in our family." I release him and step back, then take a deep breath to steady myself. "We have a lot to talk about."

"No shit," Callan says. "Where's Kassiel?"

He's gone. Probably gathered darkness around himself to escape as soon as we returned. I don't blame him. The others are going to have a lot of issues with the news about who and what he is.

"Are you actually banging him?" Araceli asks, then sees the truth of it on my face. "Daaaamn, girl. I mean, I get it, he is crazy hot, but he's also a teacher."

"He's also the *son of Lucifer*," Callan practically yells.

Marcus yanks the couch back into the center of the room, since we pushed it aside for the portal. Then he plops down and grabs one of the pink unicorn stuffed animals I left for them. "Forget Kassiel, I want to know what the hell Jonah's been doing in Faerie for two years."

"Yes, tell us everything," Bastien says, pulling up his armchair.

We all sit close together, and find some cheese, crackers, and wine, which we spread out between us. Eveanna sits stiffly to the side of us, glancing around in wonder.

"Let me start from the beginning," Jonah says, as he pours himself some wine. "I was recruited into the Order, along with Grace and the other Princes. We were just initiates, but Grace had inside knowledge because her uncle Nariel was the leader."

Was being the key term. We left him for dead in Faerie. Even though he led the Order, my gut still tightens at the thought of him being gone. He'd been my teacher for months now. He taught me a lot about my powers. And then he called me demon spawn and tried to kill me. It's a lot to wrap my head around.

Jonah continues, interrupting my thoughts. "A few years ago

the Order found out that the Staff was being kept in Faerie, but everyone they sent to retrieve it ended up dead. Once my Archangel power emerged, Grace wanted me to volunteer to get the Staff." He stares into his wine glass. "Grace was a true believer in the Order's tenets. I should have seen her betrayal coming."

"We all thought she was our friend," Araceli says. "It's not your fault. She even passed Bastien's lying test."

"Yes, using careful words," Bastien says, his eyes narrowing. "I suspect she planned everything from the beginning. She knew Olivia would try to stop the fae being tortured, so Grace made sure she had no part in it, and then she knew we would go to Faerie and use the feather to find the Staff. All she had to do was come with us."

I close my eyes as I remember things she said, both this year and last. "She's been manipulating us this entire time."

"Yes, I see it all clearly now," Jonah says, with a sigh. He really loved her, so it must be killing him to know their relationship was all a lie.

"Who is her father?" I ask.

"Her father?" Jonah frowns. "An Ishim named Malcolm. He dated her mom for a short while, but otherwise hasn't been in her life much. Why?"

Curious. I'll have to find out more about this guy, and why he might want the Staff. "Just something she said. Sorry, go on."

Jonah nods. "I knew if the Order ever got hold of the Staff, Liv would be in danger. They were going to keep sending people to get it, which is why I volunteered...with the intention of making sure they never got it."

"How did you manage to stay alive in Faerie?" Araceli

asks. Then she offers her hand with a smile. "I'm Araceli, by the way. Liv's roommate."

"It's nice to meet you," he says with a warm grin. "I managed to fool the fae for a few days. Longer than I expected." Eveanna rolls her eyes at this, but doesn't respond. "But eventually they caught me and threw me in prison. I explained who I was, and why I was there, and they weren't sure what to do with me. As the son of two Archangels, they didn't want to kill me. They also didn't feel they could send me back. Eventually I won over the High King and he let me stay in Faerie as long as I helped guard the Staff."

"You're lucky the High King was amused by you," Eveanna says.

Jonah winks. "Everyone is amused by me. Even you."

I glance between the two of them. "Are you..."

Eveanna wrinkles her nose. "Definitely not. I have no interest in men."

I hold up my hands. "Sorry, had to ask."

"No, I've been faithful to Grace, much good that did," Jonah mutters.

"Why didn't you send word to us?" Bastien asks.

"I was too afraid the Order would find out and know I was still alive. Or worse, be able to track me down somehow."

Tears fill my eyes again. "You have no idea how hard it was for all of us, not knowing what happened to you. If you were alive or dead. Your parents have both been distraught."

"I'm sorry," Jonah says. "I never wanted to hurt everyone. I was just trying to protect you." He glances at the other Princes and his eyes harden. "I even made my best friends promise to keep you away from this school, but that didn't work. And now you're sleeping with Callan?"

"All three of us actually," Bastien says, like it's an obvious fact.

Jonah's jaw drops. "What the fuck?"

"Sorry." Marcus looks down with shame in his eyes. "It wasn't something we planned, developing feelings for your sister."

"Feelings?" Jonah half yells. "What do you mean, *feelings?*"

"Speak for yourself," Callan snaps. "I only slept with her to protect her."

"You were supposed to protect her by keeping her far away from this school and from the Order!" Jonah says, shaking his head. "Now that they know what she is and have the Staff, Liv is in more danger than ever."

"What do you mean?" Araceli asks.

Jonah runs a hand through his hair, but he looks anything but calm. "The Staff requires both an Archangel and an Archdemon to activate it's full powers, but they have to work together. If they wanted to send the demons back to Hell, for example, they'd both have to agree to do that."

"That's good," Marcus says. "That means Grace doesn't stand a chance of using it. Unless she has both an Archangel and Archdemon in her pocket, anyway."

"And no Archdemon is going to agree to send everyone back to Hell," Callan says.

Bastien rubs his chin. "No, but it also works for anyone with Archangel or Archdemon blood."

"Exactly." Jonah leans forward and meets my eyes. "Olivia, you have both."

I have both. The idea sinks in slowly, leaving me reeling.

I have both.

"You understand now?" Jonah asks. "You're the only person

alive that can use the Staff by yourself. That's why I never wanted it to leave Faerie, and why I asked these idiots to keep you far away from this life. If nobody knew you existed, they couldn't try to force you to use the Staff."

"Shit, Olivia is in more danger than we realized," Callan says.

"Yeah, especially since you exposed her as a half-demon," Marcus mutters.

"You did *what?*" Jonah asks.

"We have many things to catch up on," Bastien says. "But the most pressing matter is to figure out how to get the Staff back."

"Agreed," Araceli says.

I nod, trying to focus. "We need to look for Grace, Cyrus, Jeremy, and anyone else who came back. They could still be on campus, although I doubt it."

"If they are, I'll find them," Bastien says. "I need to speak with my father about all this too."

"We have a lot to do." I stand up slowly. "But first, Jonah needs to see our dad."

The group splits up with a loose plan to look for Grace and the Staff. Marcus, Callan, and Eveanna are going to scour the campus for Order members, while Bastien consults with Uriel, and Araceli finds out what happened while we were gone from Tanwen. I have no idea what Kassiel is doing—probably reporting to Lucifer what happened.

I want to join the hunt too, but family comes first. I take Jonah to the house in Angel Peak, where our father opens the door and drops the cup of tea he's holding. As it shatters, Gabriel rushes forward to embrace his son.

"You're alive," he says into Jonah's hair. He looks up at me with proud eyes. "You brought him back."

Dad gestures for me to come closer, and I join their group hug, all of us holding each other tightly. Our little family, reunited at last. I may have failed in every way regarding the Staff, but at least I did something right.

*J*onah sits beside me as we stare at the stage where all the graduates line up. Callan, Marcus, and Bastien stand tall in the front, wearing all white caps and gowns. I didn't go to the ceremony last year, and I'm surprised to find it's almost exactly like a human graduation. Uriel is in the middle of a speech, but he lost me about three minutes into it. My mind keeps drifting to the events of the past few weeks.

We were in Faerie for two days in Earth time, but luckily it was a weekend, so no one was too worried about us. Tanwen managed to cover for us as needed, though she couldn't stop the Order from coming after us. I think she feels guilty about it, because she's announced she's staying in Angel Peak during break to help protect the town and the school from the Order or the Duskhunters. Some of the other Valkyries are staying too. They've offered to train some of the students who stay behind too, like me. Tanwen seems way too excited about that. She's going to kick my ass, but I suppose it'll be good for me.

The Order should have had its final meeting and initiation for its new members a few days ago, but we never saw any hints of it by the lake, in the forest clearing, or in the cavern. With Nariel dead and Grace missing, I have no idea what the state of the Order is—and Jeremy and Cyrus aren't talking. Cyrus is up there now, graduating and accepting Grace's diploma on her behalf. My one consolation is that he and Isaiah broke up in the last week, as I predicted.

"Does it bother you that you're not up there?" I ask Jonah. He's not graduating since he missed an entire year of school. He talked Uriel into letting him test out of a few classes and double up on others. If he manages to keep up, he'll graduate next year with me.

"Not really," he replies. "Sure, it sucks that I'm not graduating with my friends, but I learned a lot in Faerie, things I never would have learned here." He nudges me with his shoulder. "Besides, now I get to go to school with you for the first time."

"Lucky me," I say sarcastically, shoving him back. "Who doesn't want their overprotective brother following them around?"

He gives me a pointed look. "It's not being overprotective if you're actually in danger."

I sigh and tug my jacket tighter around myself. My plan was to spend winter break searching for Grace and the Staff, but the Princes overruled me. For my safety, they want me to stay in Angel Peak with my dad while they investigate. Jonah gave me his puppy dog eyes and I couldn't refuse, but we'll see how long I manage to keep that promise before I go stir crazy.

Eveanna will be going with them on the hunt. She's staying with my dad at the moment, using glamour to make herself blend in. She leans over and whispers, "When do they prove themselves?"

"I'm sorry?" I ask, not following.

"At Ethereal Academy, all students must prove themselves by showing off their skills, whether they be talented at combat, enchanting, cooking, or sewing. If they impress the headmistress, they may graduate and move into their chosen profession. If not, they must return to school for another year."

That sounds harsh. "We're a lot more relaxed here," I tell her.

She sniffs and sits back with a disapproving look. She's an interesting one, no doubt.

Uriel finishes his speech, pulling me back to the present. He calls the names of the graduating class one by one, and they walk across the stage to receive their diplomas. I clap when Callan, Marcus, and Bastien walk across the stage. Next year it's going to be me up there.

After the ceremony, we file out to the field where the sporting events are held each year. It's been transformed under a huge tent into a big dinner for the graduates and their families. As we all head inside, I catch sight of Kassiel standing in the shadows of the forest nearby. I haven't seen him in a few days, and I tell Jonah I'll be right back, and then head over to him.

"Is everything okay?" I ask him. He cancelled all of our private sessions, and I've only seen him during the last few Angelic History classes. I've started to think he's been avoiding me ever since we got back from Faerie.

He looks down at me with his green eyes. "Yes. I just wanted to say goodbye."

"Goodbye?" I blink up at him, my throat suddenly tight. "What do you mean?"

"I won't be teaching here next year." He glances behind me, and I turn to see the Princes entering the tent. Callan stops and shoots a hateful glare at Kassiel, before slipping inside. "Now that the Order has the Staff, my mission has changed. My priority is recovering the Staff before they can use it." His mouth twists. "Besides, word got out that I'm the son of Lucifer, and some of the Archangels are very upset that Uriel's allowed me to teach here. He claims he didn't know who my father was, but I think he's simply covering his ass."

"What do you mean, word got out?"

His eyes narrow. "I'm sure Callan told them."

"No..." I shake my head. "He couldn't."

"He hates demons, and believes my father killed his father. It's fine." Kassiel tucks a piece of hair behind my ear. "This was a temporary assignment anyway. I always knew it could never last beyond my mission. I did enjoy teaching though. I will miss it. And you, Olivia. But at least we don't have to hide our relationship anymore."

"That is a relief, but will I ever see you?" I move close and slide my arms around him, making us invisible at the same time to avoid any onlookers. "I need you, after all."

He gives me a sad smile. "I'll try to visit you as often as I can. I don't want you to starve again."

"It's more than that." I can't help but speak the words I've been wanting to say to all of them for so long. Well, maybe not Callan. That asshole. "I care about you. A lot."

"I care for you too. More than you know. More than any woman in all my long years." He lowers his head and presses his lips to mine, giving me a long kiss that feels a lot like a final one. "Which is another reason I must find the Staff and destroy it."

He launches into the air with his sparkling black and silver wings, and my heart aches as he flies away. The thought of not having him as my teacher next year is terrible, but even worse is the idea of not seeing him as often. Or ever again.

How could Callan betray him? I realize he didn't know Kassiel as anything but our teacher, but we fought together in Faerie on the same side. Didn't that count for anything? The stupidest part is that Kassiel and the Princes all have the same goals. They should be working together to find Grace and the Staff.

I throw off my invisibility and stomp inside, then catch Callan in line at the buffet. I grab his arm and drag him out of the tent. "What have you done?"

He looks down at me with his arrogant eyes. "You'll have to be more specific."

"You told everyone about Kassiel," I hiss.

He crosses his arms and his face turns hard. "Of course I did. We can't have the son of Lucifer teaching at our school."

"Why does that matter?"

He drops his arms. "His father killed my dad."

"You don't know that for sure."

"No one else is even a suspect."

I pinch the bridge of my nose. "Even if Lucifer did kill Michael, that doesn't mean Kassiel had anything to do with it. Do you want people to judge you based on your father's actions?" He frowns at that, but I'm not done. I poke my finger into his chest. "I thought you had changed. That you were better than the others who saw demons as the villains. That you cared about me."

He grabs my hand and pulls me against him, his mouth so close I think he might kiss me. "I do care," he growls. "I hate it, but I do. That's why I had to get rid of him. I can't have you fucking the son of Lucifer. Just be glad I didn't mention *that* to Uriel."

I push him away and take a step back. "Wow. I get it now. You did all of this because you're jealous that I'm sleeping with Kassiel."

His eyes narrow. "I'm not jealous. I'll share you with Marcus and Bastien. But not him. Never him."

"Luckily you won't have to share me at all. We are done."

I turn on my heel and walk away, silently fuming. Why did I think Callan could change? He hates demons, and can't see beyond that. Well, too bad, buddy, because I'm half demon, and that is never going to change.

For the past two years, I've allied myself with the angels, but maybe it's time to embrace my demon side even more. I might have to, if I'm going to find Grace, stop the Order, and get the Staff back. If anyone can do it, it's me.

Because I'm not just the daughter of an Archangel.

I'm the daughter of an Archdemon too.

ABOUT THE AUTHOR

New York Times Bestselling Author Elizabeth Briggs writes unputdownable romance across genres with bold heroines and fearless heroes. She graduated from UCLA with a degree in Sociology and has worked for an international law firm, mentored teens in writing, and volunteered with dog rescue groups. Now she's a full-time geek who lives in Los Angeles with her husband, their daughter, and a pack of fluffy dogs.

Visit Elizabeth's website: www.elizabethbriggs.net

Printed in Great Britain
by Amazon